$8.00

SON ᵒᶠₜₕₑ GLEN

SON of the GLEN

Sandy Young

British Cataloguing in Publication Data
A catalogue record for this book
is available from the British Library

ISBN 1 899863 16 8

First published by House of Lochar 1996
Reprinted 1998

Printed in Great Britain by
BPC-AUP Aberdeen Ltd
for House of Lochar, Isle of Colonsay,
Argyll PA61 7YR

CHAPTER I

It was the thirtieth day of June and the sun was shining as the big Austin school car stopped at the end of the rough glen road to let out a freckled-faced boy.

'Cheerio, Willie,' he shouted cheekily to the driver and started to run, his sandalled feet kicking up small spurts of dust with every step. The boy was nine years old and very lean but wiry. He wore short trousers with a shirt and jersey and knee length socks which were pushed down to his ankles. He had left home that morning, as he did every other school morning, shortly after seven to walk the three miles from his home to the road end from where the car conveyed him and about half a dozen other pupils to the small country school.

But this was the last day of the school term. Seven weeks without school stretched before him. After running for about a hundred yards he slowed to a trot and then a walk and finally stopped to take off the jersey and stuff it into his school bag. As the track began to climb steeply the boy instinctively adopted the loose-hipped, measured walk which marks a shepherd as such, no matter where he is seen.

There were only two houses to pass on the three mile route and the first of these was occupied by an old retired shepherd and his wife. Their own family were all working away from the glen and the brief visits of the young Davie Sinclair on his way to and from school, were the highlight of their day. The old lady always had a cup of fresh milk and a piece of home made cake or similar delicacy laid out ready for the boy. As the year was nineteen thirty nine and well before the days of school dinners, this was necessary sustenance for the young Davie who had nothing other than a packed lunch during the ten hours that he was away from his home. The old man sat in a wooden chair outside the door of his house. By his side was another chair which had been occupied by his wife but the approach of the boy had sent her back inside from where she emerged bearing a cup and a plate. Davie shrugged off his school bag and flopped to the ground in front of the chairs. The plate was placed on the ground beside him and he grasped the handle of the cup and drank thirstily. A fat, elderly collie keeked out from behind the old man's legs.

'Is it a long lie tomorrow, Davie?' asked old Mrs. Bennett settling back in her chair.

'I don't know,' replied the boy. 'I think Dad's going to a gather at

Strathbeg so I may have to do the hill if Ian goes with him.'

The old man drew on his pipe and exhaled a cloud of smoke.

'Aye,' he said, 'at this time of year it's better if somebody had a walk round.'

He knew that the hot weather caused ewes with heavy fleeces to become itchy and that in attempting to scratch themselves they sometimes turned on their backs and then, because of the fleece, were unable to roll over onto their feet again. A ewe that was on her back was liable to have her eyes pecked out by gulls or Hoodie crows. Remembering his own childhood he saw nothing odd in a nine year old boy having to walk round a two thousand acre hill with only a collie dog for company.

'How is your dog doing?'

'Oh, he's going to be good,' the boy was enthusiastic, 'Dad wouldn't let me take him on the hill when the lambs were smaller, but I'll be able to take him now.'

'Well, it might be better to let your father take him for a couple of turns first,' advised the old man. 'A young beast like that could gather the whole of the moil if he got away. His father was a glutton for work when he was young. Weren't you, boy,' he said fondly.

He bent to pat the head of the collie which thumped its tail.

The boy stood up with the lithe movement of the young.

'I'd better go,' he said, then turned to the old lady whose knitting needles had been clicking steadily since she sat down. 'Can I leave my school bag until the cart comes down with the hogg wool?' he asked. 'I won't need it for a while now.'

'Of course, Davie. Whoever is with the cart will stop by for a cup of tea and we'll give it to them. Don't work too hard in the holidays. You'll give us a visit sometime. We'll miss you,' she added.

Here she spoke no more than the truth. Even at the mouth of the glen the boy could be their only visitor over a period of several days and she knew that three miles up the glen young Davie's mother, could go for weeks at a stretch without seeing another female face.

'I'll be down for the Games,' he promised and added with the gravity of an adult. 'Keep well, both of you.'

The track took Davie high up round the shoulder of a hill, before dropping down to follow the river, which provided the gravel for road maintenance. At the top, Davie paused to look around. To the south the hills of Antrim were a blue haze in the distance and to the east, beyond Sanda and the massive bulk of Ailsa Craig it was just possible to discern the line of the Ayrshire coast. The grass fields beneath him were dotted with brown and white Ayrshire cows now beginning to move nearer their parent farms for the evening milking and in the brown of the turnip fields, squads of people were crawling on hands and knees to single the plants.

The huge bulk of a liner, outward bound, appeared as though it had sailed out of a cove in the cliffs a little over a mile away and as he stood, the heavy note of its siren in the clear summer air told him that someone local was aboard, either as an emigrant or as a member of crew.

The beauty of the scene was partially lost on this young boy who tended to take it for granted. He was happily unaware that far away in Europe a sequence of terrible events was already under way which was destined to horribly and prematurely end the lives of some of the young men who were now working in the peaceful fields below him and that neither the liner nor most of her crew were to see another summer. As the sound of the siren died away it was replaced by the rasp of a corncrake and as Davie turned to follow his route a pair of skylarks took their song into the blue sky above his head. The liner was by this time approaching the headland round which it would disappear and already beginning to lift a forefoot in response to the swell of the Atlantic. For a moment more the boy watched, then broke into a jogtrot which would eat up the remaining two miles to his home.

Davie's father, Donald, was a tall, lean, quiet man in his late thirties. His family had been shepherds in the area for centuries and although his formal education had ceased when he was fourteen, he was a voracious reader and this appetite was sustained by a library which had been established in a now disused classroom in the school by a philanthropic local laird. Every month the post van dropped off a small bundle of books with the Bennetts, in the last house before the road end, and took a similar bundle back to the library. This was an arrangement considered not worth mentioning to the Postmaster General. It was through his interest in reading that he had met Marie, his petite and pretty dark haired wife who had administered the library as a voluntary duty while she was a teacher at the school which her son now attended. Although she had been born in Glasgow she was of Highland parentage and had no complaints about living the isolated life of a shepherd's wife.

The only other member of the household was Ian, the single shepherd. Ian was a stocky, broad shouldered, red haired, cheery extrovert who had reached the grand old age of twenty-two. He loved his dogs, his button key melodeon and girls, in that order and with a corresponding degree of intensity. He had come to the Glen on leaving school as a boy of fourteen. Young Davie had been ten months old, which meant that Ian was a big brother to him. In the eight years that they had worked together the two shepherds had never exchanged an angry word and it was Ian who taught Donald's son how to heat and shape a ram's horn so that it could be made into the head for a shepherd's crook, and how to lie on a river bank, taking care that his shadow did not fall on the water, and gently curve his fingers beneath a trout or salmon so that it could be flicked onto the bank.

Bedtime, not just for Davie, but for the whole family, was just after the nine o'clock news on the wireless. Visitors were almost unknown, so the only exceptions to this rule might be when because of mist, or rain swelling the river, it wasn't possible to start gathering sheep at daylight, which meant a late finish to the day's work.

CHAPTER II

The following morning Davie wakened with his mother's hand shaking his shoulder. 'Half past six, Davie,' she said. 'Time you were up. Your father and Ian went away to Strathbeg at four.'

As the boy had had to rise at this time since going to school just before his sixth birthday, the early hour was by no means unusual to him and by the time he came down the narrow wooden stairs and had washed his face quickly at the cold tap at the door, his mother had his breakfast on the table.

'Did Dad take Glen with him?' he asked. Glen was his young dog.

'Yes,' replied his mother. 'He left Gem for you. He said that you are not to go down to the shore yourself, but to stop at the Eagle's Rock and send Gem down. If she finds a ewe on its back she'll bark and wait with it, 'til you climb down. Ian was going to gather the north side of Strathbeg so he took an extra haversack with him and he was going to leave it at the Smoker's Knowe for you. There's a flask of tea, some sandwiches and a piece of cake in it.'

Davie knew the Smoker's Knowe to be a small hill at the far west of the ground that he would have to cover and that even if he found nothing to delay him it would take almost three hours to get there, so this was welcome news. Gem was a smooth haired collie with upright ears and was only six months younger than the boy. She was an animal of excessive intelligence and good nature and Marie knew that she had little cause to worry about her son even in the vastness of the hill, as long as Gem was with him. Davie had been following the men to the hill since he was old enough to toddle and often came back perched on the broad shoulder of one or the other. He had the inborn sense of the country boy.

Although a dry spring had helped to delay the growth of bracken, it still made it difficult for the boy to see in some places on the lower ground but after he had climbed higher the bracken gave way to heather. Every year in the spring, the older heather was burnt off in rotation to keep the plants from becoming coarse and in this way grazing was improved, both for sheep and grouse. It also meant that walking was easier and it was much easier to see.

Gem ranged at an easy trot, about fifty yards on either side of Davie.

Suddenly she stopped and uttered a sharp yelp. Davie hurried over to find a lamb looking with fear and suspicion at Gem. The dog was stand-

9

ing beside a ewe which was lying on its back in a small hollow, all four legs kicking feebly in the air. The fact that there was no dung behind it told the boy that the plight of the ewe was short lived and, all that was needed was to roll it on to its feet and hold on for a moment until balance was restored, and it was able to run off followed by a bleating lamb. Davie watched as the ewe stopped and the lamb dived beneath her to suckle.

A little over an hour later he stood at the highest point of the hill looking out over the sea which lay some 1,300 feet below. To the north, Islay and the Paps of Jura were plainly visible with a hazy outline to the west of them which was Colonsay. Ireland and Rathlin also lay to the west and as he watched there was a sudden boiling in the sea less than a mile from the shore. Aware of something unusual, Gem whined softly on a high note. A faint rumble was now audible to the ears of the boy and at the same time the conning tower of a submarine rose from the sea to be followed by the dark, cigar-shaped hull.

The vessel was close enough to the shore for Davie to be able to see a long U painted on the conning tower but he wasn't able to pick out the number which followed. No other ship was in sight and after a few moments men began to emerge on the deck to stretch in the sunshine. Davie was fascinated by the sight and couldn't understand why, when he told the story in the evening, his parents and Ian showed signs of anger.

'They're lurking out there all the time,' said Donald. 'If war does come, or rather *when* war does come, they'll pick off the merchant ships like flies.'

Only then did Davie realise that the submarine had been German and a potential enemy.

Most of Davie's summer holidays were spent helping his father and Ian, but whenever possible Marie allowed him to lie on in the morning.

'He'll be into full time work soon enough', she told Donald.

'Aye, ' agreed Ian, 'and after we've tied a knot in Hitler's tail I hope he goes into something more profitable than herding sheep.'

At the age of nine, however, and knowing nothing else, Davie thought that herding sheep was the best job on earth and his proudest moment of that summer came at the dipping gather at the beginning of August. Glenamoil Hill was, at that time of year, covered in parts by bracken which made gathering sheep difficult. For the first time Davie and his own dog, Glen, joined his father, Ian and a neighbouring shepherd on the gather, and, both of them being young and enthusiastic they acquitted themselves well.

All too soon the school holidays were over and the boy found himself trotting down the hill past the Bennetts' cottage to the school car. At school all the talk among the children was centred round the rumour that the Territorial Army were to be called up for active service and anybody who had either a father or a big brother in the 'Terriers' found himself something of a local hero.

Then came the Prime Minister's speech on that wet Sunday morning at the beginning of September.

'It is a sad day for us all, but for none is it sadder than for me,' said the voice of Neville Chamberlain. 'All that I have worked for, and all that I have prayed for, has crashed in ruins.'

As they sat round the table listening to the crackly voice from the radio Davie looked round the faces of the adults. His father was looking straight at his son. The hands of the big man were clasped in front of him on the table and the boy could see the white of the knuckles. Marie stared straight ahead. As Davie looked tears began to well from her eyes and roll down her cheeks to splash on the table. Donald saw the expression on the boy's face and turned towards his wife. Without speaking he covered both her hands with his own strong right hand. Marie could no longer choke back her sobs. Ian's eyes were bright and Davie thought that there was the hint of a smile on his face.

The end of the week brought the war to Glenamoil. As Davie came in sight of the house on his way home from school on the Friday evening he saw Ian coming off the hill from the direction of the shore, and he appeared to be carrying something in his arms.

When he saw the boy he laid his burden in the heather, and, after standing for a moment, walked on so that they met at the gate to the house. The front of his clothes were wet although it was a dry, early autumn day and there was an expression on his set white face which frightened Davie.

'What's wrong, Ian, what were you carrying?' he asked.

Ian put his arm round the boy's shoulders.

'It's a wee girl, Davie,' he said. 'A bonny wee fair haired lassie, not any older than yourself.' His voice broke in a sob.

'She was floating in the water and Roy swam out and drew her to where I could catch her.'

Davie knew that Ian, like many men who had been brought up close to the sea at that time, had never learned to swim.

'What happened, where did she come from?' asked the boy.

'The Germans torpedoed a ship that was taking children to Canada. She must have been on it. I only wish that I could get my hands on the bastard that gave the order.'

At that moment Marie came out, attracted by the voices. At the expression on Ian's normally cheerful face she gasped and her hand went to her mouth. David broke from Ian and ran to her.

'Donald's in the house, Ian, I'll send him out,' she said without waiting for an explanation and turned to lead her son inside.

After a few moments Donald came back into the house. 'We'll take her body up to Ian's room for tonight,' he told his wife, 'Ian can sleep in Davie's room. I'll go down the glen and phone the police and tell them that we'll take her down with the cart in the morning. They'll have to organise to meet us.'

'Has Ian any idea of who she is?' she asked.

'I don't think so. He's pretty upset. I've never seen him angry before.'

'Well, much as I dislike the idea, I'd better see if there's any identification on her clothes before you go to the phone.'

Donald ruffled his son's hair before going out and in a few moments the men could be heard taking the body up the narrow stair.

After a few minutes they came down to the kitchen. Marie filled whisky into two glasses and handed one to each of them.

'I'll go up now,' she said quietly.

When she came back down she was crying.

'My God, how could anyone kill a lovely wee girl like that?' she said. 'Her poor mother.'

'Did you find a name?' asked Donald.

'Yes, her first name was Kay. It's embroidered on the pocket of her blouse.'

For the next week Ian was quiet and withdrawn, then on the Friday evening he announced that he intended going to the town on the following day to volunteer for the armed forces.

'I know that I am in what's called a 'Reserved Occupation', he said 'but I could never live with myself if I didn't do something to help to shorten the career of the fellows who killed wee Kay.'

Davie waited up late on Saturday night, waiting for Ian to come back. He seemed to think that Ian would return dressed in uniform and was disappointed when this wasn't the case.

'What did you join?' he asked eagerly.

'The Royal Air Force.'

'Why?'

'Well, I've tramped hills all my life until now and could do with a change so that ruled out the Army. I've felt seasick just standing on the cliff looking out to the sea on a rough day so I didn't want to risk the Navy. That only left the Air Force as I didn't fancy being a spy.'

Donald and Marie laughed. The idea of the frank and honest Ian being a spy seemed ludicrous enough to be funny, despite the potential seriousness of the situation.

But Davie was persistent.

'When will you be going away? When will you be back?'

'Well, they told me that I would be going quite soon, but the coming back has still to be decided.'

'Bedtime, young man.' Marie terminated the interview.

While the thought of Ian going off to war had been exciting to Davie, the reality, when it came, was a sad occasion. On a clear autumn morning, Ian said goodbye to Donald and Marie and accompanied Davie down the glen to catch the school car in which he got a lift to the bus which would enable him to catch the bus to Glasgow.

Tears rolled down the boy's cheeks at the school gate as he watched the bus swallow up his hero and he took little comfort in having been given the important job of looking after Ian's dogs in their master's absence.

In mid January, there was a light fall of snow and as Davie was walking home he found footprints crossing the road less than a mile from the farm. He mentioned this at supper time.

'I wouldn't have expected anyone to have been out there today unless Strathbeg are still missing some tups,' said his father. 'Are you sure it was human footprints?'

'Oh, yes,' said Davie, 'I could see where they crossed the road going down towards the burn, then they turned off towards the shore, but there were no tracks of any dogs.'

'Well, nobody would go out looking for stray tups without a dog. The only other person I can think of is old Archie, the gamekeeper, but he usually calls for a cup of tea when he's this far up the glen.'

The following day was a Saturday and Davie wanted to take his own dog Glen and one of Ian's to the hill.

'All right,' agreed his father. 'You can follow the ridge out to the shore and if any sheep are over the top, send out a dog to turn them back into the glen, but if there's any sign of a snow shower head down to the bottom and follow the burn home.'

When the boy reached the top, the air was clear and frosty and he could see for miles around. As he stood, a double winged Swordfish from the nearby aerodrome flew over the north and the pilot waved from the cockpit. He carried on along the ridge sending out the dogs alternately to nudge back any sheep that were straying off their home ground. As he reached the peak above the sea it was Glen's turn. At a word of command the big black and white dog loped off to the right and gathered about a dozen ewes. A convoy of ships was passing through the North Channel towards the open sea and Davie watched them at the same time as he kept an eye on Glen's progress with the ewes. As the sheep were passing a large rock, they suddenly scattered. Instinctively, the dog swung to bunch them together again. As he himself came to the rock Davie heard him growl and a man rose from the heather with binoculars in his hand.

'Oh, I'm just out for a walk, I was watching the birds,' said the man packing the binoculars into a case. 'What are you doing here?'

'My dad's a shepherd and this is part of his hill. Ian, the other shepherd, has gone to the RAF and I help my Dad on a Saturday. Where do you live?'

The question was unexpected and the man seemed to hesitate before answering. 'Oh, I live in the town' was said with a vague gesture towards the north.

'Campbeltown?'

'Yes, that's right, Campbeltown.'

'That's a long way to walk.'

'Oh, I like walking.' The man took a few steps forward and again the dogs voiced a protest which made him stop.

'Aren't these brutes dangerous?' he asked angrily.

'Not really, they're working dogs, but they don't like strangers.'

'Keep them clear of me then.' There was a guttural harshness in the voice which puzzled Davie.

'They won't touch you, but anyway I'll have to get on. My parents get worried if I'm later on the hill than I should be. Goodbye.'

'Goodbye,' Echoed the man.

As Davie topped a rise about a hundred yards further on he glanced back to see the man still standing looking after him. Had Davie been able to hear and understand German he would have heard the man mutter to himself: 'What am I doing here? That boy is the same age as Karl and Freya. Why should I be trying to destroy him and his parents?'

Karl and Freya were his twin children. Not for the first time since embarking on the life of a spy, he found his mind returning to them and their pretty fair haired mother. It took little effort to recall the sound of their laughter in the foothills of Zugspitze in far off Bavaria.

'That explains the footprints in the snow,' said Donald when Davie told his story that evening.

'Shouldn't we report this to the police?' asked Marie.

'Yes, I think you're right. I'll go down the glen to the phone, but I doubt if he'll hang around now. It sounds as though he wouldn't have shown himself if Glen hadn't driven the sheep so close to where he was hidden.'

Early next morning two policemen arrived and Donald, with two of his dogs accompanied them to the shore at the far end of the hill. There, in one of the small sheltered caves at the foot of the cliffs, they found a rough bed of dry bracken and the cold ashes of a fire. Something white caught Donald's eye and he picked it up. It was a photograph of smiling children, a boy and a girl, both about ten years old, obviously twins.

The men came out to the mouth of the cave and stood looking out to sea. The dogs were clambering over the rocks between the caves and the water when suddenly one of them stopped and gave a low growl. Donald moved down and found a knitted woollen glove wedged in a crack in a rock just above the water mark.

'Well, we can forget about this lad,' said one of the policemen. 'After he saw young Davie he must have thought that it was time to go. We know that they have submarines lurking out there in the hope of picking off a straggler from a convoy and one of them probably picked him up. If he had still been here and offered resistance I'd have shot him, but anybody who carries a photograph of his kids even on a spying mission can't be all bad. In a way, I'm glad that he isn't here, so long as he doesn't come back.'

For Davie, the most exciting event of the late spring was Ian's first leave. He had been in Canada training to be a fighter pilot and was sporting his wings and pilot officer's insignia. Somehow he seemed much older than the carefree young man who had left the glen during the previous autumn. To his dogs, however, after an initial sniff he was no stranger and most of his leave was spent helping with the lambing on the hill.

'What's it really like?' asked Donald one evening as they were sitting round the supper table.

Ian was silent for a moment.

'Exciting at first. It was all so new. Then homesickness sets in. Going out to Canada we sailed from Liverpool. We passed out here just before mid-day and I actually saw you on the skyline above the shore. That was the worst time.' After another pause he went on. 'Thank God it was too far out for me to recognise which dogs were with you. If I had seen any of my own pair I think that I'd have tried to swim back. Swimming is one of the things they've taught me. Now I find it easy. It isn't only what the other fellow can do to you, but also the power you have to hurt him. It seems to be different for someone who is used to violence. There were two Czechs and a Pole in Canada with us. These fellows had seen so many horrible things that they would disembowel their grandmother with hardly a second thought.'

He glanced at Davie, and went on.

'We were a real mixed lot on that course. There were some from practically every Dominion and Colony. Many of the British lads were from fairly well-off families and had interrupted a university education to join up. Mostly they were a grand bunch with a great sense of humour, but there was one real nyaff. He seemed to have endless money but wasn't all that bright. He had a loud, three dimensional voice and spent a lot of his time making fun of some other accents. I was the only teuchter so I came in for my share, but he really went to town on the Czechs.'

'One night we were wakened by the sound of squealing from the ablutions which were at the end of the hut. We found this character lying naked on the floor with his hands tied together. He had obviously laid on the last straw and Prague pride had demanded appeasement. Not only had they tied him up but for good measure they had tied a string round his testicles, passed it over a beam and hung a one pound weight on the end of it. If we hadn't heard him he would have been singing soprano for the rest of his life. We were all really sick of him so nobody had all that much sympathy, but the point is that the Czechs didn't really care. They would have left him trussed up there for a week and never given it a thought. I've been trained now to kill people and I know that in the heat of battle I will do it, but for the rest of my life I will have to live the knowledge that I will have caused some child to be fatherless or some mother to lose her son.'

He looked at Marie for a moment.

'I've spent lot of time thinking about wee Kay,' he went on quietly. 'When I do that I find it easier to understand men like the two Czechs.'

On the day when Ian's leave ended Davie stood at the meadow gate and watched him disappear down the glen. As Ian had passed the kennels, one of his dogs had howled, a high keening note and Ian had spoken reassuringly to it. Now it started up again and with a lump in his throat Davie turned back to quieten it. At the side of the kennels there was a gate leading out to the hill. There David found his father. The big man was leaning on the gate, quietly drawing on his pipe. As his ten year old son drew alongside, he reached out an arm to encircle the boy's shoulders. Together they stood in silence looking up towards the hill where sheep grazed in the sunshine. Suddenly Davie realised that tears were cascading down his father's cheeks.

CHAPTER III

During the summer of 1940 the news seemed always to be getting worse and on many nights Davie was aware of the voices of his parents in earnest discussion after he was in bed. Ian's letters were scarce and short but as the Battle of Britain raged it was obvious that he was involved in it. At this time Davie, young as he was, became aware of strain between his normally happy parents. The late night discussion were becoming noisier and some of the days contained long silences.

On two occasions Davie had to miss school to help his father to gather the sheep, once to take off wedder lambs and once cast ewes as there were not enough good fields to hold sheep for any length of time.

One evening he arrived home to find Ian there. He was sitting at the kitchen table with his back to the door and turned round when he heard Davie behind him. But this was a different Ian. His eyes had a wild and starey look. His eyebrows and lashes had disappeared and his whole face looked red and sore. The boy stopped in shock; then Ian spoke.

'It's all right, Davie,' he said. 'I'll soon be as handsome as ever.'

'What happened?'

'My plane caught fire but I managed to parachute down.'

Davie became aware that both hands were bandaged.

'What caused the fire?'

'A German bullet, I'm afraid. Now don't you be worrying. I'll look different tomorrow after I've had a night's sleep and the good news is that I have twenty-eight days leave to look forward to.'

After a few days the angry colour faded from Ian's face and his eyebrows and eyelashes began to grow. He went to the hill with Donald for the ewe hogg gather and the day of normality on the open hill with his dogs seemed to have a calming effect on him. On the Saturday, Davie and Ian went to the hill to look for any hoggs that had been missed at the main gather. Apart from the sheer enjoyment of being on the hill with him, David was glad to go for two other reasons. The tension between Donald and Marie seemed to have increased since Ian's return and since previously, the one had never had a cross word for the other, the boy was mystified. He also wanted to show off Glen's prowess which Ian found impressive. At just under three years old the big strong collie was just coming to his peak. All he needed, and indeed wanted, was work.

'You'll have to watch him on the rocks,' Ian warned, 'a dog as fast and keen as Glen can easily run over a cliff and hurt himself badly.'

The man and the boy made their way out along the ridge of the hill and by the time they were above the cliffs, looking out to sea, they had turned half a dozen ewes and lambs well into the glen to be picked up on the way back. With the grey sea beneath them they sat in the shelter of a rock to eat the sandwiches which Marie had prepared while the dogs sprawled waiting for the crusts. Davie questioned Ian about his life in the Air Force and almost an hour passed before Ian, sensing a change in temperature, stood up suddenly to find that while they had been sitting, a mist had gathered behind them on the top of the hill and was now almost down to their level.

'We'll have to move, Davie,' he said. 'If this mist gets down much farther we'll lose the sheep we turned in and have to do it all again another day.'

Just then two ewes with three lambs appeared round a rock about fifty yards away. The leading ewe stopped in surprise for a moment then, with a snort, turned and charged back down towards the shore closely followed by the others. Davie turned to send out Glen but Ian stopped him.

'No Davie,' he said. 'No matter what Glen does that old ewe won't stop until she reaches the water and by the time we could get them back up here the mist will have closed in. Now that we know that the bunch are here I'll come back out on Monday and round them up.'

'Will you take Glen? I'll be in school.'

'All right. He'll maybe not work as well for me as he does for you, but I'll gladly take him.'

On the Monday morning, Davie was at the end of the meadow on his way down the road to school when he heard a noise behind him and turned to find Glen loping after him. Then Ian appeared round the corner from the kennels.

'He picked up your scent when I let him out.' Ian called. 'If you wait a minute I'll come down and slip a lead on him 'til you get away. Once he knows that he has to follow me he'll be all right.'

As Davie turned to close the meadow gate, Glen whined softly and wagged his tail, but in response to a gentle tug on the lead he followed Ian back towards the hill.

As Davie passed the kennels on this road to the house that evening, he saw that Glen wasn't there and assumed that he and Ian were still on the hill. When he went into the house, however, he found not only Ian but also his parents and immediately sensed something terribly wrong. Long into middle age Davie was to remember the tableau into which he had stepped then.

His father spoke first.

'It's Glen, Davie' he said. 'I'm afraid he's dead.'

'What happened?' he asked as his mother moved towards him. Ian took up the story.

'We were coming up from the shore with the sheep that we saw on Saturday. Suddenly the sheep broke back. Glen ran out to stop them, I whistled to him to sit, but it wasn't your whistle which he's used to. In the heat of the moment he ignored the command and went over the cliff. He was dead when I reached him.'

David swallowed the lump in his throat as his mother's arm came round his shoulders, then the practicality of the country boy took over.

'Has he been buried yet?'

'Yes.' It was his father who answered. 'Ian and I went back out. We carried him up and buried him beneath the rock where you took your sandwiches on Saturday.'

The boy clung to his mother for a moment then he nodded, turned and walked out the door. Ian started to follow but Donald stopped him.

'No, Ian,' he said 'leave him on his own for a wee while. The first thing that he needs is a good cry and for that he may choose his own company. Leave it for half an hour then take a walk down the burn side. I'll be surprised if he hasn't taken old Roy with him.'

And so it was that when some time later Ian casually walked down the water side he found a composed boy sitting on a rock with the big black collie resting its head on his knee while he threw some stones at a tree on the opposite bank. As the man sat down beside them the boy spoke with a wisdom beyond his years as the fingers of his left hand ruffled the ears of the dog.

'It's a bit silly, isn't it to be crying over a dog when you have to go away again so soon to fight and kill men?'

Ian felt a lump in his throat as he answered.

'Davie, even when you are an old man you will remember Glen and feel that you gained something from having known him. When the carcass of Hitler is thrown to the crows, the whole world will feel relief and shame that he belonged to the species of man. Now, young fellow, tea time.'

The time-old trio of man, boy and dog made their way back to the house.

When they got there they found Donald and Marie standing close together by a window looking onto the hill and during the meal Davie learned what had been disturbing his parents during the previous weeks. Donald was the first to break the silence.

'Are you coming to the sale with me on Thursday to help me to pick a few shearling tups?' he asked Ian.

Ian looked first to Marie then back to Donald.

'You're going to be here to put them to the hill then?' The statement was a question.

'Yes, Marie and I have talked it over.' Then to his son. 'Since the fall of France and then the Battle of Britain I've been wanting to join up. Your mother was dead against it partly because of my age. It took a lot of discussion, but in the end Glen's death has a lot to do with my decision to wait here.

'Glen died doing what he did best. The job I know best, as Ian told me when we were walking back home this afternoon, is herding sheep. Britain needs food and will need food after this war is won. Your mother and Ian both tell me that I will do most good here.'

As autumn receded into winter, Davie found himself leaving home for school in the morning before daylight had properly arrived and not arriving home until darkness had fallen. Nevertheless, he still made time to call on the Bennetts, the old couple at the mouth of the glen, and have his customary cake and glass of milk. One evening he found difficulty in finishing the cake which did not escape the notice of Mrs Bennett.

'Are you not feeling well, Davie?' she asked anxiously.

'Och, yes, just a wee bit hot. I ran from the car up to here, I'll be all right once I get outside.'

'Are you sure? You look a bit pale.'

'Yes I'm fine. I'd better get up the glen. Since I met that man on the hill Mum worries if I'm the least bit late, especially now that the darkness is down so early.'

He stooped to ruffle the hair between the ears of the old collie as he moved towards the door.

'See you tomorrow night. Cheerio.'

'I don't like the look of that boy tonight,' Mrs Bennett told her husband after Davie left.

The old man bent to light a stick from the fire.

'Och, woman, you're always looking for something to worry about. He's a growin' boy. He's probably been eating snashters at school.'

'Well, maybe.' She wasn't convinced. 'I just wish that he hadn't to go all the way up that glen on his own.'

Her fears would have been increased if she had been able to see Davie at that moment, being violently sick at the side of the track. The rest of the journey home was a nightmare. He was sick seven times and a pain which had started as merely a nagging ache low down on his right side became more intense to the point where he cried out aloud as he retched. About half a mile from the house he staggered into the arms of his father who had come to look for him. Before they reached home, even a supporting arm wasn't enough and for the last few yards Davie had to be carried in the arms of his father.

'I'll go for the doctor,' said Donald as he gently laid his son on the bed.

'No, wait a minute,' his wife commanded.

She placed her hand low down on the boy's abdomen and pressed gently. He yelped with pain. The parents' worried eyes met across the bed and she motioned towards the kitchen.

'I'm pretty sure it appendicitis,' she said when they were out of earshot of their son. 'I've seen it twice before; when I was teaching.'

'What are we to do?'

'We can't afford to wait until the doctor gets here. You yoke the horse, put some hay in the bottom of the cart and bring it round to the door. I'll strip and sponge Davie then dress him for the journey. We'll both take him down to the Bennetts, the ambulance will manage up to there. One of us will have to come back to feed the dogs and the cow in the morning.'

Mercifully, Davie seemed to sleep after he was laid, heavily wrapped in blankets, on the loose hay in the cart, but there was no such relief for his mother. Every stone and pot-hole sent an exaggerated jar through her body. Worry made her want to tell Donald to whip the horse into a trot, but common sense told her that the extra jolting might cause her son's inflamed appendix to burst and let the poisons flood into his already tortured body.

About a mile from the Bennetts' house, she called to her husband to stop. Davie's face was hot and clammy to the touch of their cold hands and he moaned gently with every breath. The three-quarter moon shining in the clear, frosty night enhanced the greyness of his skin.

'I think you had better hurry ahead and leave us,' she told her husband. 'Warn the Bennetts that we're coming and then go on to phone the doctor.

'Tell him,' for a moment her voice broke, then she steadied herself, 'tell him he'll have to hurry,' she finished.

Marie reached the Bennetts' to find the old couple at the door. As is the way with older country folk, they displayed neither panic nor excitement. The old man removed the door of the cart and, displaying a strength which belied his years, gathered the boy gently in his arms and carried him into the cottage. As he laid his burden on the bed his wife brought a basin of water and a soft cloth to wipe the sweat from Davie's face and hands. At the touch of the cool cloth he opened his eyes.

'Hullo, Mrs Bennett,' he said quite calmly, then, seeing his mother he reached out his hand which she took in both hers. 'I'll be all right, Mum. Don't worry.'

'Of course you will, Davie,' she told him with a confidence she was far from feeling. 'Your Dad's just gone for the doctor. He won't be long.'

'I'll attend to the horse,' said the old man and made towards the door.

Shortly afterwards, the doctor hurried into the house. He had been long enough in the district to have delivered Davie, with the assistance of Mrs Bennett. Less than five minutes completed his examination. He nodded to Mrs Bennett to remain with Davie, whose eyes were again closed, and gestured to the parents to follow him through to the kitchen. His face was solemn.

'It's his appendix and pretty ripe too, I'm afraid,' he said.

'What can you do? He'll have to go to Glasgow.' Marie moved close to her husband.

'Yes. Normally I would send for an Air Ambulance but these aren't normal times. There's no guarantee that I would get one before daylight and maybe not even then.'

'What can you do?' Marie asked again, this time with a catch in her voice.

'I won't try to disguise the fact that Davie's a very sick boy. Any delay is dangerous and I don't want to increase the risk. You may know that the local hotel has been commandeered as a naval hospital.'

Both parents nodded. 'Well,' he went on, 'the surgeon dropped in about a week ago to introduce himself and say hullo. He is a civilian who has joined up with rank of Surgeon Commander. I'd heard of him but never met him. He's good. With your permission, I'd like to ask him to operate on Davie in his hospital. I'm sure that he'll do it.'

'What's the alternative?' Donald's voice was quiet.

'There's none. Tomorrow will be too late.'

'How will we get Davie there? Did you send for the ambulance?' Marie asked.

'No, the regular driver has been called up and I thought the new man would take too long to find this place in the blackout. My own car's up near the door. If you wrap Davie in the blankets again we'll lay him on the back seat. It's only four miles. Hurry now.'

The doctor was closing his bag as the parents carried their son to the car. The old lady came into the room.

'Well, doctor?' There were tears running down her experienced cheeks as she asked the question.

'At the moment, sixty forty, the wrong way I'm afraid, but if this surgeon is as good as they tell me, we may win yet.' He squeezed her arm as he hurried out to his car.

'I'll pray,' she said simply and sincerely.

'I'm afraid that at this point it's more up to Him than to medical science.'

Fortunately, the doctor's reply was lost in the darkness of the night as he hurried to his car. He meant no irreverence, being wise in the ways of country folk, but he always found it disturbing to have to fight for a life which he had known from its beginning. At the car he found Donald and Mr Bennett standing quietly in the moonlight which was just strong enough to let him see that Marie knelt on the floor in the back beside her son.

'Try not to worry,' he said to Donald as he tossed his bag onto the other front seat. 'this surgeon is one of the very best. I'll get word back to you as soon as I can.'

'Now don't you bother about me,' Donald's voice was controlled. 'I'll go home now and attend to things; then come back down in time to catch the school car in the afternoon.'

'Right, I'll make sure that Marie gets some sleep.'

The two men watched the car disappear slowly down the bumpy road and speed up after it turned the road end. The old man placed his hand on Donald's arm.

'A dram and a bite to eat before your go,' he said and led the way back into the house.

The hotel had been given a coat of grey paint and looked ghostly in the moonlight. As the doctor's car stopped at the door a male sick-bay attendant hurried out.

'Commander Graham?' said the doctor without waste of words.

'Turned in, sir. Do you want me to call him?'

'Yes, and could you ask him to hurry please.'

'Will he need to operate, sir?'

'Yes.'

'Right, sir I'll alert the theatre as well.'

He disappeared inside and his raised voice was heard.

'Stretcher to the door, on the double.'

Within seconds two men appeared. One carried a canvas stretcher.

'Any fractures?' he asked the doctor.

'No, but he has acute appendicitis. Be as gentle as you can. It'll be a bit awkward getting him out to the stretcher.'

'All right, sir. Leave it to us.'

The other man looked at the car for a moment before opening the passenger door and bending inside. There was click and a sliding sound and the seat was deposited on the ground. A quick run round to the driver's side and that seat too came out. Like many professional men, the doctor's mechanical knowledge stopped at the fact that without petrol his car wouldn't go.

'My God, that's like a conjuring trick.'

'No' really, sur.' The accent was broad Glasgow. 'Ah wus a mechanic afore that wee nyaff, Hitler, got goin'. Ah huv varicose veins an' the wee bugger Ah goat oan ma medical widnae let me join up proper so here ah am. Ah'll tell ye this, but, if ah get near enough tae Hitler tae get him by the goolies ah'll alter his singing voice quicker than ah took oot thae seats!'

As he finished speaking he opened the back door and saw that what he had thought in the dim light was a man, was really a woman.

'Aw, Ah'm sorry hen,' his voice was really contrite. 'Ah juist never took the time tae look.'

In spite of her anxiety, Marie giggled.

'It's all right,' she said. 'The word is from the Hindi word 'goli' meaning ball or bullet.

'Och, Ah'm sorry onyway hen. Ah shouldne huv said it. Oot ye come an' we'll soon huv yer man fixed up.'

Just then a nurse came out with a torch and shone it inside the car.

'Och, it's yer wee laddie. Here Charlie, back-in yer kert.'

The stretcher was passed through the car so that the poles rested on the door frames, then the men reached in from either side and lifted the boy on to it.

'Right, Charlie, canny ahead. Shine yer licht in here so that ah can see whit tae trip over.' The last was said to the nurse.

The stretcher was lifted, Charlie followed instructions, and, without jolting the patient the other man crouched his way through the car and the procession passed into the foyer. Davie opened his eyes to the light.

'Where am I?' he asked.

'It's aw right, son ye've just joined the navy.'

'Well, I'm going to desert. I want to join the R.A.F.,' and he dropped into unconsciousness.

Marie made to follow the stretcher party, but the nurse with the torch stopped her with a hand on her arm.

'There's nothing more you can do for him just now,' her voice was soft and full of pity. 'Come through to the kitchen and we'll find a cup of tea.'

They brought their tea through to a small comfortable sitting room where a coal fire glowed. Like Marie the nurse had been a teacher, but had turned to nursing at the beginning of the war and the two found much common ground for conversation. It wasn't until the fire began to die down that Marie realised that almost two hours had gone past since their arrival at the hospital.

'I'm sorry,' she said in genuine apology, 'am I keeping you from your work?'

'No, not at all. I had just come off duty.'

'Shouldn't you be sleeping then? I'll be all right now.'

'All in good time. I don't work again until 1400.'

It took Marie a second or two to work this out to two o'clock in the afternoon.

'I'll make up this fire.'

The fire was burning brightly again when the doctor came into the room followed by a tall man of around Marie's own age. Both were in theatre green and Marie gasped. Their faces seemed grey and tired against the dark green gowns.

'This is Mr Graham, Marie,' the doctor introduced his companion. 'He has already operated on Davie and Davie is now in a side ward.'

'Is he going to be all right?'

'I would say so,' it was the surgeon who replied. 'He's a healthy young lad and that is very much in his favour.'

'Can I see him?' she saw his hesitation. 'Please?'

'All right, but he's still under anaesthetic and the next stage is deep sleep and the longer the better. It's all part of the healing process.'

'Will I take Marie through?' asked the nurse.

'Yes, then do you think you could find her a bed?'

'Easily. Nurse Galbraith who shares my room is on leave and won't be back for a few days yet. Marie can have her bed.'

'Good,' he turned towards Marie again. 'Try to get some sleep. I gather that Davie has had a healthy open air life. That will help him more than anything we can give him.'

'I know, and thank you very much.'

'Not at all, I've got one that age of my own.'

'I'll wait until you've seen Davie,' said the doctor as the surgeon left the room.

When she came back Marie had her lower lip firmly clenched between her teeth. 'He looks so small and vulnerable,' she sobbed.

'That's another thing in his favour.' The Doctor realised that tiredness was making his own voice gruff and went on more gently, 'If he was a big fat boy the operation would have been much more difficult.'

'Yes, I know,' suddenly she noticed how tired the doctor looked.

'How long is it since you were in bed?'

He smiled and glanced at a clock on the wall.

'About twenty-six hours. I was called out at midnight and delivered a baby boy in a tinker's tent at Pass Bye at five o'clock yesterday morning.'

The nurse was shocked.

'My God, will it survive in this cold?'

'Oh yes. Nowadays, we hear much about natural immunity. That baby has been born immune to everything except Foot and Mouth disease. The real danger in a lot of these cases is to the doctor. The parents are so grateful that they often name the child after him. That has already happened to me three times and every time I meet my namesake I am expected to dip into my pocket. It can be an expensive business.'

'Now girls,' he went on, 'get you to bed and I'm going to do the same. Marie, do you want something to help you to sleep?'

'No, I think I'll sleep without it. I feel exhausted and I know that Davie is getting the best of attention.'

'Right, I'll leave word that you're to be called if he wakes up before you do. I'll have a last look at him, get out of these clothes, and then go home. I'll call back after morning surgery.'

CHAPTER IV

Marie awoke with a hand shaking her shoulder and opened her eyes to see the nurse.

'What is it, Jean.' she asked, startled. 'Is it Davie?'

'Yes, he's awake and asking for you and Commander Graham has seen him. His temperature is down and he's going to be fine.'

'What time is it?'

'Just before twelve.'

'My goodness, I went to bed thinking that I wouldn't sleep and I've slept for seven hours.'

'Well, just take another ten minutes for a quick wash and freshen so that you are looking your best for Davie. I've left out clean underclothes of my own for you and I'll go and tell Davie you won't be long.'

Ten minutes later Jean returned to find Marie dressed and brushing her hair before the mirror. A good sleep had washed much of the worry of the night before from her features. When the two women went through they found Davie propped up with pillows to a half-sitting position. His face was very white but he smiled when he saw his mother. Marie placed a hand on each of his cheeks and bent to kiss him. Davie spoke before she had a chance to say anything.

'Hello, Mum. Did you know that Jock has a ferret?'

'A what?' Surprise raised the tone of her voice. 'And anyway who on earth is Jock?'

Jean laughed. 'The Glasgow SBA. He keeps it in a hutch down behind the engine room. We're always telling him that he'll land himself in trouble with the local farmers. He's always out after rabbits.'

'He promised to take me with him when I'm better. The ferret is called Benny and he's yellow with black spots. Jock says that he'll bring him in so that I can see him.'

'Uh huh, that remains to be seen as the pup said when he piddled behind the door. I'll have a word with Jock.' Unnoticed, the surgeon had stepped inside the door and heard what Davie said. 'Now then, young man, it's too soon for you to be getting excited.' He turned to Jean after looking at his patient for a moment. 'It's almost lunch time. Do you think you could rustle up a little custard and a glass of milk.' Then to Marie, 'When do you think your husband will be here?'

'Oh, late afternoon. Around five or so.'

27

'Good. Now then, Davie, after you've had your pudding, I want you to rest again. We must have more colour in your cheeks before your father comes.'

When Marie looked in again after her lunch, she found Davie sound asleep. His breathing was regular and there was indeed more colour in his cheeks. Jean was going on duty so Marie walked down from the hospital to the shore and walked along the sand in the winter sunshine. Here the weather was clear and frosty but on the east side of Ireland, away from the Gulf Stream, the hills had a thick covering of snow. Between, on the blue sea, a convoy of merchant ships, having survived the Atlantic crossing were lumbering south. As Marie watched, some of them veered to port toward the Clyde while the rest carried on towards the Mersey. She found her thoughts going towards the womenfolk, the mothers, wives and sweethearts of the ships' crews. So recently she had thought that she was going to lose her own, and, as the doctor had firmly told her he must be, her only son.

She thought of big, kindly Ian, whose father had died in the '14–'18 war and whose mother had then succumbed to a mixture of grief and flu, leaving him to be brought up by an aunt. Now this man, who had to steel himself to do some of the necessary jobs of a shepherd because they inflicted temporary pain on his sheep, had himself been trained to kill and maim men and thereby make other children orphans. With a sad smile to herself, she remembered 'Wee Bella', the aunt who had reared Ian. On the day when he had come to the Glen she had insisted on travelling up in the cart with his 'kist' to see him settled.

'Ye're little mair than a lassie yersel' but ye've been a school teacher so ye ken how tae rear weans,' she told Marie. 'Juist gie him a skelp on the lug when he needs it an' a pat on the heid when he disnae and he should-nae gae far wrong.'

Marie smiled. 'I'll send for you to do that.'

The wee fat woman with the ruddy face looked around to see that nobody else was within earshot. 'Ah, well, that's juist the snag. Ah'm no' gaun to be here much langer. Ah've goat gallopin' consumption. The doctor has a fancy name for it but ah ken that's whit it is.'

She saw a tear glisten in Marie's eye and placed her hand on the younger woman's arm. Marie saw that the hand was hacked and pitted like that of a man.

'Now dinna you be daft. Ah'll be mair comfortable up there than ever ah wis on this earth. It's juist a dampt nuisance havin' tae go saw soon. Ah wantit taw se' that boy tae University, he's clever enough an' ah've goat a shillin' or two pit by, but noo ah'll be content juist tae see him in a steady job. There'll aye be sheep on thae hills an' they'll aye need men tae look efter them.'

'Does Ian know all this?'

'Naw, an' dinna you be tellin' him. He's a saft big lump an' he'd want tae wait at hame tae look efter me, then when ah went he widnae ken where taw turn an' micht juist gae wrong.

'This wey he's got a job an' a good home an' he'll no miss me a' that much. The young soon forget an' get interested in other things. If it wisnae that wey the world wod hae sunk in bairns' tears lang ago wae so many wars an' ructions. An' there's gaun tae be another. Ah read the papers. Auld Hinderburg should hae drooned that wee Austrian pup when he was still fit.'

'Will you be all right?' Marie was concerned. 'Will you not come up here?' She hesitated. 'Nearer the time' she added. The older woman laughed.

'Ach, naw, lassie, it's bad enough travelling that kert when leeving an' Ah'd huv tae go back doon it when deid.' Then she became serious.

'It's kind o' ye tae offer, really it is an' it tells me that Ian has got a good hame. Ye've nawe idea the comfort that is tae me. But dinnae you be worrying, the summers comin' on an' ah'll no be here for the winter. If ah linger a wee bit the doctor kens tae get me intae hospital. Ah can afford it. Ah wis aye fearfu'. But ah'd rather go quick.' She looked upwards. 'Him an' me huva blether whiles. Ah juist hope He's been listening' but mind you, efter the day ah think He must hae been.'

On a clear summer's morning some two months later, Marie had been out with Davie who was just finding his legs. As they rounded the corner of the house she saw a man on horseback coming through the meadow gate and as he came nearer she recognised the doctor.

'Hello, folks,' he said as he dismounted. 'Is Ian about?'

'They're away for a gather and not back yet, but they should be in sight soon,' Marie replied. 'What's wrong? Is it Bella?'

'Yes, how did you guess?'

'She told me the day Ian came here, but asked me not to tell him. She also said to keep him busy so that he wouldn't see her ill. Is she dead?'

'Yes. She was always an early bird. This morning I was coming in from an early call when I noticed that her 'reek wisnae up' as she would have said herself and got suspicious. I found her dead in her bed. She must have died of an embolism in her sleep.'

Marie brushed away sudden tears with the back of her hand.

'Well. He must have been listening after all.'

'What's that?' the doctor asked.

'Oh, just something she said. Will Ian need to go down to make arrangements?'

The doctor smiled. 'She had left five letters propped up on the mantelpiece beside the clock, one for me, one for the minister, one for the undertaker, one addressed to the local hotel and a sealed one for Ian. I have it in my pocket.'

'Mine was just a letter of thanks, in case she didn't have time to say it at the end, and to tell me to send her bill to the lawyer. I couldn't help comparing Bella to the other call-out I had this morning. It was to an old bitch who was simply needing a good fart after too much gin, but her maid who phoned had explicit instructions that I must come at once. If I had been attending a case such as a confinement which I couldn't leave immediately she would have given me dog's abuse when I got there whereas old Bella would have risen from her deathbed to "gie me an extra pu' on the string" as she said.'

'I only met her once but she was a person I could never forget,' said Marie.

She looked back towards the hill. 'There's the first of the gather coming into sight. Put your horse in the stable then come into the house. I'll put the kettle on. The men will be in the fank in about twenty minutes.'

Donald came into the house first and stopped when he saw the doctor.

'I thought I heard a noise from the stable,' he said. 'What brings you up so early in the day?'

'It's Bella, she died in her sleep. Where's Ian?'

'Just gone to kennel the dogs. He won't be long. Poor Ian, that young dog Roy worked so well for him this morning that he was walking on air, but this will set him back.'

Just then Ian came in.

'Hello, Doctor,' he said, 'I saw the estate pony in the stable and guessed that it might be you. It's Aunt Bella, isn't it?'

'Yes, Ian, she died peacefully in her own bed. I found her this morning just after six.'

There was silence for a moment. 'Yes, I knew that she was ill. I overheard you and her talking.' His voice faltered for a moment then he brought his head up. 'I just didn't quite know what to do but then I thought that either you or the minister would come for me when I was needed. She hated to be fussed over.'

The doctor drew an envelope from his pocket and held it out.

'This was on the mantelpiece. It's addressed to you.'

The boy took the envelope, turned without a word and went out into the sunshine. Marie served food to the two men and they ate in silence.

30

After a time she rose and handed Davie to his father.

'I'll go out now,' she said.

She found Ian sitting on a clipping stool beside the stable wall. His head was back in the sunshine and tears streamed down his cheeks and splashed on to his shirt front. Marie sat down beside him and put her arm round his shoulders. For a moment he drew away, but then turned and dropped his head on to her shoulder.

'I'm sorry,' he said with a sob, 'I thought I was too old for this.'

'Ian,' she said, 'there are two things that we never outgrow, one is laughter and the other is tears.'

He lifted his head and looked at her for a moment. 'It's not that I'm sad. Really, I'm not. She was a good woman and she's happy now. It's just that she did so much for me, she was the only parent that ever I knew and now I'll not be able to pay her back.'

Marie had let the silence lie for a moment before speaking. 'Well, Ian, the length of time we are given in this world is not for us to decide. Bella was tremendously proud of you and in that pride she found great pleasure. There are many parents who would give a lot to have a son like you. By being as you are you paid Bella back in greater measure than you'll ever know.'

Marie was brought back to the present with a sensation of cold. With a start she realised that the sun was becoming lost behind the hill and that she had wandered quite a long way from the hospital. She did not know the exact time but knew that it wouldn't be long until Donald would be there, so she turned back. The school car had a circuitous route and she wasn't sure which road would bring it to the village. She was still almost a mile short of the hospital road-end when the car drew alongside her and a tired-looking Donald leapt out. Seeing her smile and the glow of the cold on his wife's cheeks almost made him weep with relief.

'Is he all right, has he had the operation?' he asked anxiously.

'Yes and yes.' said Marie catching his outstretched hands. 'He was sleeping peacefully when I left.'

'Thank God. I hope I'll never have to put in another night and day like that, as long as I live.'

The driver of the car leaned across and poked his head out of the open door. Seeing the smiles on both of their faces brought out his own smile.

'Good,' he said, 'I'll soon have my war correspondent back.'

Marie laughed. 'Not for a wee while, Willie, but I would think that he'll have a few first hand stories for you when he does return.'

'I'll look forward to that. Do you want a lift?'

Donald looked at Marie for a reply.

31

'No thanks, Willie, I think we'll walk. The longer Davie sleeps the better and it's a lovely evening.'

'Fine. I have to take the minister round to the estate for eight o'clock this evening for a christening. Is a lift back of use to you?'

Again Donald looked at his wife.

'So long as you are fit for the rest of the journey that would be a good idea,' she said. 'Davie is out of danger now but I'd like to wait for another couple of days or so just to keep him company.'

'Right, Willie, I'll be at the hospital road-end at twenty to eight.'

'Remember me to Davie,' called the driver as he moved off.

Walking back in the early evening dusk, Marie told her husband about Commander Graham and Jean and about Jock's embarrassment on realising that it had been a woman in the back of the car. As they entered the foyer the surgeon came from the direction of the wards and seeing Marie with her husband he headed towards them.

'Hello, nobody needs to tell me that you are Davie's father' was the greeting as they shook hands.

'Yes, although I didn't think it was so obvious,' laughed Donald. 'I don't talk so much for a start.'

'Well, I've just come from your son so I could agree with that.'

'How is he?'

'A wee bit sore, but much less than I expected. He's a tough citizen. I'll give him something later on to make sure he sleeps tonight and by tomorrow the pain should be almost away provided he doesn't cough or laugh.'

'I really don't know how we can repay you,' began Donald, but the surgeon cut him short.

'You're not even going to try,' he said. 'I'm quite sure that you don't leave a sheep to suffer if you can help it. Besides it had a nice feeling of normality for me to do something that wasn't complicated by bullets or burns. Now, if you'd like to go and see Davie and then meet me back here in, say,' he glanced at his watch, 'about twenty minutes, I'd be pleased if you and Marie would join me to eat.'

Like many folk of his era and area, Donald had never been inside a hospital and didn't quite know what to expect. They had to pass through a ward of male patients first. Several of the beds had cages over leg wounds and one man, who was sitting up in bed reading, had lost part of his right arm.

'Hello, Dad,' was Davie's greeting when they reached his side ward. 'Did Mum tell you about Benny?'

Donald laughed with relief and felt tears spring to his eyes. 'Yes, she did, but don't you get any ideas, young man. We have enough of a menagerie already, without adding a ferret.'

'Are you staying here tonight with Mum?'

'No, I'd better go home but your Mum will stay. Willie is giving me a lift back later on. He sends his regards and says that the school car is very quiet without you.'

The same question was put by the surgeon over their meal.

'We can easily find you a bed if you want to wait,' he added.

'It's kind of you but I'd better get back,' Donald told him. 'Apart from the stock, I promised the Bennetts, the old couple at the end of the road, that I'd get word back to them before their bedtime. I don't think that they went to bed at all last night.'

'Well, you know best yourself.'

'How long do you think that Marie should wait?'

'Clinically, Davie is out of danger, but the better he settles the quicker he'll recover. After another couple of days he should be used to us. He's quite an extrovert boy and that helps.'

Suddenly he laughed. 'I have nightmares about Jock and that damned ferret of his getting into the wards, but the tales that he tells of their various adventures do as much good for the patients as I do with a scalpel. Like most of his kind he is a tremendously kindly wee man and Davie seems to have taken a shine to him which can only be a good thing.'

By the time Donald was ready to leave, Davie's eyes were heavy with sleep.

'That will be him for the night,' said the surgeon. 'He's only had a mild sedative, but it should be enough to dull the pull of the stitches if he moves in his sleep.'

'Thanks again for everything,' said Donald as he and the surgeon shook hands.

'I'll come down again the day after tomorrow and, all being well, Marie can come back with me then.'

Marie clung to her husband as they waited at the gate.

'Oh, Donald, I was so frightened,' she said. 'I know that the surgeon is brilliant but it was Jean and wee Jock who did most for my morale. They seemed so calm that I felt nothing could possibly go wrong.'

CHAPTER V

On Donald's next visit he found almost as much change in the appearance of his wife as in that of his son.

'Gosh, you look as though you've been on holiday for a month,' he told her as they met at the hospital door.

She laughed, 'Jean and I have been for a long walk each morning when she is off duty. Then in the afternoon when Davie is asleep I do the same again. The weather has been so lovely.' She went on more seriously. 'Donald do you realise that we have never been away from the Glen together, even for a single night, since our honeymoon?'

Having been reared in the hills, this was the only way of life that Donald had ever known but, not for the first time, he realised the sacrifice that Marie had made even though she made light of it and seldom, if indeed ever before had he heard her complain.

'Yes, we'll have to do something about that,' he replied, going on to ask about their son.

'He's fine, really he is and he's in the main ward now so he has plenty of company.' She squeezed his arm and went on with a twinkle. 'Are you going to take me home with you tonight?'

He laughed, 'Davie must be better if your thoughts are turning that way!'

'Jock has been great,' Marie told her husband as they walked towards the ward. 'Davie just won't miss me when I go home. This afternoon they had him up to sit in a chair for the first time. He was complaining that his stitches were hurting. 'Ma, Goad,' says Jock, 'if Ah hud kent that ye wur gaun tae mak a' this noise aboot a few steeks Ah wud huv goat Big Montrose tae put a zip in ye.'

Donald laughed at her Glasgow accent.

'Who on earth is Big Montrose?' he asked.

'The surgeon. His real name is Angus Graham but Montrose is Jock's nickname for him. They're great friends really. Angus is often called in by the local doctors to give a second opinion so he has his own car here. Jock was a mechanic before the war so he does any repairs that are needed and keeps it polished.'

David was sitting up in bed talking to the man next to him when they rounded the door of the ward. 'Hi, Dad. This is Jim. He comes from Liverpool,' he said by way of introduction.

Donald saw that his was the man whom he had seen on his previous visit and whose right arm ended just below the elbow.

'Hello, Jim,' he said stretching out his left hand. 'I hope this boy isn't disturbing the peace too much.'

'Not at all, Mr Sinclair. It's nice to have some young company for a change.'

'I must be getting old,' thought Donald as he moved round to Davie's bed. 'Jim looks little more than a boy himself.'

Davie's natural colour had come back and the flush of fever had disappeared from his cheeks.

'Is Mum going home tonight?' he asked the question of them both, but it was Marie who answered.

'Yes, I think so. You don't need me here now, do you?'

'Oh no, I'll be fine. Jock says he'll take me down to see Benny some day soon.' His voice became slightly petulant. 'Big Montrose says he can't take Benny into the ward.'

'Davie,' Marie was shocked. 'You're not to call Commander Graham "Big Montrose".'

'Why not?' said the voice of the surgeon behind her. 'It's more complimentary than some of the names I overhear occasionally.' Then to Davie: 'I hear you were out of bed for a wee while today. How do you feel now?'

'All right, but I can't walk straight.'

The surgeon laughed at the indignant tone.

'Well, I didn't put a tuck in your belly.' Then he was serious. 'Don't worry about it, Davie, that's just the pull of the stitches. They have to be firm so that your wound will heal properly. We'll take them out in about a week, or less, and then you'll be as straight as a Guardsman.'

'Actually I should now let Davie go to the local hospital,' he told Donald and Marie over their meal, 'but so long as you are agreeable I'd like to keep him here. He and Jock have struck up a friendship which means that he has settled well, but apart from that his presence in the ward is doing a lot of good. A lot, far too many, in fact, of our patients are hardly out of their teens. Davie is a stuffy wee lad and hasn't shed a tear. This means that the other lads don't want to lose face and tend to make a better job of keeping the stiff upper lip.

'Don't get me wrong. I'm not being hard. Some of their wounds are quite horrific, but attitude and determination do play a tremendous part in recovery.'

He stopped for a moment then looked from one to the other.

'I'm sorry, this is a bit of a hobby horse of mine. I often think that wee

Jock's humour does more good here than my scalpel. Anyway, the gist of all that is – please can we keep your son here until he is fit to go home?'

The parents looked at one another in some bewilderment and Marie answered.

'Honestly, Angus, if you hadn't brought it up we wouldn't have dreamt of having him moved.' Her voice broke suddenly and she dissolved into floods of tears. After a few moments she regained some of her composure and raised a tear-streaked face to look at the surgeon.

'I'm sorry,' she said. 'It's just that I can't help thinking of what would have happened if you and your hospital hadn't been here.'

'Well we were, and I wouldn't dwell on the alternative. How are you two getting home tonight? Don't tell me you're going to walk all the way? I know there's a full moon but that's carrying romance a bit far.'

Donald laughed. 'Willie's coming to our rescue yet again,' he answered. 'He says that he has to go round our way anyway, but to be honest I don't know why. He said to be at the road-end just after nine.'

Davie took their departure so cheerfully that Marie was slightly disappointed.

'I feel as though my baby has grown up and left me,' she told the Bennetts when they called there on the road home. 'He was more interested in something Jock was telling him than in the fact that we were leaving.'

'Well, it certainly made it easier than it would have been if he had cried for you to stay,' said the old lady. 'It's a good thing that children nowadays get the chance to leave home and spread their wings. Old Hugh, who was in the Glen before you, never slept a single night out of that house from the day that he was born until he died.'

On the Saturday of that week, Marie was helping Donald to bring some sheep in to the fank when they say a man on horseback coming up the road. As he approached they saw that it was one of the estate farmworkers.

'This is the laird's own pony,' he told them. 'The second ploughman has gone to the army. I'm taking over his job and the laird is taking mine himself, so he hasn't the time to exercise him properly. My orders are to leave the pony with you to use while Davie is in hospital and for as long as you want afterwards. The first day the cart is over you can pick up more feeding.'

'Oh, that's great,' said Marie. 'I haven't been on horseback for years and don't fancy going up and down that road bareback on old Tommy the Clydesdale.'

On the Monday, Marie took advantage of a clear, crisp winter's day to ride down the glen for a visit to the hospital. The pony was enthusiastic and clearly enjoying himself but because of the roughness of the road and patches of ice there were few places where she could allow him the luxury of even a trot far less a canter, but after a cup of tea at the Bennetts' she kept him to the softer side of the better road and let him have his head for a time. Going up the road to the hospital she saw Davie waving at a window and waved back. After tieing the pony she entered the foyer to be met by Jean.

'We have two patients for you to visit today,' Jean told her.

'Oh,' Marie was surprised, 'who is the other one?'

'You'll see in a minute,' she was told with a smile.

When she entered the ward she found Davie sitting on the bed of another patient whom she recognised on getting closer.

'Jock, what happened to you?' she asked.

'Aw, hullaw, hen,' he glanced at Jean, then spoke to Marie again. 'D'ye mean tae sae she hasnae tellt ye?'

'Oh no, Jock, ' said Jean 'You tell it much better.'

Marie noticed that both Jean and Davie seemed to be suppressing laughter as Jock started his story.

'D'ye ken auld Erchie, the gamekeeper?' he asked first.

'Yes.'

'Well, Benny an' me wis oot for rabbits when ah saw the auld deevil comin' roon a knowe. He didnae see me an' ah hid Benny's box in a bunch o' whins so ah juist shoved Benny in ma trouser pocket an' hid ahint a rock. That wis fine, but when he got nearer ah hud ta crooch doon an' that wis when it happened.'

'What happened?'

'Well, when ah crooched doon ah must hawe squeezed Benny an' he got a fright. The wee bugger bit me.'

'Where?' The question was out before Marie could stop it.

'Well, ah could say 'ahint the rock', but ah ken that's no whit ye mean. Whit ah wull tell ye is that ther's some bits o' masel that no keen tae lose an' Benny bit wan o' them.'

'Oh, Jock, I'm sorry. I really am. That must have been very painful.'

'Well, aye, it was a bit sore, but the real pain wis havin' tae come back here an' tell Big Montrose whit heppened. He said tha he didnae ken whether tae gie the anti tetanus jag tae me or Benny.'

Marie was glad of the joke so that she could join Jean in laughter.

'Will you be laid up for long?' she asked presently.

'Ach, naw hen, ah'll be back workin' in the morn, but ah'll go tae the kirk on Sunday juist tae mak sure that ah still sing bass. Onyway, gled it heppened here an' no in Glesca. Ah'd never huv lived it doon there. Besides,' he went on, 'if ah've tae be stuck the gither wae catgut ah'd sooner it wis done by Big Montrose than some o' the butchers ah've kent. Och, aye, it could that. Ah could huv smothered poor, wee Benny when ah crooched doon.'

Ten days later Davie got out of hospital. His first night was spent at the Bennetts and then on the following day, his parents picked him up with the cart, well cushioned with hay, for the journey up the glen.

'We're really sorry to see him go,' the surgeon told Marie, 'but after a month's rest he should be fit for anything. Youth is a fine thing to have.'

'Ah'll be up in the spring time tae see the eagles' nest. Ah've never seen wan,' Jock said as they were leaving the hospital.

'Okay and bring Benny,' said Davie. 'There's lots of rabbits at the Glen.'

CHAPTER VI

By the early spring Davie was completely back to normal. Part of Donald's wages was the income from the annual cull of rabbits, something which was necessary for two reasons. Rabbits stole grazing from sheep and tended to stick to the better and sunnier areas. In that part of the country they had few natural predators so they had to be controlled. In this, the Sinclairs had new-found allies in Jock and Benny. Jock was able to borrow a bicycle and most of his time off was spent at the Glen where he could pursue his hobby without fear of old Archie, the gamekeeper. Despite his veneer of coarseness, Jock was a clever and entertaining man and the whole family enjoyed his company and his stories of Glasgow during the long years of the Depression.

'My Auld Man was a riveter in the shipyaird,' he told them. 'Ma Mither cleaned offices. Then cam the strike an' the Depression an' the Auld Man wis laid off. Ye ken, there's naethin worse for a man than tae want tae work, be fit tae work, an' no' be able tae find work. It killed the Auld Man in the end. He widnae gae oot, juist sat lookin' oot the windae. He died o' consumption six years ago. God kens, the shipyaird could dae wi' him noo, but he's no' there an' many mair like him.'

'Is your mother still alive?' asked Marie.

'Oh, aye she's toug, the Auld Yin. She's got a job as a cleaner in a hoaspital noo an' she enjoys that.'

'Were you always a mechanic?' asked Davie.

'Aye, ah wis lucky. Ah got a job in a garage when ah left the school. The Auld Wife wanted me tae stey at the school an' go tae university. It disappointed her when ah' didnae, but there wis nae wey we could afford the money for that. She wanted me tae be a doctor so ah telt her that ah'd dae doctors' cars instead.'

'When did you get Benny?' This question also came from Davie.

'Oh, he's juist a boy like yersel.' Jock laughed. 'Ah, had his granny first. When the Auld Man wis ill ah got her. Money wis scarce an' ah used tae go oot at the weekends an' catch a couple o' pairs o' rabbits. Ah never took mair than a couple o' pairs because that wis aw we could keep fresh, but it made an awfy difference tae how we ate.' He went on after a moment's silence. 'Noo ah bring in four pairs a week tae the hospital an' the cook maks a stew. It's funny when ye think aboot it. Ah started catchin' rabbits because o' poverty. A lot o' the patients are fae well off folks, but efter a wound or an operation, the rabbits are the first thing that'll tempt them tae eat.' He laughed suddenly. 'Big Montrose says that if he gets struck off the Medical Register for allowin' me tae catch them ah'll huv tae train him as a poacher.'

Ian arrived on leave just after Easter and spent a week helping Donald with the lambing.

'I'm going to change to Bomber Command,' he told them. 'I've had a good run in fighters and think I'd like a change. Bomber Command is crying out for pilots so I think this is time.'

'How much longer is this dreadful war going to go on?' asked Marie.

'A while yet, a good long while, I'm afraid. That's one of the reasons why I want to get into bombers. If we can knock out Hitler's factories it would go a long way towards bringing him to his knees.'

'I suppose you're right, but it seems so savage to drop bombs on people.'

'Well, wee Kay changed my attitude to that. There must be innocent folk in Germany, no doubt about it, but anybody who would do what the commander of that submarine did, doesn't deserve any form of mercy. I've shot down German planes so I know that I've killed men, but if the world is going to be safe for children like Kay, than I have to do it.'

On a Saturday towards the end of June Jock arrived up to find Davie in rebellion.

'He has brought home his form for entry to the Grammar School,' Marie explained. 'His father and me want him to take a professional course, but he doesn't agree.'

'Explain this tae me afore ah meet him,' Jock pleaded.

'Well, we feel that if he takes the professional course, which includes languages, he has a wider choice of what he wants to do in later life. If, when he is older he decides that he wants to herd sheep or take a trade then he will be doing so from choice and not from necessity. We feel that the other course would narrow his field before he is old enough to decide what he really wants to do. This is all the world he has known up till now.'

Jock was silent in thought for a time 'Aye, that sounds like a sensible argument,' he said. 'Ah'm never in favour o' forcin' anybody tae dae onything but it seems like wee Davie is in danger o' puttin' himsel' in a poseetion where in later years he'll find that he has forced himsel'. Ah'll let him hae a blether wi' me.'

When Jock reached the fank he found Donald clipping the last of a batch of hoggs and Davie rolling fleeces.

'Is that a job weel done?' he asked as Donald loosened the strap which tied the sheep's legs to prevent it from kicking, and let it jump off the stool.

'Not quite,' said Donald. 'There's still three hoggs on the north side just over the top. They must have been outside the March at the gather and somebody has knocked them back. I saw them the other day, but lost them in the mist.'

'Can I go for them now, Dad?' Davie was eager. 'It's clear enough today and Jock can come with me.'

Donald looked at Jock who nodded slightly.

'Alright,' he said. 'Take Gyp and old Roy. Gyp will bring them to you and old Roy will make sure that they won't get away this time.'

'Oh, great. I'll go and get Mum to make up a haversack with a flask in case we take a while to find them.' and the boy ran off towards the house.

'I hope you hadn't any other plans,' Donald said ruefully to Jock.

'Och, now, certainly nane better, an' it's a gran' day for a picnic.'

As man and boy climbed out to the hill it was indeed an idyllic day. There was hardly a cloud to mar the blue of the sky and soon they were both sweating in the heat. The dogs, also enjoying the day, snuffling and smelling, ranged in an arc to either side. Suddenly, Roy stopped, ears forward in pointing position.

'He's spotted somethin', Davie,' said Jock. 'We'd better take a look.'

Cautiously they approached the quivering dog but for a time couldn't see anything. 'Don't move yer feet, Davie,' said Jock quietly. 'Juist look wee bit tae yer right.'

'Where?' Davie's voice was equally soft.

'In the heather, juist aboot a yerd oot, atween you and Roy.'

Davie looked more closely and saw a grouse chick looking back at him.

'There must be more. I doubt if that's the only one.'

'Weel, just stay quiet for a meenit. We don't want tae staun on wan.'

After a minute Davie pointed. 'Look,' he said. 'At the edge of that clump of heather just in front of us.'

'Ma Goad, there's camouflage for ye.' Less than six feet from them an adult grouse crouched with five other beady-eyed chicks beside her. 'We'd better slip awa,' said Jock. 'We're terrifying the poor wee bird bae bein' here. Juist watch yer step.' They moved back a few yards and Davie said quietly 'That'll do, Roy,' and the old dog turned to follow them.

When they reached the top, the panorama of the Inner Hebrides, Rathlin, Ireland and the Wigtownshire coast was there for a mere turning of the head. The village could be seen over the tops of the hills and about a mile from it, the hospital, where Jock worked and Davie had disposed of his erring appendix, was just discernible. As they moved along the ridge, Jock pointed towards three sheep which were grazing just off the top.

'Is that no' whit we're looking for?' he asked.

Davie laughed. 'Good for you, Jock,' he said. 'How did you know that they were hoggs?'

'Weel allowing that we were lookin' for that number o' sheep it hardly took a genius. Besides, that's the only sheep ah can see that hauvna goat lambs. Ur we gaun tae tak wir piece afore we disturb them.'

'Well, I suppose Mum told you,' Davie broached the subject when they were seated on a rock.

'Ay,' the reply was non-committal.

'And what do you think, Jock?'

'Me?' Jock took a bite out of a sandwich. 'Ah think that we're a daft wee laddie.'

'Oh.' Davie was clearly taken aback. 'Why?' he asked.

'Weel, it's a simple metter o' lettin' yersel' be either a volunteer or a conscript.'

'What do you mean, Jock?'

'Juist whit ah say if ye'd gie me the time tae explain. Juist noo a' ye want tae dae is come hame tae they hills an' be a shepherd.'

'Yes.'

'Fine, an' there's naethin' wrang wi that. But that's juist noo when this is the only life ye ken. Try tae think forrat a couple o' score years or so. Will there still be sheep on thae hills far less shepherds tae look efter them?'

'Of course there will.' The boy was indignant.

'Well, ye may be right, but ah hae ma doots. This war is gaun tae change a lot o' things an' no least will be the attitude o' weemen tae whit they'll thole. The days are juist aboot bye when a wumman wull be gemme tae walk, three miles up a rough track tae get tae her hoose like yer mother does.'

'But women don't herd sheep.'

'No' as a rule,' Jock admitted, 'although they tell me there's some as dae. But if the weemen want oot o' the hills the men'll follow.'

He was quiet for a moment then went on. 'They tell me that auld Hugh McNeill who wis herding the Glen before yer faither never slept a night onywhere else till he died. They tell me tae that he wis a happy man. Weel they might be right, bit tae me he soonds a bit like the dug that got fleas off his mither when he was a pup an' never got rid o' them. He was only happy because he didnae ken ony better. This war has done somethin' that nae ither war has done in that it has taken young men an' weemen oot the hills in a time o' change. When they come back they'll want watter closets an' electric light and an odd nicht oot tae the pictures if they feel like it. If they bide at the back o' beyond they havena' a choice. Noo, Davie, if ye pick the wrang course, yell huv robbed yersel o' a choice. If ye tak the technical course ye can be a tradesman be it shepherd or slater, electrician or engineer, but that's as far as ye'll get. If ye tak the other course ye can be professional or artisan, whitever ye decide the choice'll be yours when ye want tae mak it.'

Davie was quiet for a long time and when Jock looked he caught him wiping away a tear.

'You know, Jock,' he said, 'if my parents had explained it like that I wouldn't have argued. I'm sorry.'

'Ach, weel, maybe ye didnae gie them ower much o' a chance. Onyway, there's nae that much herm been done that canna be sortit. Mebbe in five years time we can come oot tae this rock again an' hear whit ye've decided. Noo, we'd better gether thae sheep or yer faither'll be oot here tae look fur us.'

When Jock left for the hospital that evening, Davie escorted him for about the first mile of his journey and surprised the wee Glasgow man by formally shaking his hand as they parted.

'Thanks, Jock,' he said simply, 'I might have made a big mistake.'

'Well, Davie,' came the reply, 'there's some can work better wi' their hauns than their heid an' there's some can work better wi' their heid than their hauns. Fae whit ah've seen o' you ah think you might belang the category lake Big Montrose. They're no sae plentiful, folk that can work weel in baith heid an' hauns, an' ah feel it wid be a shame if ye didnae gie yersel a chance tae fin' oot.'

The change from a class of nine and a total school roll of sixty two, to a class of thirty four and a total school roll of five hundred and forty was strong and a bit frightening to Davie. None of the boys from his primary school had followed him into the professional course and the only familiar face belonged to a girl whose mother had returned to the village to live with her parents after her husband had been killed at Dunkirk. The girl was very brainy but the death of her father had left her quiet and introverted and the gregarious Davie was rather in awe of her. Nevertheless, he soon settled in and rather to his surprise, found that he was enjoying the new area of learning that was opening up before him. After having had the same teacher for every subject in primary school, he found that having a change of teacher sometimes half a dozen times a day meant that the time passed much faster.

To the delight of them both, Ian's next leave coincided with the school

Christmas break and the two spent several happy days on the hill towards the end of tupping time. On the day Ian's leave ended, Jock arrived just as he was leaving, dressed in his uniform.

'When did ye get yer D.F.C.?' Jock asked on seeing the ribbon on his chest.

'Och, about a month ago,' The reply was careless and off-hand.

'What's this?' said Marie who had come on the scene. 'You always change out of you're uniform so quickly that I never even noticed. Why didn't you tell us?'

Ian put his arm round her shoulders.

'Marie,' he said solemnly, 'I happen to be in the armed forces, so I get a medal. Every time I pass through London, and it must be the same in dozens of other cities, I see folk going about their business despite all that Goering can throw at them. Believe me, they are the real heroes – they cannot hit back. I can. Anyway,' he finished, 'I'd gladly give them back the medal in exchange for a month at home during lambing time.' Abruptly he turned and his uniformed figure disappeared out the door. Jock raised his eyebrows at the abrupt exit, but Marie reassured him.

'It's always the same,' she said.

'The day before he has to go away he walks out to the north side of the hill above the shore, then when it's time to go, he just disappears without saying goodbye.'

'Ah, weel,' said Jock, 'ah canna say that ah blame him. If it wisnae for the Auld Wife ah winna even go back tae Glesca noo efter bein' here, far less tae go where Ian has tae go.'

'Oh, how I wish it was all over. It all seems so horrible. Every time I hear an announcer say on the wireless "some of our aircraft failed to return" I think of Ian. What a mother must feel as she puts her children to bed in a place where they have frequent bombing must be really terrible, especially if her husband is in the forces as well.'

One evening, towards the end of June, Jock arrived at the Glen shortly after Davie came home from school. Donald had been working at the fank all day so everyone was already in the house. The wee man looked as if he had been hurrying and had a general air of excitement.

'It's Ian,' he said without preamble. 'He came into the hospital as a patient this mornin'.'

'What's wrong?' gasped Marie, her face pale.

'Noo dinna be worryin'. He's bye the worst. They were comin' back fae a raid an' met a couple o' German fighters over the Dutch coast. There wis a bit o' stoor an' they shot doon wan an' damaged the ither an' got away but Ian got a bullet in the right knee an' a skelf oot o' the heel o'

44

his left fit. Ah hud a word wi' big Montrose afore ah left. He says the fit is nae worry but he disnae think that the knee will ever bend again.'

Everyone was silent for a moment, then Donald spoke. 'Well, that's bad,' he said, 'but thank God it's not worse.'

'How's he taking it? Is he in much pain?' asked Marie.

'Ay, a bit,' Jock admitted, then went on with the wisdom of experience. 'The pain should settle in a few days. The move will hae stirred things a bit. Hoo's he takin' it?' he was quiet for a moment. 'Ye ken Ian better than ah dae so it'll no surprise ye tae hear that he's mair worried aboot his rear gunner than he is aboot himsel'. It seems somethin' exploded in the turret juist as he hit the second Jerry. The gunner's lost his eyesight. He wis an art teacher before the war.'

'Oh, my God,' gasped Marie and burst into tears.

'When can we see him?' Donald asked.

'Certainly no' the night an' ye might be better tae let the morn slip by as weel. Ye must mind that Ian sterted this day in some hospital in the sooth o' England an' he's gey tired.'

'Why is he up here in your hospital anyway, Jock?' Marie had recovered her composure.

'Quite simple. The power o' a good Scots tongue – his ain. He wis in hospital close tae his base an' his navigator cam in tae see him. This wis yesterday, an' pert o' the blether wis that for some reason or another a plane wis comin' up tae the aerodrome at Machrihanish today. Ian managed tae persuade the surgeon tae get him on it. It seems the surgeon kent Big Montrose an' said that he wid be in good haunds.'

'Well, we can certainly endorse that,' said Donald with feeling.

A couple of days later, a Saturday, the family Sinclair made the journey down the Glen. After a visit to the Bennetts' for a cup of tea they were able to cross the river which was low after a prolonged spell of dry weather and take a short cut over the hill to the hospital. Jean met them at the door and brought them into the ward where they found Ian with his right leg in traction. The greyish look on his normally healthy complexion was evidence of the pain and shock through which he was passing but his face lit up at the sight of his visitors.

'Gosh, Davie, you've grown,' were his first words.

Marie laughed 'Yes,' she said, 'and his parents have only grown older.'

'Well, you don't hold the monopoly in that,' replied Ian.

The Sinclairs found that he was keener to learn about the spring lamb crop and how things were at the Glen than to discuss his wounds and how he got them.

After an hour Jean came back.

'Commander Graham is wondering if you would care to eat with him while Flight Lieutenant Boyd has his tea,' she told the Sinclair adults formally, then turned to Davie. 'S.B.A. Spence presents his compliments and invites you to "nosh wi' the ordinary folk whaur the grub is juist as good".'

Everybody laughed at her mimicking of Jock's accent.

'Can we come back in for a wee while after teatime?' asked Marie as they rose to leave.

'Oh, yes, and if you wanted to wait overnight and go home tomorrow we can find beds for you.'

'It's kind of you and the idea is tempting,' Donald replied, 'but there are dogs and a cow at home which will need attention.'

'Well, how did you find him?' asked Angus when they were seated.

'I think I found him better than I feared,' said Donald, with a glance at his wife. 'He's obviously still in some pain, but much more cheerful than I expected. Is the knee as bad as you thought it at first?'

'Well, yes, I'm afraid so. I think the wound would be caused by a piece of shrapnel. It went through the back of the knee from one side to the other. The leg must have been bent at the time and the metal cut an inch wide gap through the two main tendons behind the knee and took a nick out of the bone as well. That's bad enough, but if it had been as little as an inch further forward he would almost certainly have lost the leg from the knee.'

'Does he know?' Marie asked in a shaky voice.

'Yes, we had a long talk this morning. He has seen so many horrible things during the last few years that he regards having a straight leg for the rest of his life as no more than a nuisance. He's simply a brave and practical man.'

'He... he... won't be able to go back to shepherding?' Marie's voice broke to a sob.

'Maybe not in the high hills,' Donald broke in, 'but once this war's over shepherding will probably change like many other things. Places like the Glen will be considered too remote for people to live in and will probably be planted with trees. I honestly don't know whether I like the idea or not, but I'm afraid that in a few decades to come shepherding will be much more technical than the dog and stick of the moment.'

The surgeon laughed.

'A case of "How you gonna keep them down on the farm after they've seen Paree?"' he said.

'Something like that,' Donald agreed. 'Anyway, Ian was never impetuous and always thought things out. Once his mind gets adjusted to the idea

I'm sure he'll work something out.'

When the family went back into the ward, Ian made no mention of his condition except to say that the worst of the pain now seemed to be over and when they left he appeared cheerful and unworried.

'The worst of the pain really will be over,' Jean told them as she walked them part of the way down the road from the hospital. 'The worry now will be his reaction when he tries to walk. For somebody who was as active and fit as Ian it is never easy to adjust to a dot and carry one method of climbing the stairs.'

Thanks to an arrangement involving the grocer's van and the post van, one or other of the Sinclairs was able to visit the hospital quite frequently during the next few weeks. On one occasion, Marie arrived to find Ian sitting on a chair beside his bed which was covered in papers.

'What on earth are you doing?' she asked.

'Well,' came the reply. 'After Angus first told me that my leg was going to be straight I spent a lot of time thinking over what I was going to do. Obviously I won't be fit to herd a hill such as the north side of the Glen, but I don't want to lose my connection with the hills and animals. 'When I was at school, Aunt Bella always talked about sending me to University and I suppose that has helped me to make up my mind. I'm going to take a degree in agriculture and then I can take a job as an estate manager or even as an Agricultural Adviser. What do you think of that?'

Marie grasped his hand in both of hers.

'Oh, Ian, I think that's just marvellous. Donald and I have been so worried about you.'

'Yes, isn't he the clever boy,' said a laughing voice behind her as Jean came in.

CHAPTER VII

Making a decision about his future seemed to give Ian a morale boost which speeded his recovery. On the next occasion that the Sinclairs were able to visit him as a family, they found him outside walking on crutches under the guidance of Jean and Angus.

'Once he masters the use of crutches there's no reason why he should-n't get home.' Angus told the Sinclairs after Jean had taken Ian inside. 'mind you,' he went on 'You may find that he may not be too keen to leave here.'

'What do you mean?' Marie asked.

'Ach, don't mind me. It's maybe that I've been too long away from home myself.'

A fortnight later Ian came home.

'I never knew how much my legs meant to me until now;' he said, after a journey which had involved Willie's car for the first part and the horse and cart for the second. He was still on crutches so a bed had to be prepared for him downstairs, but luckily the ground round about the house was fairly level which made it easier for him to take exercise. After a few days he was even able to get as far as the fank and operate the shed-der gate when the hoggs were being taken off.

'If only I had an autogyro I would manage the hill as well,' he joked.

Marie had told Jean that Ian's own room was vacant if she wished to spend her nights off at the Glen and she arrived up that afternoon.

'My, you do look healthy,' she said when she met Ian. 'But,' she wrin-kled her nose, 'you smell of sheep.'

'I'm glad of that,' he laughed. 'When I came home smelling of hospi-tal my dogs wouldn't come near me.'

The following morning was one of a kind that is only found in the north and west of Scotland. The slanting sun brought out the soft brown of the dying bracken and an autumn gale had disturbed the trees to the point where the leaves ranged in colour from a deep russet, through yel-low, to green, depending on the degree of shelter.

'We're going for a hike,' Ian told Marie as he and Jean stood outside.

'It will be more of an amble than a hike,' laughed Jean. 'If he gets tired I'll come back for the wheelbarrow.'

They still hadn't returned when Donald came in at lunch time, but came in shortly afterwards.

'I didn't think that there was enough wind to put that amount of colour in your cheeks, Nurse Black,' Donald teased. 'In fact, I would even go so far as to say that that was rather a guilty shade of pink.'

Jean blushed even deeper and held out her left hand. A piece of light fence wire was encircling the third finger.

'What on earth's that for?' Donald was puzzled.

'You gommeril,' cried Marie. 'It means that they're engaged. Oh Jean, I couldn't be more pleased.'

Donald rose, embraced Jean and shook Ian's hand warmly.

'Careful with my man,' protested Jean. 'You'll topple him off his crutches.'

'When are we going to have a wedding?' Marie asked when everyone had settled down.

'Not for a while yet,' It was Jean who answered. 'Ian is going to have to spend the next three years at college and nobody knows how long this war is going to last. I'm doing as much, if not more good at the hospital here than I would anywhere else so it makes sense for me to wait here.'

While they were still in excited discussion, Davie came into the house.

He was by now progressing from lean boy to gangly youth and shared the general lack of interest of his age group in the excitement of his elders.

'Ian and Jean are engaged, isn't that great, Davie,' cried Marie.

'Oh, yes, Jock told me over a month ago that this was going to happen.'

'How did Jock know when I didn't?' Ian demanded indignantly.

'He said that the Big Montrose told him that that was the way the wind was blowing.' Davie answered calmly and everyone burst into laughter.

A side effect of Ian's decision to go to college was that young Davie showed much more interest in his school work. Like many before him he found that secondary school became more interesting and challenging the longer he was there and Ian's ready acceptance of the idea of college gave education a meaning to which previously he had given no thought.

'What's college like?' was the first question when Ian arrived back for his first break.

'Not at all what I expected,' Ian told him. 'I had thought that it would be like school were you sit at a desk all day, but there is much more variety. Certainly there are lectures which you must attend, but after that it all depends on the amount of effort you want to put into it. I've become friendly with a fellow from Perthshire who also was a shepherd, but went into the navy and lost his left foot. On good days we sit and study in the shade of the trees in the park.'

'I never thought that university would be like that,' said Davie. 'I thought that it would be just like school, cooped up in class all the time.'

'Oh you won't escape the classes entirely, but the difference lies in the amount of choice that you have. There is much more self discipline required if you are going to make a success of it. There's a very good sports ground run by an old boy who was once a football trainer. He can give you a cure for everything from dandruff to gout. Unfortunately, some folk are inclined to spend too much time there to the extent that it affects their studies.'

'That's silly.'

'Well, yes, so it is but it's something which comes up more in people from the country areas. The city boys grew up with sports clubs and training grounds and if they had athletic ability they had a chance to develop it. If I wasn't lame I might easily have fallen into the trap too. Man is a competitive animal. It's quite funny to hear the old groundsman trying to sort out somebody who he thinks is neglecting his studies. I was sitting behind a tree one day when nobody knew I was there and I overheard him talking to one fellow.

'An' whit are ye gaun tae be if ye graduate?' he asked.

'Oh, I'm going to be a lawyer.'

'Ur ye, bae Goad. Weel wid ye mind tae gae me a copy o' yer graduation photo.'

'Of course,' the fellow sounded flattered. 'But why?'

'Och ah juist want tae show it tae ma grand weans. Ye'll be the only lawyer ever ah kent wae mair smeddum ablow the waist than above it!' It worked too. I only see that fellow at the sports ground on a Saturday now. Anyway enough about me. How's school going with you?'

Davie was quiet for a time before he spoke.

'Quite well really,' he said. 'At first all I wanted was to be old enough to leave and come home despite what anybody said. Now I think that I should stay on and go to university. Mum and Dad both would like that and of course Mum's been there already so she knows what it's like.'

'Have you any idea of what you'd like to do?'

'Not really. I keep changing my mind. At times I think that I'd like to be a surgeon like Angus, but that means that I'd be inside all the time and I don't fancy that. One of the other boys wants to be a civil engineer. His father is working on the extension of the aerodrome. He says that his dad spends more time out on the site than he does in the office. I'd like that.'

'Well, Davie, if you want my advice it is to think seriously about civil engineering as a career. Even without the damage that this war is doing, the day is coming when more and more families are going to own a car of their own, so roads will have to improve, not to mention dams for fresh water and hydro electricity. The list is endless.'

'Jock told me the same thing,' said Davie. 'He said that picture painters and civil engineers were the only people who left something behind by which they would be remembered a hundreds time after their death.'

Ian laughed.

'Well,' he said. 'In both cases it depends on how good a job they made when they were alive.'

Early in the New Year a letter arrived addressed to Mr and Mrs Sinclair.

'My goodness,' gasped Marie when she opened it. 'This is from wee Kay's mother. Her name was Kay Stark and her mother has traced us through the Red Cross. She wants to come here to meet us and see where Kay was found,' a sob caught her voice. 'Kay was only seven years old,' she finished.

'When is she wanting to come?' asked Donald.

'She doesn't mention any particular time but I would imagine it would be fairly soon. She has another daughter who is eighteen months older than Kay but she was ill and couldn't travel at the time. Kay was going to her grandmother in Canada. It's terrible to think that if the other girl had been fit to travel they both might have been lost.'

'Where is she writing from?' Davie asked.

'Ipswich, but the family are moving to Edinburgh soon. The address she gives for a reply is an Edinburgh address.'

'Well, she would be better to wait until into the spring when the weather is better. To somebody who isn't accustomed to the hills, this place can look pretty bleak on a cold winter's day.'

'Yes, I'll write and tell her that she's welcome here for as long as she likes but that it would be better to wait until the day is longer.'

Several letters passed to and fro and it was arranged that Mrs Stark and her daughter, Elaine would come during the Easter holidays. Marie had warned them to travel as light as possible and that the one essential was stout footwear. When she and Davie met them at the road end, she was pleased to see that they had taken her advice and that each carried a haversack as their only luggage and were what Jock would have described as 'weel shod'. They were obviously mother and daughter, both being fair as Marie remembered Kay and with Elaine, in her early teens, already looking to be tall like her mother.

Davie shouldered Mrs Stark's haversack, but Elaine insisted on carrying her own as they made their way up to the Bennetts'. Old Mrs Bennett now required a stick even to get about the house, but this did not prevent her having a tea table set with home-baking on a snowy white tablecloth.

Mrs Stark was enchanted with the old couple and their tidy wee home. While the chat was still in full flow, Davie and Elaine set off up the glen carrying the haversacks and leaving Marie and Mrs Stark to follow. Davie tried to set a steady pace but Elaine forged ahead and by the top of the first hill her face was shining with sweat and he suggested that they should rest and allow their mothers to catch up with them.

'What do you do here, Davie?' she asked a little petulantly when she got her breath back. 'It's so quiet and there are so few houses.'

Davie laughed. 'Wait till you get up to the Glen then you can't see any other houses at all,' he told her.

'But what do you do? Do you play football or cricket... or anything?' she finished.

'I play football sometimes at school but I can't join the school team. All the matches are on Saturdays and I can't get to them. Anyway, after Ian went to the Air Force I had to help Dad on Saturdays and during the holidays and now, of course, Ian has gone to college after he was wounded and Dad is on his own.'

'Don't you want to see the cities?'

'Not really, but when I go to university I'll have to live there whether I like it or not. I've been in Glasgow twice. Mum's parents lived at Milngavie and we went on the boat from Campbeltown to visit them but they're both dead now.'

By this time, Marie and Mrs Stark had caught up and the four of them continued up the glen. Katherine Stark was a tall, fair, anxious woman, but ready to smile. Marie learned that her husband was a metallurgist involved in some research and that though they were both Scots they had lived in Ipswich from just before the war.

'That's why we decided to send the children to my mother in Canada,' Marie was told. 'I have a sister in Winnipeg, but she took Infantile Paralysis shortly after the birth of her son in 1934 and lost the use of her legs. When our father died mother decided to go out to help her and it seemed a good idea to let the girls go too until after the war. We just never thought that anyone would sink a boat full of children.'

The following day the four walked and climbed to a spot above the shore where Ian had found Kay's body. There had been a white frost in the bottom of the glen but they climbed into sunshine and clear still air. By the time they were able to look down on the sea all of them had shed clothes but were still sweating. They sat on a rock looking down to the water and for a time nobody spoke, but eventually Katherine broke the silence which had only been disturbed by the lap of the sea on the rocks.

'I'm just so relieved that her body was found,' she said quietly. 'I don't think that I could have borne the thought of her being missing.'

Again after a silence, she turned to Marie.

'How did she look?' she asked hesitantly.

'She still had all her clothes on and there wasn't a mark on her face at all. I never disturbed her clothes except to look for her name and that was on the pocket of her blouse, but Ian carried her in and he never mentioned any broken bones. She was clear of the rocks in fairly deep water when Roy got to her and drew her in to where Ian could catch her.'

'I had to ask and I'm so glad that I did,' said Katherine, 'and I just had to come to see where she was found.'

Ian had spent the first few days of his Easter break with Jean at her parents but arrived back on the evening before the Stark's departure. Seeing where Kay had been found and meeting the people who had cared for her body seemed to help Katherine and she greeted Ian warmly. Later that evening at the tea table, the conversation turned to Jock and his ferret and she laughed heartily.

'I haven't heard my mother laugh so much for a long time,' Elaine told Davie as they parted at the road end on the following day. 'I just wish that Dad could find the time to come here too.'

'Does he take holidays, or is he like my father?' asked Davie.

'He hasn't taken a whole day off since the start of the war. Even when we were moving to Edinburgh Mum and I travelled in the van with the furniture and he came up the following day by rail so that he could work in the train. It's sickening. He's an old grey man – and he's only forty-one. I wish this horrible war would end.'

CHAPTER VIII

The war in Europe ended on the day before Davie was due to sit the first of his third year exams. Helping his father with lambing at the weekends and evenings had cut into his study time, much to the annoyance of his mother and the celebrations caused a welcome postponement of the exams.

'He's going to use the time to study,' Marie insisted to Donald. 'If the exams had gone on as planned he would have been in school and not on the hill so his normal school time will be spent on study. The sheep can have him at the weekend.'

Donald was feeling the strain of tackling a rather difficult lambing time virtually single handed, but found himself unable to argue. If Davie had been going to follow him into shepherding it would have been different, but for some time now Donald had felt guilty that so much of the boy's time was being consumed by his need for help on the hill. One evening towards the end of June he came in to find Marie with a letter which she handed to him to read. It was from the Director of Education offering her her old job back in the local school.

'I knew that Mary Brown was leaving to get married,' she told Donald, 'but I thought that there would have been no difficulty in filling the post.'

'What do you think?'

'What do you think?' The question was thrown back at him.

'Well, I don't think that it would work well in the long term if we were to wait in Glanamoil but,' he hesitated, 'I'm now forty-five and won't be able to keep up to this pace indefinitely. The way things are going, I don't see us getting another shepherd to replace Ian so now could be the time to make a change. Anyway, you've had a couple of hours to think it out. What's your own thoughts?'

'Oh, Donald, I'd love it. I miss the children so much especially now that Davie is growing up and in a couple of years will be off to University. And do you see the salary? It's more than you're getting just now and you could do something else.'

'We'll wait until Davie gets home then talk it over properly,' said Donald.

'I would need to wait here until the November term to allow the laird to get somebody else. He's always been good to us and I wouldn't want to let him down.'

Davie was more enthusiastic about the prospect of a move than either of his parents had expected him to be.

'Well that's all settled then,' said Donald finally. 'I'll go down to see the laird on Saturday.'

'We'll be sorry to lose you, Donald,' said the laird, 'but I have to admit that I've been expecting you. I had heard that Marie was to be offered the job at the school. Have you given any thought to where you're going to go?'

'Not really. We don't particularly want to move into the village, but it'll need to be somewhere that's on the route of the school car or within reasonable distance of the school.'

'Maybe I can help you then,' said the laird. 'I know that the Smithy Croft is coming vacant. So many farmers are buying tractors that one blacksmith is soon going to be more than enough for this district. The croft is a bit small for a full time living but it would make the bread and butter and you would be able to get plenty casual work to provide the jam. Would you like me to speak for you?'

'It's very good of you and I'd be most grateful,' confessed Donald.

'Glad to help, very glad. Our family connection goes back a long time. Your grandfather was shepherd on Strathbeg when my grandfather came to the estate.'

Suddenly, he gave his bark of a laugh and went on, 'The only thing was, your grandfather was there because he was an excellent shepherd. My ancestor married my grandmother, whose family owned the estate and whose only brother had been killed in the Crimean war. The other old roué survived the war which, from all that I hear was rather a pity. Apparently he was in an advanced state of impecuniousness when he married and all this affluence went to his head. Happily, he was able to sire my father before expiring as an alcoholic eunuch.'

Donald laughed. 'I'm glad that he managed that anyway,' he said.

'Yes. Isn't it strange the tenuous and sometimes ignoble links to which we owe our existence. We'll have a dram before you go and before we get too morbid.'

The first thing that Ian announced when he returned for the summer break was that he and Jean had set a date for their long awaited wedding.

'The hospital is closing at the end of the summer and going back to being a hotel,' he told Marie, 'and anyway I'll have to start looking for a job. We're getting married in the church here on the last Saturday in September. Jean says that she now has more friends here than anywhere else and anyway, this area will always be home to us.'

'That's great,' said Marie. 'Jock has been telling us for a while that there was talk of the hospital being wound up soon, but he didn't know when. The bad thing is that we are going to lose you, Jean and Jock more or less at the one go. He tells me that he would like to wait here, but as long as his mother is alive he would have to go back to Glasgow.'

'Well, Jean and I don't want to move to anywhere else either but where we settle will depend on where I can get work.'

'It's just that so many things seem to be happening at once,' said Marie. 'We've been seventeen years in Glenamoil and that's a fair lump our of a lifetime. Once Davie goes to University, Donald and I will feel like the original idea for Granny's Heilan' Hame.'

The laird proved to be as good as his word and on the day of the milk clipping at the Glen, he arrived up to say that not only were the Sinclairs to be given the tenancy of the Smithy Croft, but that he had found a shepherd to take over Donald's job when the ewe hoggs went to wintering at the beginning of October. This meant that by the time winter took a grip, both Marie and Davie would be picked up and deposited by the school car right from their own door and would no longer have to face the long, dark walk from and to the Glen.

Ian and Jean were married in the village church on a beautiful soft autumn day. Jock was best man and Marie was matron of honour. The local hotel made the best they could of rationing to provide a meal for the thirty odd guests. The following Friday morning, Davie left the Glen for school on his own as Marie had been given the day off for the flitting to Smith Croft. On his way down the road Davie met the estate tractor and trailer which had been loaned by the laird for the occasion.

On the previous day Donald had walked the two cows and their calves over the three miles down the glen and the further mile to the croft and left them grazing there. Of the dogs only Gem, Ian's bitch, now 63 in human terms and beginning to show her years, was going with them. Old Roy had died peacefully of old age earlier in the summer and the two young dogs, both offspring of Roy and Gem, were being sold to the incoming shepherd. By the time that Davie got home, the tractor had gone and his parents, with the help of Jock, were erecting beds and placing furniture. In the 1940s, carpets were not part of the possessions of a shepherding family and the main living quarters were all concrete floored with linoleum and the odd rug in bedrooms. One major advantage which the new house did have was a shower fixed over the bath.

This had been constructed by the blacksmith and involved rubber hosepipes which could be connected to both the hot and cold water taps and which in turn conveyed the water, by means of a galvanized pipe fixed to the wall to a home-made overhead rose. To Davie, and indeed to his father, this was the height of luxury which was only rivalled, but not superseded by the black telephone which sat coyly on a shelf in the small entrance hall. In the early evening as they were having their tea, this jangled into life and Marie picked up the receiver.

'It's the hospital for you, Jock,' she called after listening for a moment.

When the wee man came back to the table his face had paled and Marie noticed the sparkle of tears in his bright blue eyes.

'What's wrong, Jock?' she asked anxiously.

'It's the Auld Wife,' he said, after a moment's hesitation. 'That wis Big Montrose. He's juist had a phone call fae the hospital in Glesga where she worked. This afternoon, they thocht that she wisnae lookin' weel an' made her sit doon while they got her a cup o' tea. When they cam back wi the tea she wis deid in the chair. The doctor is a pal o' big Angus. He said that it wis her hert that juist gaed oot. She never suffered nor laid as an invalid an' that's the wey she'd huv wanted.' His voice faltered, then he went on in an even tone. 'It's no easy the noo, but gi'n a week or two has gaen by ah'll huv gethered the sense tae be gled that she got her wish.'

'What do you want to do just now?' Donald asked.

'Juis gaither ma braith fur a wee while then ah'll go back tae the hospital. Angus is arrangin' for the van tae tak me tae the seven o'clock bus for Glesga in the mornin'. There's nae relatives in this country as far as ah ken. Ma mother had only wan brother an' he was killed in the Clydebank blitz an' hud never merrit.

'There's a sister who went tae Australia wae her man aboot the time when I was born. Her man's deid, but she an' the Auld Wife wrote regularly tae one anither. Her two sons are wi' the Australian army in Burma an' that's the lot. Ma mother had some fine neebors. Man they were great, an' ah'll never forget them, but ah cannae see me ever gaun back tae Glesga tae live noo. Angus telt me juist this mornin' that he's been asked tae keep the hospital open for another year an' he asked if I was willing tae wait wae him. Noo that the Auld Pair are thegither ah've got nae ties and when the place closes ah can please masel'.'

'It seems terrible that we can't do more for you,' said Marie.

'Lassie, ye've done mair than enough for me these past few years an' if ah kent ma mother there'll be a letter o' instruction as long as yer erm left somewhere for me. Juist noo, ah'd better get back an' try tae get some sleep. Ah've got seven days' leave startin' fae the morn so ah should see ye next weekend.'

Ian and Jean arrived back from their honeymoon at the beginning of the following week and the news that the hospital was to remain open delighted Jean.

'By the time it closes, Ian will be ready to take a job so I might as well stay on and earn some money,' she said. 'Ian will probably study better if I'm not around to distract him particularly on the run up to his finals.'

Nevertheless, when Ian went back to college, she suffered badly from loneliness and both she and Jock spent all the time they could at the croft. Davie was finding that fourth year work was much harder but the school car now dropped him at the door which meant that he was home more than an hour earlier in the evenings and had this amount of extra study time. As the croft had been neglected for a few years previously, Donald found that there was much to do to repair drains and fences and he was glad to have Jock's help and also that Marie's salary came in at the end of each month.

One thing that delighted Jock was that both the croft and the surrounding farms were over-run with rabbits and he and Benny spent a very busy and lucrative winter. The next door farmer had decided to keep some four score of Blackface ewes for crossing with a Border Leicester tup. This was a new venture about which he knew little, so in return for help and advice, Donald was able to borrow a pair of horses and any implements which he required. Having little skill with a plough, he knew that his first efforts would cause quite a bit of local amusement and this was indeed the case. If practice did not make perfect however, it did make possible and the end of the spring saw him with about an acre and a half of potatoes and another two acres made up of cabbages, carrots and turnips all doing well. Much of the success of this part of his enterprise depended on Jock keeping the rabbit population under some form of control.

One day, Jock was pursuing his efforts close to the main road. It was a day in early spring and one of those, alas all too infrequent, when the west of Scotland climate can favourably be compared with any other place in the world. Peewits were soaring above the fields giving their mating call, primroses were peeping shyly from the more sheltered banks and the smell of new turned earth was everywhere. Jock had slipped Benny beneath the net which he had placed over the mouth of the burrow and was sitting down to enjoy the sunshine while awaiting developments when a booming empty barrel type of voice hailed him over the fence.

'Hullo there. Isn't this a beautiful day?'

At this particular point in the operation Jock was keen to avoid noise in any form so as not to alert the rabbits and a rhetorical question, delivered as through a megaphone, was neither helpful nor desirable. Benny was expert at his trade, however, and as Jock rose to his feet a rabbit scurried out of the hole and into the net. This Jock despatched quickly and humanely and the appearance of the ferret at the mouth of the hole told him that there was nothing of interest left inside.

After Benny had been slipped into his box, Jock turned to address himself to his visitor. While agreeing that it was indeed a pleasant day, he saw that the man had a shiny, dairy-fed look and gave no appearance of the type to be enjoying a cycling holiday despite the bicycle. His clothes, from the shiny black shoes, up through the clerical grey suit, past the silk tie to the Anthony Eden hat were well fitting despite a distinct corpulence and told of a skilled and expensive tailor.

'What are you doing?' The decibels hadn't decreased.

Jock explained quietly.

'Oh. Was this your part of the war effort?' The tone was three dimensional and superior. Jock had spent the early years of the war being resentful of his failure to get into the armed forces, but after many patient talks Angus Graham had convinced him of the importance of the job which he did. This now helped him to view his oafish companion with more amusement than rancour and his reply of 'Ach, well, it helped, och aye, ah suppose it helped' was a masterpiece of vacuity.

'Have you been here all through the war?'

'Aye, mair or less.'

'Oh, well, at least we should be able to count on your support now.'

'Support for whit?' Jock was puzzled.

'Oh, well,' the tone was condescending, 'you must know that we will soon have to have a General Election. After spending the war in a peaceful place like this the least you can do is vote for us when the Election comes.'

'Ur you a candidate?'

'No, but I'm a party worker and a very good friend of the candidate.'

'Well, ye might be right aboot the former, but ye're awfy far mistaken aboot the latter.'

'What do you mean?' The man's face had assumed a colour akin to a Victoria plum.

'Weel, if ye go roond the country talkin' doon tae folk the wey ye've done wi' me, baith ye an' yer candidate could find yerselves gey scarce o' freens. When ah meet folk lake you ah whiles wunner if Guy Fawkes wis a' that far wrang. Ah'll bid ye good day.'

As Jock gathered up his ferret box, his nets and his rabbit and moved to the next burrow which was some fifty yards down the turf dyke from the road, he left a very apoplectic gentleman gazing after him.

CHAPTER IX

For the Sinclair family, the year of 1946 was marked by a series of events, all of which were to prove significant in the future. Donald did his first lambing for his farmer neighbour and it was so successful that the two other farmers in the glen decided to put on sheep and employ him to look after them. This was going to have a marked effect on his income. Ian gained his B.Sc. in agriculture and landed a post as an Agricultural Adviser in Perthshire. This meant that giving specialist advice on his beloved Blackface sheep was going to be a large part of his duties. Jean's parents had left her a small sum of money and this, together with the nest egg which his Aunt Bella had 'pit by' for Ian, meant that they were able to buy, and substantially pay for a small bungalow in a delightful, inquisitive wee village.

'She's put me into debt for over a thousand pounds to buy and furnish this house,' Ian told Marie in front of Jean.

'Of course I did,' his wife reposted, 'I've got faith in you.'

After a short run-down the hospital closed in mid summer. Angus Graham moved back to his former hospital in Glasgow but, after some deliberation, Jock accepted the offer of a job in a garage in the nearby town.

'When ah came here ah didnae like the place. It wis far oer quiet,' he told Donald and Marie, 'but noo its taken a grip o' me an' ah don't really want tae go back tae the city. Besides, noo that the Auld Yin's away, there's naething left in Glesga tae draw me back.'

Entry into fifth year of secondary school forced Davie to think seriously of what exactly he wanted to do with his life. He was now as tall as his father and despite adolescent acne was obviously going to inherit his mother's clear skin and dark good looks. The move to the Smithy Croft had meant that on Saturdays a walk of little more than a mile took him to a bus route and he was able to be a member of the school football team. The compulsory pedal exercise of his earlier years had endowed him with an excellent pair of lungs and sturdy legs and the new sports master, recently demobbed from the army, was quick to spot a potential middle distance runner. His parents were happy that he had his sights set on university, but wanted his choice of career to be his own.

'I'm not qualified to advise you and it would be unfair of me to try,' Donald told him. 'Your world is going to be a much bigger place than mine has been and that is how it should be. The one thing which I would like you to do is to conduct your life so that in fifty years' time you can look back, without shame, and honestly tell yourself that you enjoyed it.'

On a beautiful Sunday morning in early September, Davie and Jock walked to the top of Crocan Lin, which was a hill immediately behind the croft. This hill was in no way a Scottish mountain, but because of its situation and the clear air of early autumn the view from the top was breathtaking. For a time they sat in silence behind a pile of stones which were all that remained of some long ago building. The curve of the river, sparkling in the sunshine, meandered to the sea a little over a mile away and the harvest fields, by now stripped bare of their bounty stood out in golden relief against the dark green of the grazing fields in the rich alluvial soil. The light breeze was easterly and a roe deer hind and her calf, their light limbs whispering through the heather, came round the hill from the north side and stopped less than twenty yards from the man and the boy. For a time surprise seemed to anaesthetise fear in the animals and they stood for more than two minutes with their only movement being a faint quivering of their nostrils. Suddenly a flock of field fare thrummed low over the top, swerved suddenly when they sensed a human presence and broke the spell. Jock was the first to break the silence as the deer bounded back the way they had just come.

'Weel, Davie, ah can tell ye this, ye'll no' see many sights lake that in Sauchiehall Street.'

Davie laughed.

'But you're the one who always tells me that I should go to university,' he teased.

'Och, aye, but that's juist a means tae an end. Ah'd hate tae think that juist because ye went tae university ye ceased tae be a countryman. Ah wid hope for the opposite in that a good education wid help the better tae appreciate sights lake we've juist seen.'

'Don't worry, Jock,' the boy was suddenly serious, 'the talk you gave me years ago at the top of the Glenamoil hill has long since sunk in. I'm going to try to take a degree in Civil Engineering and then maybe go abroad for a few years.'

During the October school holidays, Katherine Stark and her daughter Elaine came to stay for a week. Katherine Stark's fair hair was settling into a quite becoming grey and she was much more cheerful and relaxed than on her previous visit to the Glen.

'John has taken a post at the university,' she told Marie. 'Although he still works late for several nights a week, at least we now have him at weekends. It makes such a difference and Elaine has so many friends who are always in and out of the house that the place seems so much brighter.'

While Katherine had brightened, her daughter had bloomed. Once she had been tall and gangly, now she had filled out. The petulance of earlier years had disappeared with adolescence now sitting flatteringly on her shoulders. She and Davie found that they had much in common and spent a lot of time together. Her ambition was to go to Vet. College and she hoped to get into the Royal Dick in Edinburgh.

'What makes you want to become a vet?' Davie puzzled.

'When Kay and I were little, the family moved around so much because of Dad's work that Mum said it wasn't fair to keep a pet. After we went back from here last time I got a puppy which had been abandoned. It was a beautiful wee black and white terrier with a snub nose. None of us knew anything about animals but for more than six months he was well and bouncy. Our house backs on to fields and I used to take him for long walks. He was lovely. Then just after Christmas I noticed that he no longer seemed so lively. After a couple of days he started to be sick and to mess the floor. By the time we got him to a vet, he had a deep-seated enteritis and he died the following night.'

David noticed a tear trickling down her cheeks.

'He had a lot of pain for the last few hours. I can still hear him whimper and I couldn't do anything to help him. That won't happen again.'

Suddenly she sprang to her feet. 'As we were coming out I saw your Mum putting a bramble pie in the oven and it should just be about ready. Come on, I'll race you home.'

The winter of 1946–47 was long and cold. In early spring there were a few fine days and it seemed that the worst was over. One evening Donald came in to announce that the first lambs of the spring had been born.

'Surely you weren't expecting them so soon,' Marie said.

'Yes, I was expecting a few,' he admitted. 'One of the tups broke out more than a week before the rest. I found him the following day and brought him in again, but there may be a few lambs yet at this time. It depends on how well he used his time of freedom.'

The following morning they woke to a shock.

'It's not worth your while getting up,' Marie told Davie when she came to waken him at his usual time. 'There's been more than a foot of snow during the night and it's now drifting. There's no chance of either of us getting to school today.'

Donald, however, could not be persuaded to wait at home.

'I don't understand what good you can do in this weather,' Marie protested as he donned oilskin coat and leggings. Snow was piling up against the window as she spoke.

'You won't be able to see the sheep, far less do anything to help them.'

All day it continued snowing and drifting and when Donald came home in early afternoon he confessed that he was only able to do so with considerable difficulty.

'I found two ewes and each had a live pair of twins,' he told them. 'I was able to get them into shelter and hopefully the snow won't cover them. Of two more, one has a dead pair of twins and another a dead single lamb. The lambs just never took to their feet in the cold after being born. It's frustrating. The two ewes with twins would be better with only one lamb to rear and the mothers of the dead lambs are both fit sheep, but by the time this clears it is going to be too late to foster them.'

His predictions proved all too accurate and there was little let up for the next two days. Finally, the sun shone and work began on cleaning the roads. After three days traffic was moving, albeit slowly, and lorries were able to collect the milk which had accumulated on the dairy farms and grocer, butcher and mail vans were able to do their rounds. The respite was brief, however, for late on the Sunday afternoon a gale developed and by the following morning the roads were again feet deep in drifted snow. To Donald this was disaster. Lambing had now begun in earnest in two of his three farms with the third one due to start in less than a week. The few areas of grass which had been blown clear of snow were in the iron grip of frost. Ewes were lambing with little or no milk to feed their lambs and any ewe that had difficulty in lambing had little hope of survival in the extreme cold. Even when the snow finally cleared away it took a long time for a cold dour spring to stagger hesitantly into summer.

The strain of attending to the sheep in his care combined with trying to catch up with the spring work on his croft took a heavy toll from Donald. He had always been a lean man, but by the time the sun began to shine in earnest his leanness had deteriorated to gauntness.

The one bright spot for the family occurred in late June when the parents attended the school prize giving to see their son collect the Dux Medal. Apart from the pride which they inevitably felt, this achievement meant that a substantial bursary would now be available to help their son through his student days. Davie had been offered a job in the local hotel, but Marie was becoming worried about Donald's health and, now that the bursary was easing the finances, she prevailed on the boy to spend his summer helping his father both on the croft and with his shepherding.

In the middle of July, the weather dried up and turned hot. Grain crops which had been a dark green, promising a late harvest, suddenly began to ripen and in a very short time the rattle of the binders was to be heard late into the still evenings. Only one of the farms on which Donald worked had facilities for dipping sheep and consequently the sheep from the other two farms were gathered and taken there for the summer dip to prevent them from being infested with maggots. Because of the sudden rush of harvest work, this job was delayed until the break between cutting and stacking the crop. The hot weather had brought out the maggot fly in large numbers. This had meant extra work and worry for Donald and did nothing at all to decrease Marie's anxiety about his appearance.

The dipping was finally finished and that evening Donald arrived home exhausted. During the night Marie awoke to find him hot and restless beside her. The following morning, his eyes were hot and fevered and his body hot to touch. All that day he tossed restlessly and spent another disturbed night. By the next morning the fever was with him and he complained of a stiffness in his limbs. Really worried now, and suspecting that this was more than a summer 'flu, Marie telephoned for the doctor. After spending some time with Donald he came through to the kitchen with Marie.

'Well?' her question was short and anxious.

He hesitated a moment, 'I'm really not sure,' he said finally. 'If you don't mind I'd like another opinion before I commit myself.'

'What do you suspect?' her voice trembled.

'I'd rather not say at the moment and please don't press me. I promise that I'll have an answer for you in less than an hour. Luckily an old friend from my college days is staying with us on holiday just now. He was reckoned to be the best diagnostician of our year and hasn't lost his touch. Now.' he went on kindly, 'you put on a kettle and make your man a cup of tea while I run home and pick John up. That'll be easier than giving him directions to here and I'll be back as quickly as I can.'

When Marie brought the tea to Donald she was shocked to find that he had difficulty in sitting up in bed.

'My legs seem to have gone useless,' he told her. 'It's almost as if they weren't there at all.'

She was sponging Donald's face and hands when the doctor and his friend came back and after being introduced she went through to the kitchen to wait. After little more than ten minutes, the doctor came through. 'John confirms what I thought,' he said before Marie had a chance to question him.

'Donald has Infantile Paralysis.'

Marie gulped and her eyes filled with tears.

'Now, you're not to take this as a signal for the end of the world,' the doctor went on. 'John has seen a lot of this disease over the last few years and the treatment has advanced tremendously. First of all we'll have to get an ambulance and get Donald moved to Glasgow. I'll leave John to talk to you while I use your phone,' he went on as his friend joined them.

'Where on earth could Donald pick up something like this?' was Marie's first incredulous, slightly tearful question.

'Well, it's a disease which has always been around. Basically, it is caused by an infectious virus first isolated by an Australian called Landsteiner and in the past few weeks there's been a quite dramatic surge of cases. Donald is the fourth that I have seen in the past fortnight.'

'How badly will it affect him? Just before you came he seemed to be losing the power of his legs.'

'At this point it is impossible to say and it would be deceitful of me to pretend otherwise. On two points, however, I can offer you comfort. One is that your husband seems to be a very determined man and in recovering from a disease like this that is a very important factor. The second is that there has been a tremendous advance in the treatment of the after-effects of Infantile Paralysis, particularly the use of hydropathic treatment. I know that it's a trite thing to say, but at this stage try not to worry too much. It's a waste of good thinking time to worry about something that worry is not going to solve. It shouldn't take more than a few days until the extent of the paralysis is known and then it can begin to be tackled.'

With that they heard the doctor replace the telephone receiver and go back to Donald's room so they followed him through. Marie sat on the bed and silently took her husband's hand.

'I've been in touch with the ambulance and he'll be here just after one o'clock,' the doctor told them. 'I don't yet know which hospital, but they'll phone back soon and let us know. Oh, that may be them now,' he continued as the phone rang.

But when Marie picked up the receiver it was Jock she heard.

'Whit's wrang, Marie?' his voice was slightly shrill. 'Ah've juist heard that the ambulance is tae tak Donald tae Glesga.'

Marie had completely forgotten that the garage where Jock worked also provided the ambulance driver on a need basis.

As quickly as she answered Jock's question he asked 'Ur ye gaun tae trevel up wi' him?'

'Honestly Jock, I haven't had time to think yet.'

'Well dinna bother. Ah'll go noo an' get washed an' shifted then ah'll be doon wi' the driver. Noo dinna worry, we'll soort this oot alright.'

She got back to the bedroom to find the doctor and his friend ready to leave. 'Well, Donald couldn't be in better care,' said the former when she told them the result of her telephone call. 'Angus Graham told me that that wee man was one of the best that ever he worked with and, believe me, that is real praise. By the way, where's Davie?'

Marie gasped. 'Oh, isn't that terrible, I completely forgot that he doesn't know yet. He's working at the harvest on the first farm along the road. I'd better phone and ask them to send him home to see his father before he goes away.'

'No, don't phone. We're going that way anyway and I'll stop and tell him. It'll be better than hearing something like this over the phone.

'Now we'll have to be off,' he continued to Donald 'and don't you be worrying about Marie and Davie while your away. Davie's a young man now and besides there's plenty of us here to keep an eye on them.'

'Well I'm glad that at least I got all the sheep dipped before this happened. I'll need to be fit again before it's time for the tups to go out.'

John laughed. 'That's the type of spirit that will take you through this,' he said.

Jock phoned from Glasgow in the early evening.

'Donald travelled really well,' he told Marie. 'He's a bit tired noo, but that's only tae be expected. Ah'll see him again afore ah leave here. Noo, you an' Davie get a night's sleep an ah'll run doon an' see ye the morns' nicht.'

Surprisingly, both Marie and Davie found that they were able to put Jock's advice to effect and Marie phoned the hospital in the morning to find that Donald had also passed a comfortable night. For the next three days the hospital was non-committal and austere with information, then came the first glimmer of hope offered by the cheerful West Highland voice of the ward sister.

'Mr Sinclair had a visit from the consultant this morning,' she told Marie. 'It's thought that the paralysis won't progress any further and indeed there seems to be some movement in his legs.'

For the first time Marie broke down and wept uncontrollably. On the Sunday, Jock borrowed a car from the garage and took Marie and Davie to Glasgow.

They were surprised to find that Donald was the oldest patient in a ward of twenty beds. Most of the other patients were of late teenage or in their early twenties. Donald was propped up on pillows and quite cheerful but Marie couldn't help noticing how quickly his healthy outdoor colour had faded to a hospital grey which was enhanced rather than off-set by a bright spot of colour on each cheekbone and a feverish sparkle in his eyes.

'I'm not getting much treatment yet for the paralysis,' he told them. 'I still have a bit of a temperature and they tell me that I have to get rid of that first.'

'What's the grub like?' asked Davie with the blunt practicality of youth.

'Surprisingly good really and it's still hot by the time it gets out here which can't be easy.'

Jock, who was sitting on the opposite side of the bed from Davie and his mother, had a view of the ward and suddenly Marie saw his face brighten.

'Ach, it's the auld sawbones himsel'.'

'I think I prefer Big Montrose,' said the laughing voice of Angus Graham behind her.

'How did you know we were here?' Marie asked.

'I actually saw you arrive. I was called in to see a patient who may have to come to me for surgery and was studying an X-ray against the light of the window when I happened to glance out,' he explained, 'Why didn't you phone me?'

'Yes, I know that I should have done and I'm sorry,' Marie apologised, 'but I just haven't been thinking too straight for the past week.'

'When did you come in?' the question was addressed to Donald.

'Monday afternoon. Less than a week ago but it seems a lot longer.'

The surgeon laughed.

'Yes,' he said, 'hospital does tend to have that effect on a lot of people. How long are you staying?' he added to the visitors.

'We'll go for something to eat soon then come back for a while.' It was Jock who answered after a glance at Marie.

'Fine. If you just let me go and phone my wife to expect us, I'll come back for you and drive you out to our house. I want to come back and see this patient again.'

'We can't impose on your wife at such short notice,' Marie protested. 'She'll kill you.'

'You can and she won't. Besides, I have an ulterior motive.'

As they emerged through the hospital gates, his car seemed to hesitate and be slow to pick up and after a short distance Jock leaned over from the back seat and tapped the driver on the shoulder.

'Are there any hills atween here an' yer hoose?' he asked.

'Why?' the reply was straight faced.

'Juist that ah think we'd huv tae push this jalopy if there was.'

'What do you think is wrong?'

'Well, at least ye're only firin' on three cylinders an' whileson only the two. That's the symptons an' if ye can persuade it tae tak us as far as yer hoose ah'll gie ye a diagnosis an' prescribe treatment.'

While Jock peered at the car engine, the others went in to meet a rounded, cheery wee dark haired woman who was Angus' wife. There was a daughter of fifteen, tall like her father and triumphantly emerging from adolescence into womanhood.

'Where's Jock?' asked Mrs Graham as she led them into the sitting room. 'I've heard so much about him over the years that I'm dying to meet him.'

'Working at the car,' her husband told her.

'Well, I only hope that he can fix it. You've complained so much about it for weeks now. Why you don't take it to a garage for repair I can't understand.'

'Because I only remember when I need to use the car and then I haven't time.'

'It's a good job that men only rule the world and not the house,' Mrs Graham said to Marie. 'Otherwise they would only remember to cook the dinner when it was time to sit down and eat it.'

As they were laughing over this, a shirt sleeved Jock appeared with something dark and dirty looking in his hand.

'Ah'll no' shake hauns, ah'm kinda greasy,' he told Mrs Graham when they were introduced. 'Huvin' worked wi' yer man fur years ah've aye felt sympathy fur you who hud to live wi' him.'

'What vital organ of my car have you got there, you rogue?' asked Angus.

'The distributor cap. There's a crack that's lettin' the spark run to earth.'

'What can you do about it?'

'If Mrs Graham can gie me either a wee, sharp poker or a heavy knittin' needle ah'll heat it in the fire an' bore two holes, wan at each end o' the crock an' as long as you keep the holes clean an' dry that should keep the spark fae jumpin.'

'If the efter care is as good as the surgery yer car should go like a wee burd.'

'Would it not be better if I just went to a garage tomorrow and got them to fit a new one?'

'It wid. Nae doot aboot it. There's juist the wan snag in that plan.

'Since the war, spares canna be got an' for a lot of things we huv tae rely on bits off cars that are bein' scrapped. Every mechanic in oor garage keeps a box o' junk. Ah'll huv a rake roond when ah get back an' if ah find wan ah'll sen' it on or tak it up the next time we're comin, an' fit it on for ye.'

Jock's medicine proved effective and the car went well on the run back to the hospital. Donald had slept for a little while after his lunch, but was bright and cheerful by the time they arrived at his bedside. Angus left them and went to see his patient, but arrived back in time to walk out to the car with them. Jock, besides being an entertaining companion, was an excellent chauffeur and Marie found herself able to enjoy the journey home in the summer evening. She fell into the habit of phoning the hospital at a regular time each day when usually she was answered by the ward sister and, over the phone, they became quite friendly.

Later with the absence of her friend on holiday, Marie found that her phone calls to the hospital yielded less news than before until a day came when she found the news disturbing.

'Your husband didn't sleep so well last night, Mrs Sinclair,' came the dispassionate voice, 'and we find that he's running a bit of a temperature. Perhaps you could ring again this evening.'

The evening call was a little more informative. 'Mr Sinclair?' came a voice which she hadn't heard before. 'Oh yes, he's quite cheerful and as well as could be expected.'

That night, Marie found sleep impossible and she sat up in bed reading and listening to the even breathing of her son in the next room until eventually exhaustion forced her to blow out the light. The insistent ringing of the telephone woke her.

'Mrs Sinclair?' she heard when she picked up the receiver. The voice was a man's.

'Yes.'

'This is the hospital, Mrs Sinclair. I'm sorry to have to tell you that your husband, Donald died a few minutes ago.'

Through in the kitchen she heard the clock strike five times.

CHAPTER X

Days pass and are forgotten. Weeks filter and fade through the waste disposal system of memory, but some moments are indelible. Marie was aware of Davie behind her. She turned and threw her arms round him. No words were spoken; herself unable even to cry. After a time the boy led her through to the kitchen and sat her in a chair. He poked the grey corpse of the previous night's fire, discovered a spark of life, and, by adding dry sticks, soon had a blaze going to boil the kettle. Drinking the tea helped. It was something to do. It still wasn't six o'clock on a quiet, late summer morning. Marie felt that she ought to be doing something, but wasn't quite sure what.

Anyway, what did it matter? Donald was gone. Big, quiet easy-going Donald, at the age of forty-six or was it forty-seven. It didn't really matter. Nothing mattered. What was the date anyway? That was going to be important. Forever after it would be the date on which Donald had died.

After a time Marie got up, went to the outside door, opened it and stood looking east through the glen. Donald's dogs, kennelled in the old blacksmith's shop, whined softly to get out and, still in her night clothes, she opened the door. As the dogs ran to sniff in a nearby clump of whin bushes, the sun tipped the hills and flooded the valley with light. Suddenly one of the dogs uttered a friendly 'I know you' bark and Jock appeared round the corner.

'Angus phoned me,' he explained. 'He was at the hospital to see an emergency patient. He was goin' tae operate juist efter he phoned me but hopes to be home an' gie a ring roond aboot eight or so.'

As they waited in the morning sunlight for the dogs to come back, the neighbouring farmer rounded the corner in the wake of Jock.

'I was letting out the cows when I saw Jock passing,' he explained. 'I knew something must be wrong.'

Soon two other neighbours arrived. Jock phoned Ian and Jean.

'We'll catch the boat from Glasgow tomorrow morning. Can you meet us, Jock?'

Angus phoned.

'It was pneumonia. It's often a problem with a patient like Donald who has always been active, then suddenly is forced to lie on his back.'

Davie, it was, who phoned the undertaker.

'Leave everything to me, Davie,' the calm voice was accustomed to

70

tragedy. 'I'll come and see you and your mother later in the morning.'

Mid morning the laird came with old Mr Bennett. The old man was very upset indeed and the laird little less so. The minister came, an elderly man, slow spoken and sensible. The undertaker arrived while he was there. Donald's body was to be brought home the next day with the funeral to the local cemetery on the day following.

The day passed surprisingly quickly. The night stretched endlessly. A slow day followed the night. Then Donald came home.

He was a big man, was Marie's thought when the lid of the coffin was removed. She voiced the thought and almost giggled. Jock put his arm round her shoulders.

'Aye,' he said, 'but he'd huv been a big man even if he wis only my height. The measure o' a man isnae always the distance between his croon an' his coarns.'

The day of the funeral dawned bright and sunny. Neighbour wives came to leave baking and sandwiches. Jock drove to the airport to meet Katherine and Elaine Stark.

'We'll walk past the March,' Davie decided, 'then we can get into the cars.' The older men nodded approval. The boy was sensible. He'd look after his mother. It was the way of the countryman.

The reading was from the Book of Psalms. Psalms 40, verses 1 to 11. At the fourth verse, Marie felt a surge of pride. Yes, that was her Donald. Then tears welled and splashed on to her skirt. Jean, seated beside her, reached out and took her hand. The women watched from the corner of the house as the cortege snaked its way out if the glen. Then it was time to set tables and make tea before the men came back. This, to Marie, was the first sign of normality in this period. This was what women did in times of physical or mental siege, supported and nourished their men. Directed and guided them as well, but that was done unobtrusively and with intelligence. The push from the back of the bed was the most powerful force known to man, but it was at its most effective when not advertised. After the meal the men who had stock to attend to had to hurry away. The women waited to help clear up, then they too had to leave.

Angus phoned from Glasgow. He had been unable to come to the funeral, but had kept constantly in touch. Ian's car had given trouble on the road down. Jock went to look at it with him. Marie, Jean and Katherine went out for a walk. Davie and Elaine decided to do the same but instead of sticking to the road they went through a gate and followed a burn out to the hill. The first of the brambles were turning black and they picked and ate some as they climbed. When they had gained sufficient height to have a view out to sea, they sat down on a big sloping rock which was only a few inches above ground level. The sun, which was still shining, had left the rock pleasantly warm to the touch. A stray cleg settled on Davie's arm and he squashed it with his other hand.

Neither spoke for a time. 'What are you thinking?' asked Elaine.

'We're both due to go to university soon and now I think that I shouldn't go.'

'Why not?'

'I feel that it isn't fair to leave Mum now. She'll be all alone if I go away.'

'Davie,' for a young girl her voice was suddenly hard, 'how many people have visited your house in the three days since your father died, not counting the couple of hundred who were at his funeral today?'

'Oh, twenty, thirty, I don't really know.'

'Of course you don't, because you live among people who care about other people. How many people do you think visited us when Kay was drowned? I'll tell you,' she went on, 'not a bloody one. I was only nine, but I'll never forget it. My father didn't take a single day off work. The service was at a funeral parlour. He and two of his colleagues came to the service, went to the cemetery then went straight back to work. My mother and I walked home alone from the funeral parlour. About ten o'clock that night I was in the process of crying myself to sleep when I heard him come home. He didn't even come in to see me. When I awoke the next morning he had gone off to work again. I didn't see him for more than a week.'

Davie was shocked. 'My God,' he said. 'I didn't know that folk lived like that.'

'They don't. That's not life, that's existence.' She swept her arm round the horizon. 'This is life and your friends are real people. There's nothing sham or artificial about them. Your mother isn't alone and will not be alone so don't let me hear any more of that nonsense. Donald would have wanted you to go to university and it would break your mother's heart not to carry out his wishes.'

Suddenly, as she looked at him she was aware of the signs of strain on the young features. 'Davie,' her voice was soft, 'have you cried since your father died?'

'No.'

She reached out her arms. 'Then come here and do it now,' she commanded.

Soon she felt his tears percolate through her blouse on to her breasts.

Marie went back to work on the Monday. Davie spent a couple of weeks tidying up round the croft. Then came the morning which was to mark the beginning of his university career. The ever-stalwart Jock came down to bring him to the boat. Marie was already off to work. Jock shook hands with the boy at the foot of the gangway.

'Now, you're no' tae be wastin' time worrying aboot yer mother,' he told him. 'There's plenty o' us tae make sure that she's a'right an' if ye think ye' canna pey us back, ah'll tell ye how ye can. Juist you get a good degree. We'll aw be happy tae bask in the reflected glory.'

'Thanks, Jock. I'll do my best not to let you down.'

The first few days of university gave Davie some problems in finding his way around, but soon he settled into a routine. During the writing of his first letter home to his mother he had to struggle against home-sickness to keep it cheerful. Halfway through his second letter, he discovered that cheerfulness was coming naturally. The country boy was finding the city to be quite tolerable.

He also wrote to Elaine and received in return a letter inviting him to visit the family for a weekend in their Pentland Hills home just outside Edinburgh. On a crisp, frosty Saturday morning of mid-November he took up the invitation. Davie had never seen the dark and brindle pit bings of the Lothians and the pale winter sun did little to soften their raw nakedness. The kindly green hills of his native Kintyre seemed to be of another planet and he felt a lump in his throat. As the train trundled into the outskirts of the city, the smoke from countless coal fires spread a blanket between the sun and the earth and increased his gloom. His sadness evaporated, however, when he walked up the platform of Waverley Station to find Elaine waiting at the barrier.

Their greeting of each other was awkward and self conscious at first, but after a cup of coffee they strolled along Princes Street looking at the shop windows and Davie felt the girl's hand creep into his. Rationing and the aftermath of war was still very much part of city life and to a boy who had spent all of his life in the country, the scurrying, anxious people who jostled him as they went about their business were disconcerting. He was glad when early in the afternoon they boarded a bus to take them out to the Starks' home which turned out to be an imposing two storey stone building set in a large garden surrounded by a stone wall.

They walked round the garden in the gathering dusk on a tour of inspection.

'If you look over you'll see our farm,' she laughed. 'Dad thought that we should be growing some of our own food. We have an old man who comes three days a week through the summer and one in winter. He's lovely. He has spent most of his life at sea and has a beard like the man on the Players' packet. His name's Alex, but we call him "Adam the

Gardener". Mum hasn't had to buy vegetables all summer and the tales that he tells would fill a book, but I'm not sure how many of them are true.'

A three-quarter moon was beginning to shine to the east and the sky was clear and frosty looking. As they rounded the corner towards the front of the house, a car drove in off the road and into the garage.

'There's Daddy,' said Elaine, tugging Davie forward. 'Come and meet him.'

Davie found John Stark to be something of a shock. He knew that this man was younger than his father had been and this knowledge did nothing to prepare him for this tall, thin, stooped man who held out a bony hand in greeting.

'How do you do, David,' even his voice was old and tired. 'Did you have a good journey?' Davie thought that he wasn't even hearing the answer. His head was slightly to the side as though he was listening for something else and his eyes were vague and faraway. 'Must get washed before tea,' he muttered and turned towards the front door through which he disappeared hugging his briefcase.

'Well?' Elaine's voice was sharp.

'Well, what?' Davie was uncomfortable.

'What do you think of my revered father?'

'He... he's surely older than I thought?'

'Only in appearance. He's two years younger than your own father was.' Her tone was bitter.

'Oh, yes, but their lives were so different,' Davie defended. 'Dad was always in the open air and never had a real worry in his life. Your father's job is entirely different.

'That was his choice. Your father had no choice, but made the best of what he had. My father's family were wealthy. Correction,' her tone was bitter. 'My father has plenty of money. He had one brother, Uncle Tom. He was funny. He was six years younger than my father and a doctor. He used to repair all our broken toys for Kay and me.'

Davie now saw tears dripping from her cheeks and her voice broke.

'He was killed in North Africa and wasn't married. When Grandpa died all his estate came to my father. By that time work was his God and required full time worship. When he found that he had less energy he began to top it up from a bottle. He told you he was going to wash. Of course, he is, but he'll also clean his teeth twice in the hope that you won't smell the gin that he'll have drunk between now and teatime. Oh, Davie, I'm so miserable,' and she ran sobbing into his arms.

Despite Katherine's attempts at cheerfulness, tea was an uncomfortable meal. Since Davie had been given the diagnosis the symptoms were obvious. John Stark's hand shook whenever he tried to pass anything and his jokes were explosive and artificial. As the meal progressed the food began to have effect and he became grave and pontifical.

'And what are you going to contribute to this brave new world, young man?' he asked Davie.

The boy was unused to condescension and was slightly taken aback.

'Well,' he said, 'I hope to take my Civil Engineering degree at university and then maybe get taken on by one of the bigger firms.'

'I would have thought that a shepherd's son would, if he was clever enough to go to university, have wanted to cure the sick animals of the world. Much more likely than someone like my daughter.'

'More tea, Davie?' Katherine tried to break up the conversation.

'Yes, please,' Davie was finding his mouth dry and was aware that Elaine's eyes were again glistening with tears. But the older man was not to be denied his prey.

'Well,' his voice was sharp. 'Don't you think so?'

'I've never given it much thought. I like the idea of building roads and bridges where none were before.' Then in an attempt to bring in a lighter note. 'Jock told me that civil engineers and picture painters were the only people who left something by which they would be remembered hundreds of years after their deaths.'

'Piffle. Don't you like animals?'

'Yes, I do. I've always been among animals, particularly dogs. Its just that I've never really wanted to be a vet. When I was younger I just wanted to be a shepherd like my father. It was really Jock who brought me round to seeing the benefits of a wider education.'

The atmosphere round the table was becoming more relaxed, but the respite was to be short. John Stark rose, went to the sideboard where he poured a glass of gin, swallowed half of it straight, added tonic to the rest, then resumed his seat.

'John,' Katherine began, then lapsed into silence.

'What university did this Jock attend?'

'We've told you about him, Daddy,' Elaine put in. 'He's the man who worked in the hospital during the war and is now a mechanic. He's the man who has Benny, the ferret.'

'Ah, yes,' he lifted the glass and emptied it in two large swallows. 'The street pundit. Not the most informed of educational advisers, I would have thought. Anyway, I have to work.'

He rose abruptly and left the room, his exaggerated steps advertising the fact that the recent gin had set to work in concert with its predecessors. Katherine began to cry quietly and Elaine rose and put her arms round her mother from behind.

'Don't cry, Mum,' she said. 'I'd already warned Davie. You go put your feet up and listen to the Saturday Night Play. We'll clear up.'

'You coped well with that but I'm sorry you had to,' said Elaine as they worked at the sink.

'I'm not sure that I did all that well. I've never had much experience of drink. We always had whisky in the house in case anyone called, but nobody ever took too much. I'm surprised that your father's speech was so clear. I would have thought that his words would have been more slurred.'

'When Mum and I first began to suspect that he was drinking too much it was his slurring of difficult words that we noticed first. We thought that he was just too tired as it was always in the evening. Now he speaks more slowly and his diction is clearer. It's like someone learning to cope with a chronic illness.'

'It must be very difficult for your mother.'

'Yes, she would be better to take a job to let her out of the house and meet people, but Dad just flies into a rage if anyone mentions it. Part of the trouble is that Mum has a better degree than he has and he doesn't really like it. Most men would be proud, but not him. She qualified as a lawyer here in Edinburgh.'

'My mother is a teacher with a university degree, but that never seemed to bother my father,' said Davie. 'One of the reasons for moving down to the Croft was that Mum could earn more from teaching than Dad could from herding sheep.'

'Yes, but that was their strength,' Elaine's voice was quiet. 'Your parents had to work for all that they had and shared everything that they got. Donald was a secure man and never jealous of anybody. My father started to drink when men started to come back from the war. Some of them had gone straight into the services when they finished their education and were very bright. During the war he was a big fish because people in his line were scarce. When men started to come back he couldn't face the competition. When I suggested that Mum take a job, he hit the ceiling. His argument was that after Kay's death I needed the security of her being there when I came home. The truth is that he wasn't thinking of me at all. He was thinking of himself. Not that he's ever here during the day. He only comes home to eat and sleep. Even on Sundays he goes back to the office. My big fear is that he'll have a serious accident with the car sometime. Mind you, an injury might wean him off the bottle, but it would be terrible if someone else was hurt as well.'

'This play is rubbish,' Katherine said when they went through to the sitting room. 'Let's put on some records instead. What music do you like, Davie?'

'I'll choose a programme,' said Elaine before he had a chance to reply. 'Take your seats, lady and gentleman.'

Her first record was of Father Sidney MacEwan singing 'Danny Boy'. Next, Bach's 'Jesu, Joy of Man's Desire' played on the organ filled the corners of the room. This was followed by a Scottish accordion player, Jimmy Shand, whose name was rapidly becoming known. He played a selection of waltzes followed by a set of reels.

'And now, lady and gentleman,' Elaine glanced at the clock, 'some music to count sheep by.'

The needle slowed for a few seconds, then Handel's 'Largo' crept from the radiogram. At first it was played softly, little above a whisper on the organ, then, bar by bar, the full orchestra was felt rather than heard. Strangely, the decibel level never seemed to rise, but the sheer size of the music being played seemed to be everywhere. Davie glanced at Katherine. Her eyes were softly closed and she was smiling. Gently the music diminished. As the final bars were retreating from the ear, the door of the room crashed open.

'How the hell can anyone work with that racket going on,' roared John Stark.

Davie sprang to his feet, caught him as he collapsed, and dropped him into an armchair. The sheer shock of the change of atmosphere kept everyone silent for a moment. Katherine appeared calm, but Elaine's face was white and angry.

'How could you,' she said at her father's unconscious body. 'Our lovely evening. How could you.'

Despite her mother being there, Davie put his arm round her shoulders. She pressed her face to him and began to sob. Her father began to snore softly. Moisture blubbered from his lips and trickled down his chin as he exhaled.

'Do you want to get him to bed?' Davie asked Katherine.

'Could we?'

'Yes, I think so. Just a minute.' He left the room, but was back within seconds with a towel from the bathroom. This he drew below the drunk man's legs above the knees, then looked at it for a minute.

'Yes,' he said again, 'if you two can each take an end of that, I'll take his shoulders. The stairs are wide and shallow. It shouldn't be too difficult.'

'I won't,' Elaine burst out. 'Leave him there. Let him freeze. He doesn't deserve help.'

Davie turned to face her and looked full into her eyes.

'Oh, yes you will,' he said quietly. 'It's going to be much easier for everyone if your father wakes up in his own bed. I doubt if he'll remember any of this in the morning.'

He pulled the door wide open and moved behind the chair. Elaine stood for a moment then lifted the other end of the towel which her mother was already holding.

'This is going to look a bit funny, but nobody else will see us,' said Davie. 'The only awkward bit will be the doors. All ready? Right. Upsa-Daisy.'

It certainly wasn't the most dignified of processions. Davie had to walk backwards all of the way, but slowly the master was borne to his bed-chamber in his own house.

'Do you want to undress him?' Davie asked Katherine when finally her husband was lying on top of his bed.

'Yes, but I'll manage all right,' she looked at her daughter with a mixture of defiance and apology, 'I've become quite good at it. This won't be the first time. Thanks Davie,' and she put her arms round him and gave him a quick hug.

Davie's prediction proved to be correct. John Stark appeared at the breakfast table bright and cheerful and showed no sign of the previous night's debauchery.

'Would anyone like a run out the east coast today?' he asked looking round the table. 'I want, briefly, to discuss something with a man from the Newcastle office. I said that I would telephone him this morning and tell him where to meet me. He's a keen young chap who has just joined the company and drives a big Humber. If he comes as far as Eyemouth, we could go by the main road and come back by the coast. My meeting should take less than an hour. How does that sound?'

'That sounds great, John,' Katherine was enthusiastic. 'Do you want me to fill the thermos flasks?'

'Yes, then we can have afternoon tea by the beach.'

'Fine, Dad. Just fine.' Elaine was more muted.

In the end the day did turn out well. Despite his excesses of the previous night, John Stark was a competent driver and they made good time down the main A1 road to the sleepy little seaside town. While the meeting was taking place, Davie and the womenfolk drank coffee in a small café then wandered down to look out to the North Sea. The haar of the earlier morning had disappeared but, quite close to the land, a coaster was plodding north towards the Forth in a haar of her own creation. As they turned their backs on the sea, John Stark's black Vauxhall appeared.

'Told you I wouldn't be long,' he shouted cheerfully as he drew up. 'Now the rest of the day is a holiday.'

'You can come in the front with me, dear,' he said to Katherine. 'The young folk will be all right in the back. I'll keep an eye on them in the mirror.' He had a strange bleating laugh which reminded Davie somewhat irreverently of the voice of a blackface tup. Elaine rolled her eyes at Davie as they entered the car from opposite sides.

Instead of going back towards the main road they took the quieter, country road through Coldingham and over Coldingham Moor. A stretch of nearly twenty miles of main road followed, until they made another right turn to take them back towards the coast. As they rolled into North Berwick the sands of the bay blushed golden in the winter sun.

'Oh, Dad, can we picnic here?' Elaine had contributed little to the conversation until then. 'It looks so lovely.'

'Of course. Great idea. I'll get the rug and the blanket out of the boot,' and he swung the car sharp right off the road. A bank of sand shielded them from the light wind as they sat and they found it surprisingly warm. As the picnic was finished and Katherine rose to pack things away, Davie felt something tickle his ear and thinking it was a fly he attempted to brush it away with his hand. The irritation persisted and again he swiped. At the third attempt, he glanced sideways to find that the source of his annoyance was Elaine with a long, feathery piece of grass.

'Come on, sourpuss, I'll race you to the water,' she said and sprang to her feet.

She had reached the sea by the time Davie caught up and they stood for a time looking out to the Bass Rock before turning to stroll along the water's edge. As they walked, Elaine's fingers sought Davie's hand.

'You'll shock your father,' he said a little nervously.

'No, I won't. Look.'

He glanced over his shoulder to see John and Katherine Stark walking slowly in the opposite direction. Their arms were round each other's waists and they appeared to be deep in conversation.

The grey dusk was fighting the rising moon by the time the big Vauxhall purred into its garage. Katherine and Elaine hurried off to prepare a meal and, after a wash, the menfolk met in the sitting room. John Stark went to a corner press and took out a bottle of gin. He loosened the cork and took a glass in his left hand. As he tipped the bottle he hesitated, then replaced the glass and recorked the bottle in the press and firmly closed the door. That evening the tea table conversation was animated and cheerful.

CHAPTER XI

Davie's next few letters from Elaine reported that things had vastly improved in the Stark household.

'It doesn't seem like the same place,' she wrote. 'Dad has stopped working at nights and weekends and he and Mum have been to a few shows. It now means that I come home to a home instead of just a place to sleep. Mum looks ten years younger. If this goes on… oh, Davie, I just couldn't bear it not to. I'm scared even to think of going back to the way that we lived.

'Now to something just as important. Can you come through to see us again before the Christmas hols.? Dad is quite insistent. Could you come on the Friday night this time? Please?

'If you can manage this coming weekend, drop me a quick note and I'll meet you at Waverley. Please try. If you want to study you can bring some books with you and do it here. Please.'

When Davie stepped off the train he found not only Elaine, but also her father in the welcoming party. John Stark had lost his stoop and his features had filled out. The hand which he extended in greeting was firm and dry. When Katherine came out of the house to meet them, Davie saw for himself that Elaine hadn't exaggerated the improvement in her mother. After greeting Davie, she hooked her arm through that of her husband and the four of them entered the house. When Davie came down after leaving his case in his room, he found that Elaine had gone to help her mother in the kitchen and her father awaited him. After a few lighthearted remarks, the older man became serious.

'Well, Davie,' he said, 'I'm glad that you came back after your experience last time.' Davie felt himself embarrassed, but before he could speak the other man went on. 'I never realised the hell I was subjecting my family to. I've lost the last few years entirely through my own fault. Rest assured I won't make that mistake again. I'm only glad that my family are still here at the end of it.'

It was a happy weekend. Monday morning came too soon for all of them. On the Saturday evening John insisted that Davie phone his mother and they all spoke to Marie in turn.

'Are you coming down to see us over the holidays?' Marie asked Katherine.

'John and I will wait 'til Easter when the weather is better,' Katherine answered but added 'Elaine can go for a few days if she likes,' much to the delight of that young lady.

'I'll come for New Year.' she told Marie. 'You can show me how to make black bun.'

'That'll need to be for next New Year. I'll show you how to eat this year's.'

It was decided that John would leave Elaine through to Glasgow after Christmas and she would travel on by bus. There was no boat during the winter months. Jock would meet her at Campbeltown.

'You can depend on Jock,' said Marie.

Davie found himself on the road home for the Christmas holidays in a state of some surprise that it had come round so quickly. He had expected time to drag, but in reality he found it hard to believe that almost three months had gone by since Jock had left him on Campbeltown pier. Predictably, the wee man was waiting in the cold of the raw December evening when his bus lumbered into the town. The welcome from his mother was joyful. The welcome from his father's two dogs was exuberant. Marie and Jock came to the door attracted by the noise. Davie had gone to let them out for a run before having anything to eat himself.

'They've been so good,' said Marie. 'I let them out for an hour before I go away in the morning then again whenever I come back in the afternoon. They never run away. They're such good company.'

Davie was relieved to see how well his mother was coping with life on her own.

'I found the evenings long when you first went away,' she told him. 'I was rising early in the mornings, working like a beaver, then finding myself with nothing to do when it became too dark to work outside. Now, I lie in bed a little longer and move a little slower. I really find it hard to believe that your first term is over.'

'That makes two of us, really,' said Davie.

'Do you enjoy university as much as I did? You look as though you do. You look great.'

'The first few days were horrible. I was terribly homesick. Several nights I would have quite cheerfully set off to walk home. Then I seemed to drop into a routine and the days flew past. Going to Edinburgh helped too.' he added.

'Yes,' Marie was serious. 'I understand that you helped Edinburgh as much as Edinburgh helped you.'

'You know the story then? I didn't know until I got there.'

'Oh, yes. Katherine had been very worried for a long time. He started drinking just after Kay died. I suppose the sorest loss in this world is for a man to lose a daughter. Katherine tried to keep it from Elaine for as long as she could but in the end, as Elaine grew up, it became too obvious.'

'I don't understand what made him stop so suddenly. My last visit was such a contrast to the first that I didn't want to spoil it by being curious. Everyone was so happy and he looked so well,' said Davie.

'He slept on after you carried him up to bed,' his mother said. 'Then in the early morning he was violently sick all over the bed and himself. By the time that he got back from cleaning himself up in the bathroom, he was reasonably sober and feeling ashamed of himself. By this time Katherine had cleaned up and changed the bed. She made a cup of tea and they sat up in bed and talked. When he was suitably attired in his hair shirt, she told him how you had carried him upstairs. She cheated a bit by telling him also that you had undressed him and put him to bed. Don't look so shocked, Davie. I'm quite sure that that's one lie that will be forgiven. If ever there was a lie where the end proved to have justified the means, that must be it.'

'Do you think, or more important, does Katherine think he'll be able to keep it up?' asked Davie.

'If he wants to keep her and Elaine he'll have to. Like many men poor John doesn't seem to be as strong as his wife, but by now I'm sure that he realises how much he nearly lost. What's he like anyway? I find it strange to think that I know so much about a man whom I've never met.'

'You're lucky. If he stays on the wagon the revised version that you'll meet will be a vast improvement. I knew from what Elaine had told me that he must be younger than Dad, but when I first met him he looked to be at least in his sixties. I could hardly believe the improvement on my next visit. Katherine must have had a really terrible life over the last years. I often wonder what makes men take to drink like that. Particularly clever, well-off men. You would think that he would realise that Kay's death was as big a loss to her mother as it was to him. I just don't understand it.'

'We were lucky, Davie,' his mother told him. 'Old Mr Bennett is fond of saying that alcohol is a good servant and a bad master. We've only seen it used as a servant, thank God. When John first took the post at the university, Katherine thought that he had broken the habit, but then he started to take outside consultancies on top of the university work. During the war he had been a very important man and very much top of his tree. Then younger men started to come home and he felt himself threatened. The secret of success through hard work lies in knowing when to take things easier. Despite being left a fortune poor John seems to be very insecure. "A clever man wi' a slippy grip o' common sense" as Jock would say. Whatever you do in life, Davie, always remember that contentment with your lot can be a major part of your income.'

'You sound a bit like Jock,' laughed her son.

Elaine arrived late in the evening in the middle of a downpour. Jock sent her ahead and carried in her case for her, but even so she got dripping wet between the car and the door.

'The bus had a puncture,' she explained her lateness to Marie. 'I felt so sorry for the driver. He got soaking wet changing the wheel. On top of that, some of the passengers were complaining about us being late. It wasn't his fault. The poor man did his best.'

'Ach,' said Jock, shaking the water out of his hair like a terrier, 'the world's fu' o' folk that if ye were tae save them fae droonin', wad ask ye why ye didna save their bunnet while ye were at it.'

During the next few days, Marie was to realise how much that she missed the daughter which nature had denied her the opportunity to have. Davie spent a lot of the daylight hours outside catching up on work about the croft and as a result she and Elaine spent much time in each others company. Hogmanay was not the sad time that Marie had expected. Early in the evening the dogs began to bark. Davie got up and went to the door and after a short time they heard his voice raised in greeting.

'Och, who can this be, just when we were settled comfortably.' said Marie to Elaine as she rose and laid aside her knitting. She got to the door in time to meet Jean and Ian as they entered.

'We thought we would surprise you,' said Jean. 'Ian wanted to phone to tell you we were coming, but I wouldn't let him.'

'I'm just so glad that you came,' Marie told her. 'We'll soon sort out beds, don't worry. When did you last eat?'

'Not so long ago,' said Ian. 'We stopped off in the town to see Jock. He had been working and was just in and washed. He went out and brought back fish suppers for the three of us.'

'Yes, 'a Glasgow pit by tea' he called it,' laughed Jean. 'His wee flat is shining like a new pin.

I'm often telling Ian about how useless men are on their own, but after seeing how well Jock copes, I'm not so sure now.'

'Yes, but Jock's exceptional,' said Marie. 'He's the only man ever I knew who makes a perfect job of ironing a shirt. Anyway, I know that Ian would like a dram and I'll put the kettle on for the rest of us'.

As Ian and Davie settled by the fire the womenfolk went through to the kitchen where the chatter became audibly animated to the two men in the sitting room.

Ian smiled. 'I'm going to be a father in the summer.'

'Oh, great. That will make me a gratuitous uncle.'

'Yes, it will. Now, young man, I hope that you approach this with a gravity relative to the seriousness of the duty.'

'Oh, I will. I'll take lessons from Jock. You're the nearest to a brother that ever I've had and Jock is the nearest to an uncle,' and they both laughed.

Marie was pleased.

'Oh, Jean, that's splendid news. Are you feeling all right? I must say that you look well.'

'Breakfast hasn't been much fun for the past few weeks, but apart from that I've been fine. Doctors now are much more particular about blood pressure than they used to be and I may have to go easy on the salt, but for me that won't be too big a sacrifice.'

'The sickness soon passes. I know that it did with me anyway,' said Marie. 'The only snag that I had was a craving for oatcakes before Davie was born. I used to sit up in bed at night to eat them. Donald used to get mad at me because there were crumbs everywhere.'

'Can you take through the tray, Elaine, I must see Ian and tell him what a clever boy he is' and she ran through to the sitting room.

As the last stroke of midnight dripped from the clock to herald the New Year, there was a knock at the door and Davie went to find Jock standing on the doorstep with a lump of coal in his hand. Shortly afterwards the two neighbouring farmers arrived complete with wives, and Katherine and John phoned from Edinburgh. In what seemed no time it was three o' clock in the morning and everyone was tired. The farmers, who had to rise early, went home.

Jock also rose to go.

'Oh, no, Jock,' said Marie, 'you don't need to leave us surely. It's too late for you to drive back now. I'll make a bed for you on the sofa here.'

'Och, ye've plenty of folk here, ah'll come back the morn,' began Jock but Elaine rose and hooked his arm through his.

'Jock,' she said, 'I want to see the first sunrise of the year from the top of Cnocan Lin. If you go now, who is going to take me?'

The wee man was visibly pleased. 'Ach, weel, ah suppose there's some arguments ye juist canna win,' he said, 'but if that's the case, it's time that ye wur in yer bed, young lady. We'll need to be oot o' here juist efter seven at the latest.'

'Just go quietly then,' said Ian and everybody laughed.

'We'll expect breakfast on the table when we get back at ten o'clock,' Jock had the last word.

He was up and washed with a cup of tea made when Elaine came through the following morning.

The last of the night was still lurking in the corners when they got outside.

'We'll tak the dogs wi' us for a run,' said Jock opening the door.

The younger dog which had been a farm pup given to Donald to train and then left with him, bounded out excitedly, but old Gem followed much more sedately. Jock had taken one of Donald's crooks from the house and after they went through the gate on to the hill he held it out sideways. The young dog grabbed the other end and the two of them proceeded for a time in this fashion like Siamese twins joined by an umbilical cord.

After a time the dog tired of the game and ran on ahead startling the breakfasting rabbits. As they gained height, Jock stopped for a moment beside a burn looking down at a small green hollow which sloped down towards the water. In the middle of the hollow was a scar showing where the earth had been recently dug.

'What's that, Jock?' asked Elaine.

A pause, then 'It's Benny,' he told her. 'Three weeks ago I found him deid in his box in the mornin'. We had a lot o' fun up this burn in the last couple o' years so ah buried him up here. Ah thocht that he'd like that.'

'I'm sorry, Jock. I didn't know. Nobody said.' Elaine came close to him.

'Ach, ah never said tae onybody. Everybody's had enough bother for wan year. Benny was an auld man an' he had a happy life. He died o' auld age. Ye canna ask for much mair o' this life. Come on, we'll huv tae keep gaun tae beat the sun to the top.'

At the top, the air was clear and cold with an overcast sky. 'A high cairry' Jock described the cloud. As they sat on stones in the shelter of the old building, their breath made patterns in the still air. Low to the east, the sky was clear and, as they watched, a red, angry looking ball of sun tipped the low Ayrshire hills. For about five minutes it lit up the valley beneath them picking up the silver of the meandering river through the denuded trees on its banks. The hills on the east coast of Ireland were white with snow, but a heavy shower travelling down the North Channel soon obscured them from view.

Jock dug into the side pocket of his jacket and provided a bar of chocolate which he broke in half.

'How did ye ken aboot this place?' he asked as he handed half to Elaine.

'I walked out here with Davie in the evening after his father's funeral. He was very mixed up and needed to find himself. We sat for a time on a rock at the head of the burn and then walked up here. We watched the sun going down over the Moil hills. It seemed so peaceful and permanent that I wanted to wait here forever. Things weren't too good at home at that time,' she finished quietly.

'Och, aye. But that could be a' behind ye noo.'

'How did you know about it, Jock?' she was surprised.

'Yer mother telt me,' he said after a pause. 'When ye were here for Donald's funeral she was standin' at the corner lookin' at the view. Ah walked up behind her. She didnae hear ma feet on the grass an' when ah spoke she nearly jumped oot o' a year's growth. Then ah saw that she had been greetin' an' ah thocht that wis because o' Donald, an' quite natural, but when ah spoke tae her the whole story cam oot. Whit she wis needing wis somebody wi' a big lug an' a wee mooth an' ah juist let her speak hersel' oot. Up tae then she had only telt Marie. Ower the years ah've seen quite a few folk lake yer faither – able men that the world juist became too much for. In a lot o' cases, it takes some form o' public disgrace tae let them see how far wrong they've gone. Ah telt this tae yer mother. Ah'm gled that in yer faither's case the public wis confined to young Davie.'

She looked at him startled and he went on 'Dinna worry, Davie didnae tell me. Ah've had a long letter fae yer mother.'

'You're a marvel, Jock, really you are. I don't know what we would all do without you.'

'Lassie,' he said, rising to his feet, 'see yon wee corner doon by the shore, it's full o' folk that couldnae be done withoot an' the world's still goin' on.'

As they had been speaking, the rising sun had been swallowed up in cloud and the first lazy drops of cold rain presaged the snow shower to come. The two dogs had been amusing themselves, digging without any chance of success at a rabbit burrow, but a sharp whistle from Jock was sufficient to make them abandon this futility and romp off ahead down the hill. When they got back to the house, everybody was up and the smell of frying bacon met them as they opened the door. Halfway through breakfast Jean rose and with steady step made her way to the bathroom.

The first two days of the new year passed quietly with several friends and neighbours dropping in. Ian, Jock and Davie went along to spend an hour with the Bennetts, both physically frail, but mentally as alert as ever.

'I hear that Elaine came for New Year,' said Mrs. Bennett to Davie. 'How is she and how is her mother?'

'Very well,' Davie told her. 'Katherine wasn't able to come this time, but I think the plan is that the whole family will come for Easter.'

'Good. Try to bring Elaine along to see us before she goes back this time.'

The Sunday saw Ian and Jean on their way back to Perthshire. Jock also went back 'tae wind the nock' before his work on the Monday morning. Because Davie had been doing work on the croft, Marie and Elaine had spent a lot of time together during Elaine's holiday and a terrible sense of loneliness overcame her after Jock had picked up the young folk to take them to the bus for Glasgow from where Elaine would get a train to Edinburgh. In the afternoon, she took the dogs and walked across to visit the Bennetts who were delighted to see her. Elaine's visit had pleased them greatly.

'You're lucky, Marie,' old Mr. Bennett told her in his soft West Highland voice.

'She's a lovely girl. Aye. Lovely in looks and lovely in nature.'

CHAPTER XII

The swallows came with the spring as did the Starks. John David Boyd came with the summer and Davie looked after the croft to allow his mother to travel through to see him. It was her first visit since the Boyds had moved to Perthshire.

'I'm impressed,' she told Ian as they stood at the door of the house looking back at the hills above Loch Earn. 'It's almost as nice as Kintyre. Mind you, your son is nicer than the two of them put together.'

Ian and Jean wanted to bring their son 'home' to be baptised. Marie had to arrange a suitable date with the local minister. The last Sunday of August was chosen. Elaine came for a week to include that date. She was tanned and fit looking and her fair hair had been bleached even fairer by the sun.

'Adam hasn't been well at all,' she explained. 'Our garden is really far too much for him now but it is very difficult to get him to take things easier. He's a determined old cuss. I've been working with him all summer. It's been great fun.'

'It certainly hasn't done you any harm. You look great,' Marie told her.

'Oh, yes, but wait till you see Mum. She painted all the windows and gutters herself and most of the time wore nothing but a bikini. Dad says that she looks like Marlene Dietrich.'

'Things are still good then?'

'Things are great. It's another world from what it was before.'

To Davie, his second year in university seemed to pass in weeks rather than months. The work was much more interesting, he now had a circle of friends and at least one weekend per month was spent in Edinburgh. He also took an interest in sport, having already discovered an aptitude for middle distance running, but, mindful of Ian's worryings of long ago, was careful not to let this take up too much of his time. His mother's letters were always newsy and cheerful and she always phoned Edinburgh to coincide with his visits. Elaine was finding her course more difficult.

'I wish that I had grown up with animals, like you,' she told Davie. 'I find that I have everything to learn. The people who have a head start are those who grew up on Noah's Ark farms where they had cows, horses, sheep, pigs, dogs, cats and hens. I only had Toby and even that was for less than a year. We don't do much practical yet but I find pigs really awkward. Even the big horses can be persuaded but pigs need brute force.'

'We never had any. Dad didn't like pigs, but I suppose the phrase 'as dour as a pig' had some basis in fact,' said Davie.

'I'll need to find a vet willing to let me see some practice next summer, but I want large animal experience and most of the farms around here have bought tractors and sold their horses. I just don't know what to do.'

Marie provided a possible solution when she telephoned that night.

'I'll talk to our local vet if you like,' she told Elaine. 'He was at university at the same time as I was. Some of the farmers here have bought tractors, but there are still a lot of horses and there seem to be more cows than ever. If he's willing to take you on you can stay with us. A lot of folk now go from here to work in the town so it shouldn't be difficult to arrange a lift for you.'

Marie's diplomatic skills proved equal to the task required and she had her reward during the summer of 1949 in having the company of two happy young folk every evening. Jock spent most of his spare time doing maintenance jobs about the croft.

'It's no right that that boy should hiv tae work a' through every holiday,' he told Marie. 'Ah enjoy getting oot in the fresh air efter bein' a' week breathin' petrol fumes.'

Quiet days in the veterinary practice tended to coincide with good weather days as farmers were loth to lose a good hay-making day on anything other than an emergency, so routine animal health jobs were chased into a corner by the sun. This, combined with Jock's industry enabled the young folk to spend quite a number of afternoons swimming off the sandy beach which was little more than a mile from the croft.

A large grass covered rock overlooked the beach and after swimming they had the habit of climbing up to sunbathe in a secluded hollow where they were out of sight of other people. On a particularly warm afternoon in early August, they had swum for a time then lain back on the sand letting the tide wash over them before climbing up to where they had left their clothes. Each had developed a deep tan and in Elaine's case this was enhanced by her long fair hair. As they lay in the sun, the squeals of happy children floated up to them.

Suddenly, they were aware that one squeal had become a scream and Davie scrambled to his feet. About fifty yards from the base of their rock a small boy was jumping up and down on the sand. His mouth was open in an almost continuous scream and his right arm pointed out to sea. Davie followed the direction of the pointing hand and as he looked a slim arm waved frantically before disappearing beneath the surface some distance out.

'Somebody in trouble. Come on,' he said to Elaine and without waiting to climb down, jumped from the top of the rock to the sand and ran to the screaming child. As he was moving he was aware of other people converging on the scene. Davie's approach, combined with shortage of breath, silenced the screams for a moment.

'It's Jenny,' the boy gasped with a mixture of rage and fear in his voice. 'she won't come out of the water to play.' In his left hand he held a thick rubber ring about nine inches in diameter.

Elaine had by now caught up and as she and Davie looked out to sea, they could see a small form floating about fifty yards out.

'It's not far. I'll get her and you keep this wee man calm,' Davie told Elaine.

'Be careful, Davie,' he heard as he ran into the water.

The sea was calm with only a slight swell, but when he was about twenty yards out Davie found that he seemed to be moving faster and in less time than he had expected he had reached a little girl of about seven or eight. She was making feeble motions but her face was at times dipping beneath the surface and her long red hair floated round her head like a sea anemone. As Davie caught her arm, her eyes flickered open for a moment then closed. 'It's all right,' he said, as he turned on his back and caught her beneath her chin. 'Just lie still and we'll soon be ashore.'

After his fast swim out he didn't find that too easy to say but like so many things he soon found that it was going to much more difficult to do. A glance to the shore after several minutes told him that he had made very little progress if any. The girl was making no movement and now seemed to be unconscious. Davie rested for a moment then was horrified to find that he was noticeably farther from the shore.

On the beach Elaine had been joined by several people before a tubby red haired woman and a taller man who walked awkwardly with a stick pushed their way to the front. The boy ran to the woman and grasped her round the knees.

'Jenny won't come out of the water to play with me,' he sobbed with a mixture of temper and terror as he realised that something was badly wrong.

'Don't worry, she'll be all right,' said Elaine before the white-faced woman could speak. 'Davie has got her. He's strong. He'll bring her in.'

'Oh, why did she go out so far? She's only learning to swim.' The woman was obviously putting an effort into controlling her voice.

The man didn't speak for a moment but stood looking out to sea. Suddenly he tried to turn to go back up the beach, but his foot caught in the sand and he fell.

'There's a coil of light rope in that boat,' he told Elaine as she helped him to his feet. 'Get it for me.' He pointed to a rowing boat that had been pulled right up onto the beach.

When Elaine came back with the rope, the man picked up the rubber ring which the child had dropped and fastened the two together with a couple of swift half-hitches.

'What are you going to do, Archie?' asked the woman.

'I'm going to wade out a bit then throw the rope to them,' he was gathering up his stick as he spoke.

'But your leg. You can't. You'll fall.'

'I'll go with him,' said Elaine, then to the man. 'Leave your stick here and take my arm. I'll steady you.'

'Good girl,' said the man, who obviously wasn't excitable, and together they waded into the water.

At first the slope of the sand was gentle and they had made about ten yards before the water was lapping above their knees. Then the slope became more noticeable and after about five more yards the water was up to their hips and Elaine had to cling tightly to the man to keep him steady.

'We'd better not try to go any farther,' he said. 'It isn't going to help if we get into difficulties as well. Your friend doesn't seem to have lost any ground so I should be able to reach him from here.'

'What do you want me to do?' asked Elaine.

'Stand close behind me and catch my belt. Just watch that I don't hit you when I swing my arm back.'

The slight swell was no more than six inches or so but just as he made his cast a wave reached them. This, combined with the velocity of the throw, made them both stagger and they suffered the misery of seeing the rubber ring land several feet short of Davie and the child.

'Damn,' said Archie, starting swiftly to recoil the rope. 'I should have watched the swell. Let me turn sideways a little,' he told Elaine. 'If I can swing my shoulder it will give me a longer throw. I should have wet the rope as well to make it heavier.'

When Archie had his feet positioned to his satisfaction, Elaine bent and, thrusting her right shoulder into the small of his back, she reached round his waist, grasped his belt and pulled him firmly back towards her. His body twisted, there was a quick grunt of effort, then 'Ah, that's better.' Elaine straightened and could see the yellow rubber ring rising on the swell a few yards beyond Davie.

'Don't pull just yet,' said Archie when she reached for the end of the rope which he held in his left hand. Give him time to work out how best to secure the rope. We don't want to lose hold of them now.

For Davie, the arrival of the lifeline was not a moment too soon. In order to prevent them being carried farther out to sea he had to lie on his back with his head towards the shore. A quick glance to shore had told him that people had gathered there, but until the splash of the rope beside him he did not know what they were doing to help him. Simply maintaining his position was exhausting him very quickly, but at the sight of the lifeline he felt the adrenalin of youth coursing through his veins. The wee girl had shown no sign of life for some time but when he let go of her chin to grab the rope he felt her hand grasp feebly at his wrist. 'It's all right,' he said. 'Just lie still. Someone's thrown us a rope.' As quickly as possible he passed his right arm under the rope at the shoreward side and brought his arm over to trap the rope in his armpit beneath his shoulder then repeated the manoeuvre with his left arm. Grasping the child round the waist he threw his left leg over the seaward end and allowed his body to drop in the water until he had a hold of the rubber ring and could pass it over his right hand to the crook of his elbow. Again on his back with his head towards the shore he raised his left arm and waved. Within seconds he felt a gentle pressure on his right shoulder which told him that they were being towed to safety. The little girl's eyes were now firmly closed and her little body lay inert on top of Davie.

'I just wanted to pull and pull,' Elaine told Davie afterwards, 'but Archie wouldn't let me.'

'If we pull too hard your friend may lose his grip on the rope,' he said. 'Pull gently and try not to jerk.'

Archie's policy proved wise and progress towards the shore was steady. When they were close enough, Archie bent to lift his daughter as Elaine helped Davie to his feet. Just then there came the sound of splashing behind them and Elaine turned to find the local doctor, like Archie, fully clad except for his jacket, running through the water.

'Give your daughter to me,' he said to Archie and noticing hesitation, added quickly, 'it's all right, I'm a doctor.' Then to Elaine 'You help the men.' As Davie steadied on his feet, Archie grasped his hand. Elaine saw that the father's eyes were glistening and she guessed that he was unable to speak. Quietly she moved between the two and with the father on her left arm and the rescuer of his daughter on her right arm, waded out of the water. When they got to the sand they found that the doctor had laid Jenny face down on a rug and, straddling her slight body, was applying artificial respiration. Her mother was anxiously kneeling in the sand but someone had sensibly taken the little boy away.

The doctor's stethoscope hung round his neck with the disc tucked into the front of his shirt. He glanced up as they approached and, taking out the disc of his stethoscope, he applied it to the still body. After ten long seconds he looked up again.

'Good man, Davie,' he said, 'she'll be as good as new by tomorrow.'

The mother leapt to her feet and threw her arms round Davie's neck.

That night Marie awoke to a sound from the next bedroom. She went through to find Elaine lying face down and sobbing into her pillow.

'What's wrong, Elaine?' she asked quietly, sitting on the edge of the bed. The girl scrambled to a sitting position and clung to the older woman.

'It's stupid after so long but I was thinking of Kay,' she sobbed. 'Seeing that woman today has let me know for the first time just how Mum must have felt.'

CHAPTER XIII

Both Davie and Elaine found third year at university to be much more difficult. Also, since they had spent so much of the summer together they each found themselves missing the other and, during the first few weeks, took time to settle into the discipline of study. Several times, if the weather was good, Davie found himself on the sports ground when he should have been more gainfully employed and it took a few quiet words from the old groundsman to let him see that his priorities were getting out of balance. This was to be his graduation year. He couldn't disappoint his mother.

He started to write notes to Elaine, at all times of day and in all sorts of odd places and then each evening, when he finished studying for the day, he copied them into a letter. These he posted off several times a week. Every weekend he wrote to his mother and received long, newsy letters in return.

On his last visit before the Christmas break, Elaine's parents went out to a show on the Saturday night leaving the young folk on their own in the house. It had been a pleasant winter day with the promise of frost at night and Elaine and the two men had spent the day tidying up the garden and digging for the next spring planting, while Katherine did her Christmas baking. After her parents went out, Elaine went to take a bath while Davie listened to the wireless. He sat wedged in the corner of the sofa, part of his attention on the construction manual resting on his knees and the other on the latest episode in the weekly adventures of the MacFlannels, a radio serial to which he knew his mother would also be listening.

The strains of The Glasgow Highlanders were fading at the end of the programme when Elaine came through. She was wearing a long blue dressing gown tied at the waist and had a turbanned towel covering her wet hair.

They had spent a lot of time in each other's company and their relationship had developed into a comfortable, trusting almost brother and sister habit with passion fairly well under control. Although the subject was never directly referred to, each had accepted in their own minds that one day they would marry each other. Davie hoped to graduate in the summer, but he then had to 'serve his time' for three years with an established firm after National Service. Elaine still had another two years at university before getting her degree, but would be able to practise her profession immediately after graduation. The increasing use of antibiotics in veterinary medicine at this time, was closing the gap between experience and newly qualified knowledge.

Davie dropped his manual to the floor as Elaine sat close beside him on the sofa and rested her head on his shoulder. After a moment she straightened her back towards him.

'Dry my hair for me, Davie,' she said, then, 'No, wait a minute,' she added, 'are you listening to this wireless now?'

'No, switch it off it you like.'

This she did, then turned to the record player before returning to the sofa. As she sat down, the mellow voice of Donald Peers percolated into the room. 'Now,' she said, taking the towel from her head and handing it to Davie. 'Gently, now. Just keep time to the music.'

'If I give my heart to you, will you handle it with care,' sang the rich voice and Davie followed it with slow, circular movements of his hands. As the record died he put down the towel. Elaine leant backwards over his knees and turned her face up to be kissed. The scent of her newly washed body and the warm mustiness of her still damp hair were in the boy's nostrils and the kiss became long and deep. When Elaine felt a hand inside the vee of her dressing gown she opened her eyes and caught the wrist.

'No, Davie,' she said, looking up into his eyes. 'You know we can't. Don't make it any harder. I'm sorry. I led you on.'

Davie withdrew his hand and was quiet for a moment. 'I'm not sure how much longer I can go on like this,' he said eventually.

'Neither am I, but I suppose it's easier for a woman than it is for a man.'

They sat in silence for a long time and in the end it was Elaine who spoke first.

'Davie,' she said, 'if ever it becomes impossible, really impossible, please tell me. Now I'm going to make a cup of tea.'

When she reached the door, she turned round to face him. 'Davie,' she said impishly, 'would you like me to run a cold bath for you? The cushion which he threw after her disappearing form knocked a vase off the sideboard, but fortunately the carpet cushioned its fall sufficiently to prevent it breaking.

As she had done in the previous two years, Elaine spent Christmas with her parents and the New Year with Davie and Marie. Davie had utilised his study time well between the start of the holidays and Christmas so he and Elaine were able to take advantage of some fine winter weather to go on some of their favourite walks. Elaine also visited the local veterinary practice where she was welcomed with open arms and assured that they would be pleased to have her back for the following summer. This was good news to Marie. Davie, subject to his successful graduation had the offer of a place with an international firm of structural engineers and the prospect of Elaine's company for the summer was something to look forward to.

The time between January and Easter seemed all too short to Davie. He knew that his mother would be disappointed if he didn't qualify at the first attempt and the amount of study time divided by the amount of study which he still felt he had to do was presenting a frightening equation. His first visit of the year to Edinburgh was on the second weekend of February. Elaine met him at Waverley station and was taken aback at his appearance.

'You look as seedy as a raspberry,' she told him. 'What on earth have you been doing?'

'Studying.'

'Well, you can forget it for this weekend. It won't do any good to run yourself into the ground Take the weekend off and you'll be fitter for the fray when you get back to Glasgow.'

When they got to the house, Katherine added her voice to that of her daughter. Accepting defeat gracefully and gratefully, Davie settled down to an enjoyable weekend.

'I didn't realise how much I needed the break,' he wrote to his mother, 'Studying was becoming a disease which I couldn't shake off. I'll just have to learn to pace myself better.'

He made two more visits to Edinburgh before Easter, but each time he left his books behind in his digs in Glasgow.

A surprise awaited him when he stepped off the bus in Campbeltown accompanied by Elaine at the start of the Easter break. Usually Jock was standing at the bus stop, but this time he wasn't to be seen. They stood beside their cases on the pavement as the bus drew away. It was a mild spring evening and some of the other bus passengers stood around chattering to friends. Looking down the street, Elaine became aware of someone waving from a shining wee L-plated Morris 8 parked about twenty yards away. As she touched Davie on the elbow, Marie stepped out of the driver's seat and Jock alighted on to the pavement. The expression on the face of her son made Marie burst into laughter.

'Jock has been looking out for a car for me since before Christmas,' she explained as, with Davie and Elaine in the back seat, they drove towards home. 'This one came into the garage at the beginning of January and Jock brought it down to let me see it. It's lovely. He's been teaching me to drive ever since. I was determined to be able to drive you home for your holiday.'

'You're a brave man, Jock,' Davie teased his mother. 'After seeing her with a wheelbarrow, I would have thought twice about sitting beside her in car for the first time.'

'Don't you believe it' Marie defended herself. 'I was good. Wasn't I Jock?'

'I've aye been careful no' tae get between a mother an' her dochter,' said Jock gravely. 'But ah'll risk a son. Aye, ye wurna bad, no' bad at all.'

'Have you applied for your driving test, Marie?' asked Elaine.

'I have the form, but I haven't sent it away yet. I'm just waiting for the approval of my instructor,' The last was said with a sideways smile at Jock.

'Ye could apply any time ye like noo', was the verdict. 'It takes a few weeks for yer turn tae come roond an' bae that time ye' should be ready.'

'Now, continued Jock, 'ye can reverse in here tae prove me right. But watch my car while ye're aboot it,' he added hastily.

When Jock was at work, Marie lacked a co-driver so the car was less used during the holiday than might otherwise have been the case, but Jock made valiant efforts to be there as often as possible.

Easter Sunday afternoon was spent with a picnic on the hills above the Mull of Kintyre lighthouse.

'I don't think that it was fair to ask my wee car to come up that awful road,' joked Marie as Davie and Elaine brought out the basket which had been wedged between them. Nevertheless, she was obviously proud of her driving feat in getting them there.

They walked out the hill for a short distance and stopped at a large flat rock from where they could look down on the lighthouse and over the North Channel to the Irish coast and Rathlin. The sun was bright enough to cause a heat haze to hang on the top of the hill to the south and while the rock on which they sat wasn't warm, the unpleasant chill of winter was gone from it. Several larks competed for the sound space above them and fulmars and gulls wheeled and circled from the cliffs below. Davie and Elaine rose after a short time and wandered to the north following the line of an old sheep path. The skeleton of the old settlement of Ballymontgomery nestled in its green hollow far below them.

As they rounded a large rock, they came upon a neat cairn of stones built at one end of a small patch of green. Davie, who was leading, stopped and stood looking for a moment.

'What is it, Davie?' Elaine had moved close and slid an arm round his waist.

'It's Glen's grave. Remember I told you about my dog who was killed when he went over the cliff. Dad and Ian built the cairn when they buried him here.'

Elaine turned so that they were both looking out to sea and then turned back through 180 degrees until they were looking down the glen. Although the house was below their line of vision, the smoke from the afternoon fire could be clearly seen After a few minutes of silence, she turned them back until they were looking again at the cairn. Suddenly a grouse rose from quite close to them and 'go bocked' its way down the glen.

'Do you ever regret leaving it, Davie?' she asked.

The reply wasn't immediate. 'In a way. Yes, I suppose I do, but as things turned out we were lucky. If we had still been in the glen when Dad died, I'd probably have left school and become a shepherd. That wouldn't have been a disaster for me. It's a great life, but Mum would have been my housekeeper and wouldn't have had the kind of life that she has now.' Again they turned to look down the glen for a moment before retracing their steps to rejoin Marie and Jock.

On the last day of their holiday, they had climbed out to the familiar comfort of Crocan Lin. Spring had taken a resolute grip and the day was beautiful. For almost two hours they sat close together in the sunshine. The lazy sounds of careless freedom bathed them in contentment and hardly a word was exchanged.

The holiday came to an end. The loneliness of intensive study returned. Elaine had the familiarity of home to nestle into but Davie had to return to digs.

On the evening of his first full day back in Glasgow, Davie sat at a small table in his room. He looked out at grey, sightless windows set in sooty buildings and longed for the green and soft browns of his home. He thought of his mother who by now would have finished her evening chores about the croft and would be walking the dogs. He thought of the phlegmatic Jock who had become such a steadying influence in their lives since the death of his father. He thought of his father. Big, quiet, undemanding Donald who would have been so proud to attend his son's graduation. The word graduation brought his eyes back to his books.

On afternoons when the weather was suitable, he developed the habit of taking his studies to the sports ground and sitting in the shade of a large sycamore. The quiet country boy was a favourite with the old groundsman and one afternoon, seeing Davie staring into space, the old man sat down beside him and pulled his pipe from a waistcoat pocket.

'Worried, lad?' he asked quietly.

'Yes. A bit.'

'And could you be working any harder?' the voice was gentle Islay.

'No.'

'In that case you should stop the worrying. You're working as hard as you can and you're trying your best. There is no point in wasting good mental energy worrying about something that cannot be solved by worry. No point at all.'

The implied fatalism in the older man's words had a calming effect and in the time before the exams Davie's work was more disciplined and productive. After working towards a climax over a period of three years, the day after the final exam was something of a vacuum. Davie went to Edinburgh for the weekend and Elaine met him off the train. They embraced tightly for a long moment, then she stood back and looked at him with the unspoken question in her eyes.

'I think so,' he said. 'Yes. I think so, I hope so. I hate the idea of having to do re-sits. How about you?'

'Fourth year beckons,' she replied. 'We had a practical today. A wee man with a beard. He was lovely. I'd do a re-sit with him any time.'

Marie and Elaine attended his graduation.

'Tu Quo Que' said the Principal of the university as Davie was capped. Marie wept. 'Donald should have been here. He would have been so proud.'

CHAPTER XIV

Since Ian had volunteered in September 1939, Davie had hankered to share his experiences in the RAF. He had known that conscription would follow graduation. At the beginning of September, he presented himself for service to his country and was posted to a station in Suffolk.

Primary school had been a family affair. There had been some rough and tumble during the adolescent years of secondary school before the relatively private life of the swotting student. To be catapulted into a barrack room was a shock. Since childhood Davie had enjoyed the carelessness of having his own room. Suddenly he had a bed and a locker in common with another three dozen of his species in a vast shed and with less privacy than a horse in a stable stall. The ribald aggression of some of the other men was foreign to him and he found it disturbing. As the man next to him had been unpacking he had brought out a photo of a pretty girl and set it on top of his locker. A hefty young fellow with a knuckle-curled shambling walk stopped in passing, looked at the photo and made a coarse comment. Davie had a snapshot of Elaine taken at the beach earlier in the summer. He left it in the drawer of his locker.

After the inevitable period of square bashing, life began to get better. The sorting-out process which followed made Davie think of sheep being passed through a shedder to separate one grade from another. Along with another four from his barrackroom he was selected for pilot training and moved to an operational airfield. Since he was so recently out of university and still had the habit of study, and also because he was interested, he absorbed the theory easily and quickly. His flying instructor was a good humoured Cockney who had been a wartime pilot of Hurricanes. His family of father, mother, sister and fiancee had all been killed late on in the war when the family home received a direct hit from a flying bomb. Having no home to go back to he had stayed on in the Air Force taking a drop from Pilot Officer to Sergeant. He was a man of irrepressible good humour and by now enjoyed the rank of Flying Officer. He also had a cast iron nerve.

'There's more waitin' for me in the next world than I got left in this one,' he told Davie. So long as I leave quick an' clean I'm not too worried when I go.'

Being a natural leader, rather than a driver of his men, his success rate as a trainer was excellent. 'Never ask a man or a machine to consistently do more than they are capable of,' he told his pupils. 'Everybody and everything can do the exceptional for a short time, but both metal and man become fatigued. Man can recover. Metal can't.'

Davie was to look back on his time of National Service as the most carefree period of his life. Early in the summer he was given leave and told that he was being posted to Nairobi in Kenya. Elaine had successfully passed her fourth year exams and was again going to spend the summer with Marie. The leave blinked past. Marie and Elaine drove him to catch the summer-sailing boat from Campbeltown. They were so happy in each other's company that poor Davie felt slightly out of it. He caught a train from Glasgow to Edinburgh, had a meal with Elaine's parents and travelled south on the overnight train.

On route to Kenya, they dropped at Rome, Cairo and Khartoum before flying on to Nairobi, a city which was little more than half a century old. After the south-east of England the space seemed endless. Davie was to learn that though Kenya was two and a half times larger than Britain, the population of Britain was two and a half times larger than that of Kenya. Despite their apparent poverty, he found that the native population with whom he came in contact had an endemic cheerfulness and good humour which rubbed off on the service men and made them tolerant of the heat and the dust. Despite many warnings, some of the men suffered from sunburn, but those who were careful soon found that the dry heat of the Kenyan winter was preferable to the moist, humid heat of the south of England summer which they had left behind.

During the ten months that he spent in Kenya, Davie fell in love with the country and its people. By the time he left there was an obvious undercurrent of unrest and tales of atrocities in more remote area. This saddened him, but his sadness evaporated when Elaine met him at Waverley Station on his return home. As he emerged through the turnstile, she ran into his arms almost knocking him over.

'Oh, Davie,' she gasped, 'I'm going to graduate in July! I've just found out. I haven't even been home to tell Mum yet.'

That night, after Elaine's parents went to bed, the two young folk sat down to discuss their future. Davie knew that he had a job waiting on his de-mob but, though they had an office in Glasgow, it was a large firm and he could be sent anywhere to gain site experience. Elaine was keener on a large animal rather than a small animal practice, but was shrewd enough to realise that due to the tremendous advances in treatment the latter was becoming very rewarding, both financially and professionally.

'There's a lot of locum work in the government scheme to clear cattle of tuberculosis,' she told Davie, 'but I don't fancy doing that all the time.

I'd rather get an assistant's job with a good mixed practice. Unfortunately, your Mum's friends don't need a full time assistant, but they say that they'll give me a good reference.'

The discussion, punctuated by periods of silence which were joyfully used was still going on when the clock struck midnight.

Davie broke their embrace and went down on one knee on the carpet. 'Elaine Stark, will you marry me?' he asked solemnly.

'Davie Sinclair, I'll be proud to,' she answered.

Their next embrace was broken by her laughter. 'You just asked me to marry you so as Jock wouldn't think that we might live in sin,' she said. 'There's a wide, puritanical streak in our Jock.'

On her graduation day, Davie was back with his squadron in the south of England, but two days later a letter caught up with him. Elaine had been offered a post with a practice on the southern outskirts of Edinburgh. One of their city clients was a large retail dairy which employed them to look after the delivery horses. There was also an extensive farming clientele.

'Just what I wanted,' she wrote. 'The mix of work is just right and I'll be able to live at home.'

By the time of Davie's de-mob, Elaine was settled into her job. He was to be working from the Glasgow office of his firm and his first problem was to find some place to live on a semi-permanent basis. This problem was solved faster than he had feared. On his first day with the firm he met a man who had been in his year at university and who had graduated on the same day. His name was Donald Alex MacNeill and he had been known as 'Damn'. He had been born in Glasgow but his parents, both Gaelic speakers, had the good sense to pass on their native language to their only child. He was tall with the reddish fair hair of his Norse ancestry; a great extrovert character who was instantly popular in most company. 'Damn, what are you doing here?' was Davie's pleased greeting.

'I'm your senior by two years, boy. I tried to join the navy, but the medics wouldn't pass me. They said that I had a heart murmur, I tried to explain that what they were hearing was just the intestinal activity of a curry supper, but they wouldn't listen. Where have you been for the past two long years?'

Davie explained the route which had taken him to where they sat.

'Have you been able to get back into your old digs?' asked Damn.

'No. My landlady doesn't keep well now and has gone to live with her daughter.'

'Can you cook?'

'Yes, fairly well actually.' Davie was puzzled by the question.

Damn laughed at his expression. 'Quest no more for shelter,' he said, then was serious. 'Both my parents died last year. Dad had cancer and Mum just wore herself out nursing him. A month after he died she took a bout of 'flu. I found her dead in bed one morning. She just didn't want to live any more. I still live in the flat on my own and am getting pretty fed up with my own company. If you're willing to concoct the odd pot of stew you're welcome to move in.'

The domestic arrangement proved to be very satisfactory. The flat was in a sandstone block in Hyndland Road and had high ceilinged, airy rooms. Damn had taken his Glasgow Highland status seriously enough to learn to play the bagpipes, an instrument on which he was fairly proficient. Fortunately, the old couple upstairs were slightly deaf and the flat was immediately above a shop which was closed in the evenings. For the first few days Davie was kept busy in the office learning the general routine, but then he was taken out to site work around the city. This suited him. He was not a natural office man. Damn, with the acquired wisdom of his two years experience, was his mentor. The two got on well together both professionally and domestically.

The office manager, Mr. MacLeod, was a strictly religious old gentleman of West Highland extraction. His father had been killed by bandits during a mineral expedition to India around the turn of the century. He lived a frugal existence with his corsetted and calvanistic wife in a dull tenement flat and relieved his frustrations by ruling the office with an inflexible rod of iron. Office gossip maintained that his father and the founder of the firm had been contemporaries and so the son had been taken into the firm when he left school. He was an excellent servant of the firm. His knowledge of the office was meticulous and it was certain that his monetary rewards far exceeded the meanness of his lifestyle. He wore stiff white collars and, when he administered an admonition, had a habit of thrusting his head forward. The restriction of the collar caused his face to redden and he took on the appearance of an agitated turkey cock.

Late one afternoon, Davie and Damn returned to the office after surveying a site. It had been a pleasant sunny day and they were in boisterous spirits. Just as they were settling down in their shared office, there came a tap on the door and the head of the office manager appeared.

'Mr. Sinclair,' he said, 'I think you should be aware that we are unaccustomed to blasphemy in this office.'

As the head disappeared, both young men had difficulty with suppressed laughter, but from then on they were careful not to use the university nickname in the presence of the diminutive, but formidable, Mr MacLeod.

Elaine was on call every fourth weekend. Alternately, on her free weekends, Davie spent the Saturday night in Edinburgh and she spent the Saturday night with the boys in Glasgow. On the latter nights she had Davie's bed and he slept on an old-fashioned sofa in the sitting room. Both of the boys looked forward to her visits although for different reasons. Damn's pleasure arose from the fact that Katherine always sent through a basket of baking or similar delicacies.

'Would your mother like to adopt a son?' Damn asked with a replete sigh on one particular Saturday night after they had dined off a home-made steak pie. Elaine was serious.

'Poor Mum,' she said, 'she's having a hard time with Dad just now. He's taken to working too hard again. Some nights he's too tired to get to bed. I came in from a late call on Thursday night and found him asleep in a chair.'

The following day she and Davie were out to lunch at the home of Angus Graham and his wife and she repeated this story.

'I don't like the sound of this at all,' Angus confided to Davie when the women were washing the dishes after lunch. 'John Stark, like myself, has reached an age where exhaustion can hit him hard, but I hope that he hasn't gone to the bottle again.'

'I never thought of that,' Davie admitted, 'but surely Elaine would have smelt drink on his breath?'

'Not necessarily. Since the war a lot of people have taken to drinking vodka. It doesn't leave a smell on the breath. One or two drivers have landed in hospital because the police thought them to be ill when in fact they were drunk.'

Davie took the opportunity of his next visit to Edinburgh to observe John Stark closely. The man certainly looked tired and drawn. He also seemed irascible at times but this could have been simply due to over-work. Being unsure of himself he said nothing to either Elaine or Katherine and the weekend passed pleasantly enough. The following weekend Elaine was on call and he phoned her on the Saturday evening. For a moment or two her voice seemed strange to him. Then he realised why. She had been crying.

'Oh, Davie, it's Dad,' she answered his question. 'I had to go out last night to a dog that had been run over and didn't get back until near midnight. It was windy and he obviously didn't hear my car coming back. I left my bags in the kitchen and went through to the lounge. He was pouring vodka into a cup as I came through the door. Davie, he was drunk. Stupid, bloody drunk. He had the bottle in his briefcase. It's hellish. Why does he do it? Mum was so happy. Life was so good.'

104

Shortly after seven on the following Wednesday morning the phone rang in the flat and Davie answered it.

'Davie,' Elaine's voice was calm and controlled. 'Dad's dead. We've just found him. We're waiting for the doctor.' Then her voice broke to a sob. 'Oh, Davie, he's taken Barbiturate tablets from my bag and swallowed them. He's committed suicide.'

Davie went to the office in the morning, was given a week's holiday and caught a train at ten o'clock.

Katherine and Elaine had gone to bed around eleven o'clock the night before. John had said that he wanted to finish some work. He had seemed quite cheerful. Katherine had slept and didn't notice that he hadn't come to bed. When she came down in the morning he was lying back in a chair as though he was asleep. A vodka bottle and the small brown Barbiturate bottle were on the floor beside him. Both were empty.

The body had been taken away for post-mortem before Davie arrived. Katherine was surprisingly calm, but Elaine was completely distraught. She blamed herself for having the tablets where her father could gain access to them.

'I never dreamt that he would do something like this,' she sobbed on Davie's shoulder. 'Combined with the alcohol, these tablets were lethal. How could I be so stupid?'

All afternoon she refused to be consoled. The family doctor called after his evening surgery.

'John had cancer of the liver,' he told them. 'He came to me about a month ago complaining of tiredness. I had tests done and made the diagnosis. I told him that he couldn't live for more than two months. That was about a fortnight ago. The pathologist who did the post-mortem phoned me just before I left my surgery. His prognosis would have been four to five weeks from now.' He turned to Elaine and took her hand between both of his own. 'Now, young lady, I know exactly how you feel. But one thing is certain. Your father had a much easier end than he would otherwise have had. The last few years have seen big advances in the control of pain, but we have a long way to go yet. As a doctor, I shouldn't say this, but, in a way, I'm glad that he found these tablets.'

CHAPTER XV

The funeral was on the Monday. Davie travelled to Glasgow on the Tuesday evening with a promise to be back in Edinburgh at the weekend. The doctor's talk had helped Elaine to see the situation in a different light and she had stopped blaming herself for being careless. Jock had driven Marie to Ian and Jean's house on Loch Earn on the Sunday. On the Monday, the four of them travelled to Edinburgh in two cars for the funeral and then went home shortly afterwards. Angus Graham and his wife had come through from Glasgow. Their combined presence had been good for Katherine. Several of John's colleagues had attended the service, but she confessed to Marie that she hardly knew them.

'They all seem to be so busy,' she said. 'There never was time to get to know them.'

Davie went straight from the office to the train on the Friday evening and Elaine met him at Waverley Station.

'One of my clients gave me a capon yesterday,' she told him. 'Mum's cooking it for us tonight. I saved the old boy's favourite cow when it had milk fever.'

'What's a capon?' he asked.

'It's a castrated cockerel, silly. It's done chemically. You insert a Stilbaestrol tablet under the skin at the back of its head. The tablet then dissolves slowly and is absorbed into the system. If the chicken were left alive it would revert back to being a fully fledged male when the tablet disappeared.'

Davie stopped walking and looked at her. So sudden was their halt that a worried looking young executive, carrying a red hot briefcase, bumped into them and muttered irritated apologies before scurrying off up the platform.

'You're pulling my leg,' said Davie, concentrating on the matter in hand.

'I'm not, honest,' then she burst out laughing. 'If you're not a good boy I'll put a tablet behind your ear. That would keep you calm till we get married.'

'Would I sing soprano?' Davie asked seriously.

Katherine came to the door when she heard the car. She was made up and her hair had been newly styled. A bright fire burned in the grate and the room looked warm and cheerful. Katherine motioned him to sit at the head of the table and disappeared to the kitchen from where she emerged bearing the steaming, golden brown roasted bird which she placed before him.

'Would you carve please, Davie,' she said.

After the meal had been cleared away, the three of them settled at the fire. Katherine sat in her favourite chair and the two young people on the sofa. Elaine kicked off her slippers and, curling her stockinged feet beneath her, leaned lightly on Davie's shoulder. She had put a record on the radiogram and Bach's 'Jesu, Joy of Man's Desiring' drifted in gentle eddies through the room. After the record finished, the silence was broken only by the crackle of the fire until Katherine turned to Davie.

'I'm going back to work,' she said. 'Elaine and I discussed things last night and we thought that it was a good idea. What do you think?'

'What are you going to do?' he answered with a question.

'My old legal firm are willing to have me back. The boy who was an apprentice along with me is now senior partner and it is his idea. So many people are now buying their own homes that they need someone to look after conveyancing. They will let me finish at four in the afternoon so that I can get home before the rush hour,' she ended.

'Mum said that if she hadn't had her job when Dad died she would have gone out of her mind,' said Davie after a pause. 'She could have filled a good part of her day working on the croft, but she would have had nobody to talk to all day.' He laughed. 'Jock says that a woman's tongue and a fiddler's toe should never be still. Both would be unnatural.'

'John's lawyer tells me that I don't need the money,' Katherine said. 'John was old fashioned and, I suppose, to be honest, a bit domineering about a lot of things and one was that he didn't think that wives should involve themselves in the business of their husbands. As far as his family was concerned he was always more generous with money than he was with his time. After the girls were born I'm afraid that I took little interest in the financial side of things. His father was wealthy and John was the only surviving child, but on his mother's side he was also an only nephew of a couple of bachelor uncles. Somebody, I think it was a client in my apprentice days, told me that money is only important when you've none.'

Davie rose, used the tongs to place some more coals on the fire then sat back beside Elaine on the sofa.

'I think that going out to work and meeting people can only be good for you. Are you going to keep on this house and garden?'

Katherine was quiet for a time then 'Meantime, yes,' she said. 'If we cut down the vegetable plot and let that bit go back into grass we should be able to cope as long as you and Elaine are here to help occasionally. I really don't want to make any hurried decisions that I might regret later, but if I don't move myself to go back to work now I feel that I may drop into a rut and in a month or two won't have the momentum to do it.'

The room was having a soporific effect and the conversation became lazy and comfortable. After a time, Katherine rose and stretched.

'I'm off to bed with my book,' she said. 'Don't sit up too late.'

Davie tucked his arm round Elaine's shoulders and they sat quietly looking into the fire. After a time, Elaine shrugged off the encircling arm and turned to face her companion.

'Davie, when are we going to get married?' she asked.

'If I could afford it I would say next week,' came the answer. 'My salary won't keep us very fat for another couple of years.'

'Davie Sinclair,' Elaine was indignant. 'Don't think that I'm marrying you for your money. I'm earning too. I didn't take the trouble to qualify in order to spend the rest of my life sitting at the mouth of the cave keeping the fire going till my hunter husband comes home with a carcass over his shoulder and blood dripping down his hairy chest.'

Davie laughed. 'That wasn't quite what I had in mind,' he said. 'But marriage is generally followed by children and you might find it awkward trying to calve a cow with a baby perched on your hip.'

'Another crack like that and I'll take the Stilbaestrol gun to you,' threatened Elaine. 'Now we have to be serious. When are you going to make an honest woman of me?'

'I feel that we should wait until I'm earning a little more,' said Davie. 'But maybe we should give the world official notice of our intentions. Would you like to go into Edinburgh tomorrow and we'll buy an engagement ring? Then I think we should wait for a week or two to see how your mother copes with life without your father before we set a wedding date.'

'Okay. If Mum doesn't ask where we're going tomorrow we won't tell her. It will be a great surprise for her when we get back.'

'You don't think that I should ask for her permission first?'

'Good Lord, no. That would only sadden her by underlining the fact that Dad's no longer here. If she was likely to object she'd have had you off with a flea in your ear long ago. Now, do you realise that you haven't yet kissed your fiancee.'

Elaine's judgement of her mother's reaction proved to be accurate. After the young folk had gone off, Katherine spent the rest of the mild winter's day tidying the garden and pruning back some rose bushes. Later, just as she started to prepare the evening meal, she heard the front door open followed by quick footsteps in the hall and Elaine's left hand burst into the kitchen followed by its owner.

'Well, Mum, what do you think?'

'You're engaged. Oh, Elaine, that's marvellous.' She gave her daughter a quick hug then turned to gather Davie in her arms as he came through the door. 'Oh, Davie, Davie,' she cried, 'I just couldn't be more pleased.' Then she stepped back with her hands still on his shoulders. 'Does your mother know about this yet?' she asked.

'Not yet!'

'Then go to the phone and tell her. After you and Elaine have spoken you can give me a shout and I'll speak to her. Go now. She shouldn't have to wait for news like this.'

Katherine lay awake long after going to bed that night. So many nights during her married life she had found that sleep eluded her because of worry. This had been a great day. She wanted to prolong it for as long as she possibly could.

'When are you coming down?' Marie had asked on the telephone. 'There's snow on the Irish hills today. The view from the kitchen is lovely.'

She thought of her own starched and corsetted mother-in-law who had seldom smiled and never laughed. Elaine was so lucky. She thought of Kay, but now without sadness. If it was true that everyone had a mission in this world then Kay's mission, even in death, must have been to bring the two families of Sinclair and Stark together. She hoped that Kay was happy in heaven. She must be. She had left so much happiness by her short life. Katherine drifted into a deep, dreamless sleep.

CHAPTER XVI

Damn confessed to mixed feelings when he heard the news of the engagement.

'I suppose this means that I'll have to look for a wife when you leave,' he told Davie. 'Just when I was getting used to your cooking too. It's not fair.'

'You'll be fully qualified by the summer so you should be able to afford a wife,' said Davie. 'Just don't look for one too soon and leave me homeless before I get married.'

Such is the contrariness of life that it was to be Damn who moved out and left Davie on his own in the flat. Their firm was responsible for the building of an airfield in one of the oil rich states of the Middle East. As the consumption of alcohol was against the law of the State, Damn, a teetotaller, was a natural choice to join the team for the contract period of two years. He wanted to keep his base in Glasgow so Davie found himself in sole charge. At first it was fun. Never before had he had a living area where he knew that when he closed the front door he could be entirely alone.

Damn had been a self-confessed sufferer from gadgetitis and as a result the flat was all electric. Davie liked to cook and by switching on a fire when he came in the flat was comfortably warm by the time his meal was ready. If he was cooking something which took longer, and especially if he was using the oven, he usually managed to have enough hot water for a bath while he waited. In anticipation of the Queen's coronation, he and Damn had invested in a television set and, knowing that he was alone he would go through to dry himself in front of the fire. One night, in order to catch a programme which he wanted to see he had left the television set switched on. As a naked Davie came through the door, a young and attractive female was addressing the camera in close up. In sudden embarrassment he ducked back into the hall then laughed out loud at his own stupidity.

Unfortunately, it didn't take long for his new found freedom to throw up a problem. On the first weekend, Elaine was on call during a busy period so he waited in Glasgow and brought work home to keep himself occupied. On the second weekend he travelled to Edinburgh. Normally Elaine would have come through to Glasgow on the following weekend and Davie was surprised when she expressed doubts about coming.

'No, Davie, I'll have to talk to Mum, 'she said. 'It was all right when Damn was there as chaperone, but she might not like us being in the flat on our own over the whole weekend.'

'Would you like me to ask her?'

'No, 'Elaine was definite. 'That wouldn't be fair either on Mum or you. Mum thinks that you are the cat's pyjamas and would say yes without giving the matter any thought. I'm pretty sure I'm right in saying that.

'On the other hand, if she asked you to give a promise of propriety you would give it in all good faith. Now, my lad, I feel it's only fair to tell you that I might not be able to give you much help to keep such a promise. Leave it till after this weekend and I'll phone you.'

When Elaine brought up the subject Katherine remained quiet for a time before answering the question. Then she turned to face her daughter. 'As things are in this world now I realise how lucky I am that you and Davie would think that I should be asked,' she said, then she smiled before going on. 'Also by asking the question you have provided the answer to another which I would never dream of asking you.'

Again a pause. 'Since you have asked I'll answer you as honestly as I know how. Yes, I think you should continue with your weekends in Glasgow. I have no objections and I'm sure that Marie wouldn't either. As to how you should behave when you get there I cannot be so definite. Sorry, I grew up in an atmosphere of the most hypocritical prudery and, although I hope that it doesn't get completely out of hand, the war brought a new openness which, I feel, can only be for the best. You and Davie are engaged. Neither of you have ever been involved with anyone else. You are delaying your wedding for a very good reason. I know that it is the ambition of most mothers to see their virgin daughter married in pristine white. Fair enough. For myself, I'd rather know that my daughter had a good chance of remaining happily married for the rest of her life. Have I shocked you?'

Elaine caught her mother's hand. 'No, Mum, you haven't shocked me. Quite the opposite. We'll try to behave, but I won't make any promises. I'm afraid that I honestly couldn't. Now I'd better go and phone Davie.'

Both Davie and Elaine found their respective jobs becoming more interesting all the time. Davie, as he gained experience, was being given more responsibility and for Elaine the advances in medication and technique were making the job of a vet much easier and more rewarding. Davie was to see evidence of the wonders of new vetinary medicine on his next visit to Edinburgh. Just as they were finishing their evening meal, Elaine answered the ring of the telephone and returned to the table almost at once.

'That was the wife of the senior partner,' she explained. 'There's a dairy cow ill just beyond Lasswade. The two men who are on call are both tied up. I'm the nearest to the farm so she wants me to go. Do you want to come

111

along?' she added to Davie.

'All right,' he rose to his feet and turned to say something to Katherine.

'C'mon boy. This is serious business. No time for leaning on a shovel in this job,' and she turned and ran out to her car.

By the time Davie got there she was taking something from the boot and he had barely time to settle in the passenger seat when she was in the car beside him. 'Cuddle this,' she told him as she handed him a round shouldered, pint size bottle. Sit on it, stick it up your jumper. Anything, but just get it as near as you can to blood heat before we get to the farm.'

'Why?' Davie was puzzled.

'This is a dairy cow which calved two days ago,' explained Elaine as the car gathered speed. 'She didn't come in with the rest of the herd at milking. Being Saturday night the farm is short handed and it was almost an hour before somebody could go to look for her. When they did they found her lying in the corner of the field and unable to rise. It's almost certain to be Milk Fever.'

'What's that? You've mentioned it before.'

'It's a disease that dairy cows take around calving time sometimes before, but more commonly after. Unfortunately, it's usually the better, high yielding cows which fall victim. 'If I still think that it's Milk Fever when I've seen her I want to inject the whole contents of that bottle into her blood stream. That's why I want it fairly warm when we get there. Minutes can be vital with this disease.'

'Do you know where the farm is? Is it much further?'

'I've been to it before. It's only about a mile now.'

Soon they turned into a farm road-end to see two men waving frantically from the other side of a lush green field. Elaine turned the car through the open gate and bumped across the grass towards them.

'Damn,' said Elaine when they were close enough to see a brown and white cow lying stretched out in a small hollow. 'It looks like we've lost this one.'

Almost before the car had stopped she was round at the boot, from which she emerged clutching a thin black tube about a couple of yards long with a bulbous piece at one end. 'Hold this a minute, Davie,' she said going forward to her patient.

A quick examination; 'She's still with us, but only just,' she said motioning Davie to stand close behind the cow and taking the bottle and tube from him. Swiftly she pierced the rubber stopper and fitted the bulb over the neck of the bottle before handing the apparatus back to Davie.

'Hold the bottle at shoulder height and turn it upside down,' she ordered as she bent over the inert cow. 'Let a little liquid run out then pinch the tube and be ready to hand the end to me.' Davie and the two men watched as she inserted a needle in a vein on the belly of the cow and watched the blood run for a few seconds.

'Keep the bottle inverted and hold it as high as you can without pulling the needle out,' she said as she reached for the tube.

When the liquid was running freely she fitted the tube over the end of the hollow needle and stood up. The level of the liquid in the bottle started to drop immediately. Apart from a grunt of recognition, neither of the two men had spoken and the grunt had only come from the older of the two. As the bottle emptied, she removed the needle and stowed everything back in the car. As she was walking back she saw the cow, which had been entirely still, begin to flick her left ear. Careful not to let the other men see, Elaine winked at Davie. Nothing happened for a few minutes and then the cow suddenly convulsed and struggled to a sitting position.

'My God,' said the older man. 'If that coo taks tae her feet ah'll never let anybody say a wrang word aboot a lassie vet again.' Elaine burst into laughter.

'Just you light your pipe for a wee while, Archie. It'll keep the midges away and give the cow time to make up her mind.' Archie barely had time to get his pipe drawing to his satisfaction before the cow rose to her feet, stood for a moment, then started off at a steady pace towards the farm steading. The younger man, who hadn't uttered a single word, set off in her wake.

'Don't draw too much milk from her for the next couple of days,' Elaine told Archie. 'Just take enough to make sure that her vessel isn't sore. After that she should be all right.'

As Elaine started the car Archie leaned down to the open window. 'Ah'm sorry lass,' he said 'Ah wis wrang. Awfy wrang. Ah'm sorry.'

Elaine leaned out and patted his rough hand. 'Thanks, Archie,' she said ' I was lucky this time. Your cow deserved some credit too. Not many of them are as spunky as that one.'

'What was that all about?' asked Davie when they had regained the road.

'I'm the first female ever to be employed in this practice,' explained Elaine. 'The small animal clientele were quite pleased but a lot of the farmers, particularly the older ones, weren't the least bit enthusiastic. It has to be admitted that they have a point. Because my hands are smaller I'm quite happy to tackle a difficult lambing, but when it comes to calving or foaling where strength as well as skill is a factor, then it can be a different story.'

'Has anyone ever refused to have you and insisted on one of the men?'

'Not quite refused. Some, when they phone in, have made negative noises, but the principal's wife is a blunt no-nonsense farmer's daughter who is very much on my side and she has been able to deal with the dissenters.

'The general attitude is quite funny, particularly with men like old Archie. If one of the men attends a case, the farmer expects him to be successful and takes it as a matter of course when he is. When I go, they prepare themselves for the worst and then behave as though I've performed some form of miracle when the animal recovers. Somehow it seems not quite fair to the men' she added unexpectedly.

Just before Christmas, Davie was called into his manager's office. 'We are bidding for a contract in Kenya,' he was told. 'If we get it, and it looks at this point that we are almost certain to, would you be prepared to go out there for maybe three or four years?'

'Starting when?'

'Starting with a spell of around of a couple of months in the spring to get the feel of the sub-contractor and labour market and the general lie of the land. The job itself is due to start in the early autumn. You'll be fully qualified by then. Since you've been in the country already we think that you are the natural man for the job.'

That evening when Davie phoned his mother, he found that she also had news for him. Jean Marie Boyd had joined the world weighing-in at 6 pounds and 10 ounces.

Davie and Elaine were married in Edinburgh on the third Saturday of March, 1955. As neither of them had many close relatives they opted for a quiet wedding in the manse of Elaine's church followed by a hotel meal. Jock drove Marie through on the morning of the wedding. Both of them stayed that night with Katherine and went home on the Sunday. Ian and Jean, complete with children, came from Perthshire and went home on the same night.

The young couple spent their wedding night in a small hotel in North Berwick. Their plan was to travel through towards the west coast for the following night then go to Davie's home on the Monday and spend a week with Marie. They also had a standing invitation to spend a few nights with the Boyds. Their flight to Nairobi was booked on the Comet for the sixth of April. While staying with Marie they walked out to Cnocan Lin passing the grave of Benny, Jock's ferret. Jock had selected a flat stone from the burn and this, without inscription, he had erected to mark the spot. The young couple stood at the top, their arms round each other's waist and looked down the length of the glen to the mouth of the river and away towards the Irish coast.

'Promise me that we'll always come back, Davie,' said Elaine.

'Yes, we'll always come back. I want our grandchildren to enjoy this view.'

CHAPTER XVII

Elaine, who had never flown before, had been anxious about the flight. In reality she found it fascinating. When the cabin steward came along to check their seat belts he looked at Davie for a moment.

'It's Mr Sinclair, isn't it?' he said.

'Yes, it is,' replied Davie.

'I saw you come aboard and thought it was you. I've a good memory for faces. I was at the same base as you in Suffolk when we were doing National Service. I'll have to go now but I'll come back once we're airborne.'

Seeing Elaine's tense expression, he leaned over and patted her hand. 'Don't worry,' he said. 'I fly for a living and I'm a natural coward. This bus is the best there is.'

By the time the steward came back, the aircraft had climbed through the cloud cover into the sunshine above.

'Will you manage to eat some lunch now?' he asked Elaine.

'Yes, I think that I might,' she replied. 'The earth doesn't seem to be so far away now that I cannot see all the way down. If we had to I'm sure that we could land on these lovely soft clouds.'

After the lunch debris was cleared, their friendly steward passed down the aircraft towards the flight deck. When he came back, he stopped at their seats. 'I've spoken to the skipper,' he said. 'We'll soon be passing over the Alps and the cloud is clearing. Would you like to come forward and see the view from the flight deck?'

Elaine was at first hesitant, but forgot her anxieties when she saw the sun glinting on the snow covered peaks. The reflections were throwing off shafts of light like a firework display. 'I never realised that they were so vast,' she said. 'I always thought of the Alps as a few peaks, but they seem to go on forever.'

'The whole system is a gigantic arc,' explained the pilot. 'It runs from south east France through to north west Yugoslavia and is about five hundred miles in length.'

Rome was hot and humid. Cairo was hot. Khartoum was dusty and rather horrid, Elaine thought. They reached Nairobi in the cool of the very early morning. The plane circled over the city before landing at the airfield. Despite her tiredness, Elaine was excited as they were driven to the hotel. She had never before been abroad yet here she was with her new husband just south of the equator in the heat of the African continent.

The first few days were spent sightseeing. Then Davie had to get down to work. For his first day at the site he was to be away all day. Elaine spent the morning having her hair done in a hairdressers which was part of the hotel. In the afternoon she was going out when the manager of the hotel approached her.

'Are you going out alone?' he asked.

'Yes, Davie's out at the site today. I thought that I might walk out in that direction in the hope of meeting him on his way back.'

The manager, who was English and only a few years older than herself, shook his head. 'I don't think that's a good idea. There hasn't been much trouble around here, but I'm not happy about you walking on your own nearer the edge of town. If you're going to do that you really ought to carry a gun.'

'But everybody we've met has been so friendly,' she protested.

'My father came out here to work when I was two years old. The people were so friendly and the country so beautiful that he brought my mother and me out in less than a year. My sister was born out here. Both of us were at school in Scotland when the war broke out,' he smiled. 'Although both my parents were from Suffolk, my father always said that Scottish education was the best in the world. Anyway,' he went on, 'when we got back here after being away for six years we noticed the change. Kenya, after our enforced exile, seemed even more beautiful, but the native population had obviously entered a period of change. Now I'm the only member of our family left out here. When I was at school in Glenalmond, I used to meet an old shepherd who loved to discuss the progress of the war. He always ended the conversation with the words "Ah weel, son the trouble will gae by. Meantime we'll juist hae tae work awa'." That describes perfectly how things are in Kenya at the present time. In a few years it will get back to being the lovely place to live in that it once was, but we have to survive these years first.'

When Davie got back late in the afternoon, Elaine told him of her conversation.

'There's a difference even since I was here before, ' he admitted. 'When I was given this job I had visions of us living in a quiet spot well out beyond the site, but now I'm not so sure. I don't like the idea of you being alone all day.'

By the time they were into their third week, Elaine was in an advanced state of boredom. Davie went off every morning except Sundays and wasn't home until the evening.

'I've never really fancied myself as a nest builder, but even that would be preferable to being nothing more than a kept woman,' she told her husband. 'The first day you can manage it you'll have to take a day off so that we can find a place of our own for when we come back out. I'd risk being alone during the day with something to do rather than go slowly mad just looking at the four walls of a hotel room.'

Several evenings later, Davie came back in some excitement.

'There's a farmhouse to let just about three miles beyond the site,' he told Elaine. 'The people who own it are losing some of their land to the airfield extension and let the grazing of the rest to neighbouring farms. They've gone back to Britain but don't want to sell up completely here. We can rent the house on an annual basis for at least two years, but with luck can maybe get it for the whole of our time here. We can go to see it tomorrow if you like,'

The house was on a rise and faced south west. It commanded a view over grazing land until it became lost in the heat haze. Behind, and built at right angles to the house, there was a line of horse boxes and other outhouses. The area immediately behind the house had been laid out as a patio with a barbecue grill and several large trees provided shade. Beyond the outhouses, there was an area of thick scrubby woodland. This restricted the view to the north to less than a hundred yards. A diesel engined plant provided electricity and Elaine like the whole set up on sight.

'The house is so clean,: she said. 'There's hardly a speck of dust. How long has it been empty?'

'Something like three months since the owners left,' replied Davie. 'There's a native man called Samuel who looks after it. One of the drivers at the site is his brother-in-law and he has gone to fetch him now. He lives in a village beyond these trees.'

Samuel arrived shortly and proved to be a tall, grey haired black man, grave in manner but with a white toothed smile which transformed his whole face when he produced it. He had been foreman of the labour force when the owners had farmed the place and he showed them round with proprietorial dignity. The house was fully furnished down to sheets and pillowcases and there was even, surprisingly, a well stocked drinks cupboard, which was unlocked and said a lot for the temperance and honesty of the custodian.

'We can move in for the time we have left just now and that will give you the feel of the place for when we come back,' Davie told his wife. 'Would you like that?'

'I'd love it. I used to think how lovely it would be to live in a hotel and be waited on hand and foot. The last month has cured me. Tell me, does Samuel come with the package?'

'Yes, I would think so. He'll have to look after the place for the time that we're at home anyway so we may as well keep him on meantime.'

By the time they had to go back to Britain Samuel had become part of the landscape if not quite one of the family. Every morning when they rose his grizzled grey head was to be seen among the plants and shrubbery in the front garden. He seemed to evaporate in the heat of the day then become reconstituted as the cool of the late afternoon established itself. Several time in the dark of bedtime they saw him cross the patio to disappear towards the trees. At these times he moved at a jog trot and his feet made no sound to indicate his passage. Although he seldom spoke, his English was good, almost cultured. As she slowly gained his confidence Elaine learned that he had been the son of a chief in the nomadic Masai tribe and as a small child had spoken only the Nilotic language of his people. His father had been killed in a tribal war over grazing land and the family had been taken in and reared by a mission school. He thought that he had been around five years of age when this had happened and couldn't really remember his father. He was fiercely proud of his own family of whom he had only two, a son and daughter. His son had qualified as a lawyer and worked with a legal firm in Nairobi. His daughter had obtained a scholarship to study medicine and was in London. She hoped to specialise in tropical medicine and return to Kenya to work. Samuel himself had gathered together a herd of Afrikander cows and also worked for other people. The previous occupants, still the owners of the farm, had given him their Aberdeen Angus bull as part reward for his services before they went back to Britain.

'We call him Jacob,' he told Elaine with a smile. The biblical allusion was lost on Elaine until she remembered that Jacob, the son of Isaac and grandson of Abraham, was reputed to have fathered at least twelve sons and had therefore a reputation of fecundity. It seemed a very appropriate name for a bull and, as told by the tall, dignified Masai was not in the least meant, nor sounded to be blasphemous.

They took their leave of Samuel in the third week of June with promises to return at the beginning of September. Davie had been pleased with progress in setting up preparations for the start of the work proper and was looking forward to getting his teeth into his first big job. They landed in London mid morning to a soft light drizzle but reached Edinburgh early on a Wednesday afternoon in brilliant sunshine. '

'I must say that you look well, both of you,' said Katherine when they were settled with the inevitable cups of tea. 'Kenya seems to be agreeing with you. '

118

'Oh, yes. It's really a lovely country,' said her daughter. 'We have heard the reports of trouble to the north, as I suppose you have as well, but everybody, both black and white, has been very friendly to us. With Samuel around no-one would dare be anything else.'

'Who on earth is Samuel? He sounds really high powered.'

'He's all of that,' agreed her daughter and proceeded to explain.

'How did you enjoy flying?' was the next question.

'The flight out was beautiful. I'll never forget the sight of the sun reflecting from the snow on the Alps. Coming back was all right but I felt quite queasy before we landed at London.'

They phoned Marie when they knew that she would be back from school in the late afternoon.

'I'll have to go the office in Glasgow tomorrow,' Davie told his mother. 'But I'm hoping that they'll give me a long weekend off after that. If our plans work out we'll be down to see you from Friday until Monday.'

'Would Katherine come with you?' asked Marie.

'I don't know, but I'll put her on to the phone and you can ask her yourself.'

When Katherine came off the phone she said that she would ask to be given the Friday and Monday off work so she could travel with them for the weekend. 'They're very good to me,' she explained. 'I went in early this morning and worked through lunchtime so that I could be here when you arrived. There's a bit of a lull in the property market just now anyway. Everybody seems to be thinking more of holidays than houses.'

So it was that on the Friday afternoon they found themselves driving down the long steep hill of Clachan in Kintyre. It was a beautiful clear sunny day. Rhododendron bloomed on either side of the road and when they breasted the last rise before driving down through the village, they could see the blue haze of Rathlin peeking round the dark mass of the Mull of Kintyre, the grave of so many ships throughout the centuries.

To their right the islands of Jura, Islay and Gigha squatted on a blue calm sea and in the foreground, a MacBrayne ferry, a busy plume of smoke signifying the importance of her mission, carried the mail and meal. Davie drew the car into a depot beside a pile of road chips and they sat for a time in silence absorbing the view.

Their arrival coincided with Marie's return from work and after the initial excitement, the young couple left their mothers preparing a meal and took the car to the seaside for a walk along the sands. Pairs of fulmar guarded their single young on the cliffs above the caves and small sand-nesting terns dive-bombed their heads as they walked, hand in hand, on the firm sands below the high-water mark. When they got back, the warm smell of cooking emanated from the open door, wafted by the sound of companionable female conversation. They were finishing their meal when the telephone rang and Marie left the table to answer it.

'Jock's coming for his tea tomorrow night and he'll sleep on the sofa,' she told them. 'He has a wee job that he wants to do to my car. He told me what it was, but I don't understand. Something to do with what he calls "points", so it must be outside the car and not in the engine.' Something else that she couldn't understand was why Davie and Elaine both laughed.

Jock arrived early in the afternoon.

'Jock, you've got grey hairs,' cried Elaine when she stepped back after giving him a cuddle.

'Ah never noticed,' said the wee man and then added, after looking gravely at her for a moment, 'But ah certainly don't need tae add tae them bae worryin' aboot how merrit life is agreein' wae you.'

'Wait until you see Davie. He's aged ten years,' she said, before her husband appeared at the doorway.

Marie had let the grazing of the croft to the neighbouring farmer and only retained a plot close to the house which Jock had fenced off and on which she grew vegetables. Davie spent the afternoon singling cabbages and turnips and staking up peas. Elaine sat in a chair in the sunshine and talked to Jock as he worked at Marie's car. The two mothers went out for a walk and appeared back a couple of hours later to announce proudly that they had walked the five mile round the hill to the village and back.

'Try a shaw of potatoes,' Marie called down to Davie as she passed in to the house.

'It would be nice to have them for tonight if they are ready.'

'Ah've aye thocht that naethin' could bate a broon troot straight oot the watter an intae the pan,' said Jock as he pushed himself back from the table that evening. 'But ah hee tae admit that a new tattie straight oot the grund has tae get the medal.'

'Will you be ready for an early morning walk, Jock?' Elaine asked.

'Och, aye. Ur ye comin'?'

'Yes, I'd love it. Seven o'clock?'

'Hauf an oor earlier if ye can manage it. Then we can get well up the hill before it gets too hot. Ony mair volunteers?' he looked round the table, but everyone else shook their heads. 'Och aye,' he said sadly. 'Plenty o' owls. Nae many larks.'

Elaine came down dressed for walking on the following morning to find Jock with tea and toast ready. Even so early, the sun was warm on their backs as they left the road and followed up the burnside past the grave of Benny the ferret. As they crossed the head of the burn, which would lead them onto the rough hill, Jock was aware that his companion was slowing up.

'Ur ye feelin' a' richt?' he asked anxiously. 'Ye look a bit peely wally.'

'Jock, I think I'm going to be sick,' she said going behind a whin bush where she proceeded to follow the thought with the deed. After a few minutes she returned to be offered a glass jam jar full of clear cold water.

'Where on earth did you get that? It's so lovely and cold,' she said after she had drunk thirstily.

'There's a spring here that feeds the burn,' he answered her question. 'I left a jeely jaur at it when Benny an' me used tae come up here efter rabbits. It's easier than gaun doon on yer knees and gettin' watter up yer nose. How dae ye feel noo? Ur ye fit tae go on or dae ye want tae turn back?'

'Oh no, Jock. I feel great now. I was feeling great when I left the house. I can't think what brought that on.' The slight smile on the face of her companion made her stop. 'Oh, Jock, I just never thought. Could it be?'

'Well, it's no' a field where ah've hud much experience, but ye're a pair o' healthy young folk. Ye've been merrit mair than three months an' ah dae mind how Jean wis at first in the mornins. Dae ye want tae go back an' tell yer man?'

'Och, no, we'll let him sleep, poor lamb. The shock news of impending fatherhood wouldn't be good for him so early in the morning. Come on. I'm still fit to race you to the top.'

The view from the top was, as ever, magnificent, but the slight breeze was entirely ineffective in dealing with the midges which hovered over them in a visible cloud.

'Ye ken, there's a fortune waitin' for somebody in Scotland who can utilise bracken an' kill oot midges,' said Jock. 'The soft green o' the bracken in the spring an' the warm broom in autumn at least adds tae the scenery. If there's anything attractive aboot a midge alive ah've yet tae find it.'

'That's because you're not a lady midge, Jock,' laughed Elaine.

For a time they stood together and absorbed the beauty which was laid at their feet. Elaine stood close to Jock and laid her head on his shoulder as a daughter might. The ribbon of the river in the valley floor was now partly hidden by the fully clothed trees, but in places the sun found the water. As the sun was directly behind them, the gently moving water reflected brilliant sharp needle points of light which reminded Elaine of the sun on the Alpine snow.

'Are ye goin' tae mention bein' sick when we get home?'

'Oh, yes, Jock. It's great news. I'm going to create two brand new grannies at one stroke.'

Jock was silent for long enough to be asked 'Is something wrong, Jock? You've gone quiet.'

'Naethin wrang. Quite the opposite. It's juist that ah think that ye'd be better tae mak sure that Davie gets the news furst. "An exclusive" as they say in the papers. Then ye can tell the grannies. Efter a' they've baith been mothers. It's yer man's first shot at bein' a faither.'

'Jock, you are a romantic,' cried Elaine as she gave him a quick hug.

Davie and Elaine flew back to Kenya on schedule at the beginning of September. Elaine's bouts of morning sickness had been short lived and she now bloomed in obvious pregnancy. Both Katherine and Marie were torn between a wish to keep her at home until after the baby was born and a reluctance to see her husband go off without her. Elaine herself was determined to go.

'It's a perfectly natural function,' she told her mother and mother-in-law. 'And anyway, we are only a handful of miles from Nairobi. I can get to skilled help more, much more, quickly from where we live than if we were at the head of a Scottish glen.'

In the end, a compromise was reached whereby Katherine would go out at the end of December and stay until after the baby was born.

Samuel, and the house, were shiny and welcoming. When he saw Elaine's increased bulk, his face split involuntarily in a wide, white toothed smile, but he made no comment beyond one of welcome. Davie spent a day with Elaine in case she showed any ill effects of the journey. On her insistence that she was all right, he went to the site on the day following. There he found that the contractors had been going ahead with scrub clearance and site preparation. After the first autumn nip of Scotland, the weather was hot and his previous experience told him that hotter was to come. The heavy plant operators, who were all black men, seemed oblivious to the climate and their singing could be heard above the noise of the engines.

'Are they always so happy?' Davie asked the ganger who was an itinerant Irishman called, inevitably, 'Paddy'.

'You seldom get them down,' he told Davie. 'The troubles further up country seem to be drifting nearer so we may yet have to be careful. All the fellows we have so far are good workers. As a people, they're just like white men. Some are grafters and some are as lazy as a butcher's dog. It's the same anywhere you go. Except the "Green Isle" of course,' he ended with a grin.

As her pregnancy advanced, Elaine found the incessant heat to be very tiring.

'This is when I wish that I had stayed in Scotland,' she told Davie. 'If you took a wheelbarrow home from the site I could put my belly in that and push it in front of me.'

Samuel became more solicitous as he watched her heavy stepped perambulations around the garden. Davie's firm provided medical services for their employees and immediate family when they were working abroad. At first Elaine went into Nairobi for regular check ups, but as the heat intensified the young Scots doctor told her that he would come out to her home.

'Your blood pressure is slightly higher than I would like it to be,' he told her. 'It may be just the heat but I'll keep an eye on it. Meantime, I want you to rest as much as possible and cut down on salt. And I mean cut down. Don't try to compensate by smothering everything in a salty sauce.'

'That's a bit better,' he said the following week as he closed his bag. 'But only a bit and not as good as I would like. If it doesn't settle a little more, and definitely if it goes up, I may have to move you to hospital.'

'Oh, no. I don't want that,' Elaine was startled. The doctor smiled.

'Hospitals here aren't so bad nowadays. They've improved immensely even in the time that I've been here. When are you expecting your mother?'

'Her flight is booked to land at Nairobi two weeks from tomorrow.'

'Good. I'll get her to exert some parental discipline and make you rest. Meantime behave yourself. Is there anyone who would come in and perhaps do the cooking for you until then?'

'I don't know of anyone. Perhaps I could speak to Samuel. He might know of someone.'

'Yes, do that. He's quite a remarkable man. Do you know his family?'

'I've never met any of them but he's told me of his son and daughter. One a lawyer and one a doctor. I thought that was some achievement for a family reared in the bush.'

'Oh, yes, but they are a remarkable family. The son handles any legal work needed for our practice. He's the most complete gentleman that ever I've met. The daughter came to the hospital in London where I was a houseman. She's positively regal.'

Late that afternoon, Elaine was seated in the shade of the stoep when Samuel was making his rounds.

'My daughter will come until your mother gets here,' he said. 'She is on six week's leave just now.'

'But, Samuel, your daughter is a doctor. We can't ask her to come to cook for us,' Elaine protested.

Samuel smiled. 'Better to have a doctor who is a cook than a cook who tries to also be a doctor,' he said. 'It will be good for her and in less than three weeks your mother will have arrived and be rested.'

'Well, if you sure that it will be all right I'd be grateful. It just seems to be an imposition to ask her, on her holiday, to come here to cook.'

'It is no imposition and I too am grateful,' Samuel was grave. 'This is not a good time for a young girl to be hanging about our village with nothing to do. I will bring her in the morning.'

Early next morning as Davie was ready to go to work, a gently knock called him to the front door.

'This is my daughter, Ruth,' said Samuel and stepped aside. For the first time in his life Davie found the adjective 'beautiful' to be a complete inadequacy. The girl who stood beside Samuel was tall, almost on a height with Davie who was himself just a bare inch under six feet. She wore a colourful sari type dress which was draped over her right shoulder leaving the left shoulder bare. Her skin was a burnished ebony and her sculpturesque features betrayed a distant Moorish ancestry.

Suddenly Davie was aware that he was staring – 'gowping' like a grassed fush' Jock would have said – and he still hadn't spoken.

'How do you do? I'm Davie Sinclair,' he said and extended his hand.

'How do you do.' Her voice was deep throated and as she spoke she smiled. The darkness of her skin enhanced the polished whiteness of her broad teeth. As Davie stood aside and invited her in, her father turned with a slight wave of his right hand and made his way down the steps to the garden. He had seen Davie's consternation and a slight smile of pride creased his normally impassive features.

Ruth soon proved to be as utilitarian as she was decorative. She tackled the housework with an economy of movement which surprised Elaine. Before she started jobs such as ironing or the preparation of a food dish, everything was laid out to hand and precisely in the order in which it was to be needed. She laughed when Elaine commented on this.

'One of my lecturers at medical school was a Scotsman who was near retiring age,' she explained. 'He had arthritis in both hips and suffered a lot of pain, but was a great character. "Afore ye start any job mak sure a' yer tools are handy tae yer haun" he used to tell us. "Wance ye get tae my age ye'll learn that it's no' fair tae keep askin' yer erse to be forever followin' yer feet." Somehow or other his accent meant that I remembered what he said much better than some of the other lecturers who always used correct English.'

Ruth's study of tropical medicine had included zoonoses, diseases transmissible from animals to humans such as rabies, malaria and brucellosis and she and Elaine found much to talk about. The journey of the black girl through the social spectrum from the bush to medical school had not been easy and Elaine admired her tenacity. Her main advantage had been that before her she had always the example of her brother who was four years older and had achieved his own ambition to study law.

'Your English is absolutely perfect, much better than mine,' Elaine said. 'Is that the only language you have spoken?'

'No, it isn't and it would please my father if you were to tell him what you have just told me. Until my brother and me were each five years old he wouldn't allow us to speak English. We had to speak our native language. He maintains that the purest English is spoken by people from the Western Isles of Scotland who spoke only their native Gaelic until they went to school and learned the language properly. The missionaries who brought him up came from the island of Lewis. They reversed the situation by teaching him to speak Gaelic. They said one should have a knowledge of as many languages as possible, which helps to make sure that nobody can talk behind your back in front of your face,' she ended with a smile.

'Yes, having a resident medic was all that was needed,' said Elaine's doctor on his next visit. 'Your blood pressure is back within a tolerable range. Now, when did we think that this baby would abandon comfort and make its way into this wicked world.'

'According to you it's the seventeenth of January, but it sometimes feels that it will kick its way out before that,' Elaine told him.

'Practically every mother at your stage tells me that they think that they are carrying a future footballer. I'll come to see you again next week. Keep up the good work, Ruth. When does your leave end?'

'Two days before this baby is due,' Ruth told him. 'I may give Elaine a couple of stiff gins before that so that I can be here for the delivery.'

The doctor again expressed satisfaction at his next visit and on the following day Katherine arrived.

It was the longest journey that ever she had undertaken and, like Elaine on her first flight to Kenya, she felt that her pleasure would be greater on arrival than during the journey. A cold sleety rain was falling as the passengers made their way across the tarmac to the aircraft for the first leg of the flight to London and after leaving the ground the aircraft flew the whole journey surrounded by dense cloud. At London, they announced a two hour delay in the connecting flight and this delay eventually extended itself by another hour and a half. Katherine didn't want to risk leaving the terminal in case of missing her flight. She was too nervous to take any-thing substantial to eat. The diversion of watching the motley collection of assorted human beings who were arriving and departing on other flights lost its ability to amuse her as the delay got longer. Consequently, by the time that her flight was announced, she felt more like escaping back to Edinburgh than flying to the other side of the equator.

'Is this your first flight?' asked the pretty stewardess as she helped Katherine to adjust her seat belt.

'Not exactly, but this is the first day that I have flown. I flew down from Edinburgh this morning.'

'Where are you going to?'

'Nairobi. My daughter and her husband are there. She's expecting a baby in three weeks time.'

'Oh, that's nice. I'll come back to see you once we're airborne.'

The take-off was smooth but as they climbed, Kathering felt the plane lurch from side to side.

'Good afternoon, ladies and gentlemen,' came a disembodied voice from the tannoy. 'This is your captain speaking. We are expecting some slight turbulence over the French coast. Please keep your seat belts fas-tened meantime.'

The adjective 'slight' was soon proved to be a misnomer. For what seemed like an age the aircraft bucked and plunged like a wild horse expe-riencing its first pull on a restraining halter. Katherine surprised herself by keeping fairly calm and as the rest of the cabin crew had their hands full attending to those who were physically sick, she slipped off her seat belt and rose to help the stewardess restrain an hysterical woman who was attempting to leave her seat. The girl smiled her gratitude as Katherine came forward. The woman was attempting to punch the stewardess and screaming at the pitch of her not inconsiderable lung capacity. It took considerable strength and patience from both women to calm the girl, whose manners did not improve.

'Thank you, madam,' the stewardess said politely to Katherine when it was all over. 'We should be through the turbulence now. Would you like me to bring you something to drink?'

'Is that the sort of thing a regular part of your job?' Katherine put the question when her drink was delivered.

The girl smiled. She had the peaches and cream complexion so often seen in the north-east and her eyes were deep brown limpid pools. 'Not to say regular but it does happen from time to time,' then she went on. 'We can often spot the troublesome passengers as they come up the gang-way and it's never the old couple on their first flight going to the other side of the world to see their grandchildren. We also hear tales from the cabin staff of other airlines. The reputation of the lady whose acquaintance you have just made has, I'm afraid, been well established over the past few years.'

Katherine sympathised with her readily.

'I'd better go,' said the stewardess. 'I'll try to speak to you again before we land at Rome. I hope you find everybody well at Nairobi. You look much too young to be a granny.'

The cabin crew changed at Rome. They landed at Cairo in the grey darkness of the desert night. In daylight they circled Kitchener's city of Khartoum. The last leg of the flight down the Great Rift Valley seemed to take ages until the tannoy triumphantly announced that they had crossed the equator. Eventually the engine note changed. They were losing height for landing. The heat struck Katherine as she emerged to the top of the aircraft steps.

'My goodness, you're huge,' was her involuntary greeting of her daughter.

CHAPTER XVIII

'I seem to have spread a bit in the past few weeks,' explained Elaine when they were settled at home with cups of tea. 'Until then I thought that I was quite neat.'

'You look well,' said her mother. 'Really well.'

'I should do. I'm the best looked after pregnant woman in Kenya. Davie fusses like a mother hen but Ruth is severely practical, I have had to do my exercises every day and she watches my diet like an old style hospital matron.'

'You were so lucky to have her.'

'Luck isn't quite the word. Without her I'd have been in hospital. She put up the Christmas decorations in honour of you coming too.'

Despite her tiredness, Katherine took a long time to fall asleep that night. As she lay listening to the night sounds from outside she thought of the circumstances which had eventually brought her to the heart of the African continent. She thought of Kay, the younger of her two daughters. She remembered, as yesterday, the sadness of packing her case while consoling herself with the thought that she was being sent to safety. She could still hear the voice of the radio announcer as he told the nation that the *Athenia* had been torpedoed. She remembered the strange sensation of relief that she had felt at the news that Kay's body had been found.

John had gone to identify the body. He had told her that the features were unmarked. From then he switched off, hardly taking time to attend the funeral. Then he sought consolation from a bottle. Had he been able to join the armed forces and vent his anger in physical force it might have been different. But he couldn't. His work was too important he was told.

She thought of meeting Marie and Davie and that first long walk to the Glen.

She remembered her first sight of the spot where Kay had been found and the consolation she derived from Marie's assurance that her daughter hadn't appeared to have suffered. She remembered her first meeting with Ian, the big gentle man who had himself carried Kay up the cliffs from the shore and then almost two miles over rough hill rather than abandon her body and go for help. By the time they had met Ian he was himself crippled by the same war. She thought of Donald, a paragon of clean living, who, even so, was denied the life needed to see his grandchild. She thought of her son-in-law, Davie and of Jock's words to her when first they met after the young folks' engagement. 'Katherine,' he had said. 'Ye couldna' get a better man for your dochter even if you asked John Broons tae mak wan specially for ye.'

On this happy note, smiling she fell asleep.

Next morning she awoke with the sun on her face to find Ruth at her bedside bearing a tray with tea and toast. She had finished the toast and was in the act of pouring a second cup of tea when Elaine came in, her feet encased in slippers and wearing a light cotton dressing gown.

'Did you sleep, Mum?'

'It took a wee while before I was relaxed enough to sleep but when I finally did I never moved until Ruth brought my breakfast. No wonder that you look so well on this type of attention.'

'Yes,' agreed her daughter. 'I wish that I could keep her after the baby is born. I'm going to take badly to having to cope on my own and look after somebody else after living the life of a lady for so long.'

'The first few days will be the worst and I'll be here for them. After that you'll develop a routine. So long as the baby sleeps reasonably well at night it'll be easy.'

Elaine sat at the foot of the bed with the light at the window behind her. Katherine silently marvelled at how well she looked and the sheen of her hair. She had had just enough of the African sun for her skin to be nicely tanned without the appearance of dryness common to so many women who lived in hot climates. Her father had been extremely handsome as a young man and his daughter resembled him in many physical aspects. She hoped that the baby would be a boy. Never having had a son it would be so nice to have a grandson.

Katherine brought Elaine up to date with first hand news of Marie, Jock and the Boyds who had all visited her just before she left. She told her of little Jean Marie, now just over a year old and the light in the life of her older brother and second only in his order of priorities to his vivacious young school teacher.

As they spoke a drawing pin dislodged itself from the wall and the end of a paper chain draped itself around Elaine's shoulders. Still speaking, and before her mother could stop her, she gathered up the end of the chain and stood up on the bed to replace the pin in the wall. When she had done so she turned to step off the bed to the floor. Suddenly her right foot caught in a loose fold in the top sheet of the bed and she fell forward to jack knife over the back of a chair. From there, in a horrible parody of slow motion, she slumped to lie motionless on the floor.

Katherine's scream as she scrambled out of bed brought Ruth bursting through the door. The black girl never spoke but knelt swiftly at

Elaine's side and reached for her wrist. After a minute she gently lifted one eyelid in the white face.

'It's all right, just a deep faint,' she reassured.

'What happened?'

As Katherine explained, she became aware of a change of expression on Ruth's face and following the direction of her eyes saw to her horror a spreading pool of moisture on the wooden floor.

'She's going into labour. We'll lift her onto your bed.' This was said in a calm voice. The doctor had taken over.

As they placed Elaine on the bed she murmured, blinked, then opened her eyes wide.

'What happened?' Then her hands moved to her stomach. 'Oh,' she yelped. Ruth sat on the bed and smoothed the hair back from Elaine's damp forehead as she explained.

'Now don't worry,' she ended. 'It will probably be some time before anything much happens.'

She rose to her feet. 'I'll ask my father to get a message to your husband and your doctor then I'll make some tea.'

Her movements were smooth and unhurried. Mother and daughter heard the sound of running water, the plop of the gas stove as it was lit, then her voice outside as she called her father.

After they had drunk their tea, Ruth assisted Elaine to her feet and stood beside her for a moment until she was confident of her balance.

'Walk around for as long as you can,' was the advice given. 'For one thing it passes the time while nature gets on with tackling a job which she would rather have postponed for a week or two.'

'I just wish Davie was here,' said Elaine.

'I know,' Ruth was sympathetic but then became practical. 'Really, it's maybe as well that he isn't just now. This is women's work. We don't need a big strong man. We're just going to deliver a baby, not calve a cow or foal a mare.'

Elaine forgot her pain and burst into peals of laughter at the shocked expression on the face of her mother. Two hours elapsed before Elaine announced that she thought it was time for her to go back to bed. In that time Ruth had prepared things for the evening meal, Katherine had bathed and dressed leisurely and Elaine had produced nappies, gowns, powders, soaps and sponge for the new arrival.

'What about a bottle?' asked Katherine when she had inspected the layette.

'Oh, no, Mum. Your grandchild will get the milk that the cat can't get at.'

As Elaine was preparing to get into bed, they heard a noise in the kitchen. Ruth went through and came back carrying a Gladstone bag which she placed on a chair.

'That was Dad,' she explained. 'I asked him to fetch my emergency kit.' Then to Elaine, 'I'm afraid that both of the men in your life are out of touch at the moment. Davie has gone to see a contractor and the doctor is attending a confinement out at another village. I'm afraid that we'll have to get on with our knitting on our own,' she announced.

After a brief examination, she took a stethoscope from her bag and placing the disc on the mound of Elaine's tummy she listened for a moment then turned to Katherine.

'Here,' she said handing her the earpiece, 'have a listen.'

'It sounds like someone washing a blanket by hand,' said Katherine. 'That's a good Scottish heartbeat,' Ruth assured her. 'We shouldn't have long to wait.'

Elaine adjusted her head more comfortably on the pillow and looked up at her mother. There was a faint but discernible film of sweat on the face of the younger woman.

'Stop looking so worried, Mum,' she said. 'Over the last few years I've helped a lot of young into the world. Although none of them was human they were all made by the same method and emerged by a similar route. Now, Ruth, we'd better get on with this job.'

As Ruth worked she murmured a constant stream of encouragement to her patient. Katherine knelt by the side of the bed and held her daughter's hand. The doctor seemed so capable that there was no other useful contribution to be made. As the birth progressed the murmur became more urgent. Suddenly Elaine gave a final gasp and turned her head sideways in exhaustion. Ruth straightened and ran to the kitchen clutching a tiny object in her arms. After a moment, Elaine turned back and looked at her mother. 'Well, Granny, is nobody going to tell me what I've got?'

'I don't know myself yet either. Will you be all right while I go and find out?' Katherine entered the kitchen to find Ruth standing at the table. Unbelievably enormous tears rolled from her eyes and unheeded down the beautiful ebony face.

'Oh, Katherine,' she said. 'I can't believe it. This baby is dead. It would seem to have died a few hours ago. But the heartbeat was so strong. You heard it yourself. I just can't believe it.'

Suddenly her expression changed and she ran back to the bedroom followed closely by Katherine.

'Well?' said Elaine in a worried voice as she struggled to sit up.

'How do you feel?' asked Ruth ignoring the implied question.

'I feel as though I am about to do the same again.'

The doctor snatched up her stethoscope and made a swift examination as she listened.

'Elaine,' she said suddenly. 'That is just what you are going to do. I'll explain later. Just now what you have to do is push, count to five, then push harder.'

This time the encouragement was firm, urgent and commanding. Katherine was exhorted to count to five between contractions. Stealing a glance downwards she suddenly realised the need for haste. Ruth had her left hand, palm downwards on Elaine's stomach, but in her right she grasped two tiny ankles. Any woman who had ever been a patient in a maternity hospital knew that a breech presentation baby had to be delivered as quickly as possible.

Suddenly, Elaine gave an extra push, squeezing her mother's hand so hard that the bones of the fingers ground together. Ruth sat back on her heels, snatching up a towel as she did so. After a few seconds a faint, gull like cry came from the bottom of the bed. The tall, black doctor rose to her feet and moved to the head of the bed, her expression of pure undiluted joy.

Gently she laid her towel-wrapped bundle in the crook of Elaine's outstretched arm.

'Mrs Sinclair.' she said in her rich voice, 'allow me to present to you, your son.'

Elaine looked into the tiny, puckered features.

'Good afternoon, Donald John Sinclair,' she said.

Softly at first but with increasing urgency they became aware of the sound of a fast driven car. The outside door banged open and through the bedroom door Elaine's doctor entered this rather bloody if nonetheless happy scene.

A swift look at the smiling face of the new mother and then he delighted all in the room, with the possible exception of young Donald, by folding the tall form of the black doctor in a tight embrace.

'Oh, Ruth, Ruth,' he said. 'Thank God you were here.'

Then he stepped back. 'Do you need me?' he asked.

'Not really, except for a consultation.'

'In that case, I'll go to the kitchen and make a cup of tea,' and before anyone could stop him he disappeared round the door.

Katherine cast a horrified look at Ruth and made to follow, but the latter shook her head. Fortunately, Elaine was too taken up with her baby to notice this little exchange.

A short time later Elaine, all cleaned up and with hair brushed, was settling to give her baby his first feed when the doctor came in bearing a tray set for two.

'I left yours and my own in the kitchen,' he said to Ruth. 'I thought that we could have our consultation at the same time.'

Almost an hour elapsed before the two doctors came back into the bedroom. Elaine was lying back contentedly on her pillows and the baby was fast asleep in his grandmother's lap.

'I was going to ask if you had enough milk, but by the look of your son it would be a superfluous question,' said the doctor.

'I was a bit worried about that myself, but I seem to have bagged up quite well.' said Elaine.

The doctor and Ruth both burst into laughter.

'There's no doubt about it,' said Ruth. 'Veterinary language is much more explicit than that of the medical profession.'

'I have to ask, then I'll try to put it completely out of my mind,' said Elaine. 'Was it a boy or a girl?'

'A girl,' Ruth's voice was level.

Two large tears welled from Elaine's eyes and ran down her cheeks. Suddenly she brushed them away with the back of her hand.

'That's it,' she said forcefully. 'I have so much for which to be thankful, so very much, that it would ungrateful to cry,' and she reached out for Ruth's hand. Shortly after, the doctor rose to leave with a promise to call back in the morning. As he was going out of the door he collided with Davie.

'Is everything all right?' he was asked.

'Yes, Daddy. Yes, indeed. Everything is all right.'

Sleep came late to Davie that night. After he had admired his son, caught up with the day's excitement and they had all had their evening meal, Katherine pronounced herself ecstatic but exhausted and went off to bed. Ruth had elected not to go home and had also gone off to sleep on the assurance that Davie would call her if his family gave him any cause to worry. Ruth had explained to him the cause of Elaine's premature labour and what she and Elaine's own doctor thought had caused the little girl to be stillborn.

'I would advise not talking about that with Elaine unless she herself initiates the conversation,' she told him. 'Be thankful. Live with the living. One cannot live with the dead.'

Elaine had said only three words on the subject. As she lay back on her pillows and watched Davie gingerly nursing the baby she murmured. 'I'm sorry, Davie.'

'No, Elaine,' he said. 'It is not given to us to know why it happened.

It is our job to deal with the situation as it exists.'

He leaned over and kissed her. 'Now,' he went on, 'we must put it out of our minds. This is not a time to be sorry. We can't have our son thinking that he is second best.'

Mother and baby slept peacefully. Despite his tiredness, Davie sat protectively over them. He determined that his son should have every chance in this life. Fate had decreed that the boy would have no grandfather, but he would have Jock and Ian. His thoughts, furred by tiredness, wandered. During the past twenty years, throughout the world, the carnage of wars had caused hundreds of thousands of babies to have to face the world without ever having known their fathers. Many were the children of refugees as part of the horrendous flotsam caused by man's inhumanity to his own kind. Kenya, this vast and beautiful country, was even at that time, putting itself through a form of self-evisceration with terrible deeds of terrorism. The baby murmured and was still. His father sank deeper in his chair. The whole family slept.

CHAPTER XIX

Davie had sent a telegram to his mother to tell her that she had a grandson. Her return letter finished with some sad news. The Bennetts, the old couple who had lived in the cottage on the Glen road, were both dead.

'Jock had gone over at the weekend to tidy up their peat stack and to cut some wood for them,' she wrote. 'When he came back he remarked on how cheerful they both had been although obviously getting frail. They were delighted to hear of Donald John.'

'For the past couple of years somebody from the farm has been going up with their milk every morning. This morning the blinds were still drawn. The door, of course, was never locked. Both of them were dead on the living room floor and the light was still switched on.

'The doctor thinks that Mr Bennett collapsed with a heart attack. He thinks that Mrs Bennett had tried to help him and collapsed and died beside him. We are all saddened but really it isn't sad. They were married in 1898 before Mr Bennett went to the Boer War. They had two sons and three daughters all of whom are still in life. Three grandsons were in the last war and all of them came home. In the end they died together after almost sixty years. One cannot ask for much more.'

Katherine had to go home on the day that Donald was five weeks old. Ruth had gone back to London two weeks previously with a promise to visit Edinburgh at the earliest opportunity.

Elaine was a natural mother and, while reluctant to leave, Katherine did so without worry. Davie was away from home early on all week-day mornings but Elaine found that no matter when she looked out, the grizzled grey head of Samuel was always to be seen. If she left Donald to sleep in his pram in the shade of the trees on the patio the tall old man found work about the outhouses which ran from the back of the house and if she put the pram on the stoep, Samuel was busy in the garden. Even at the weekends when Davie was at home he seemed to appear but never at any set times. Elaine mentioned this to her husband. After a moments thought, he spoke. 'If it wasn't for Samuel I wouldn't leave you out here,' he told her. 'Every day someone at the site has some tale which indicates that the troubles are coming closer. I have discussed this with the doctor. He tells me that Samuel carries a lot of weight among his own people and that none of them would risk his wrath.

'Although Samuel himself is Masai, his wife was the daughter of a Kikuyu headman. With the son being a lawyer and, of course, Ruth a doctor, they are a powerful family.'

'Do you think there's much danger, Davie?'

'No,' slowly. 'Not really. I must confess to worrying occasionally. Everybody does, I suppose. Then I tell myself there hasn't been any trouble in this area. I just hope that I'm not keeping you in Kenya for purely selfish reasons. I'd be lost without you.'

'It surely won't get so bad that I'd have to leave. It all seems so peaceful around here.'

'I hope not,' Davie was serious. 'But if it does, Madam, you go. First available plane. No argument.'

'Yes, Master,' she dropped a mock curtsey.

From time to time they heard rumours of atrocities, but life for the Sinclair family was undisturbed. Davie was pleased with the progress of work on the site. 'The whole crew are good but the drivers particularly so,' he told Elaine. 'There's one man there called Thomas. He drives a bulldozer. I'm almost certain that he could peel an apple with it if he was asked.'

At three months of age, Donald, who had been a placid baby, suddenly turned fretful and began to waken screaming during the night.

'Teeth,' said the doctor. 'The phase will soon pass. Meantime, if you feel like chucking him out of the window in the middle of the night, remember to open the window first.'

On one particular night, Elaine rose without disturbing Davie, put the baby to her breast until he settled, then walked through to the kitchen carrying him in her arms. There was an almost full moon and she didn't switch on a light. As she stood looking beyond the patio she was aware of three men emerging from the wooded area and following a route which would let them pass close to the west gable of the house and on towards the road. As they passed to disappear beyond her line of vision, she saw the moonlight glint on the blade of the panga which each of them carried. Elaine was not a nervous person, but the flash of the polished steel made her shiver and hurry back to the comforting warmth of her bed. Davie turned to encircle her with his arm, murmured in his sleep and was still.

Next morning she never mentioned what she had seen to her husband. Later in the morning she perched Donald on her hip and went out to speak to Samuel. He listened gravely, then, 'This is not good,' he said. 'Too many young roosters are starting to crow before their feathers are grown. The end may be justified but the means are abhorrent. If you see or hear anything else that disturbs you, let me know at once.'

About a fortnight later the Irish general foreman came to the hut which Davie used as an office on the site.

'Thomas hasn't turned up this morning,' he told Davie. 'He's such a good driver I don't want to upset him by putting someone else on his machine, but we can't afford to have it idle for too long.'

'Do any of the rest of the men know what might had kept him off work?' asked Davie.

'If they do they're not telling. He's a bit of a show-off and not all that popular among them. I'll let today go past, but if he's not here first thing tomorrow morning then he drives a shovel when he does turn up.'

Next morning Thomas still didn't appear and another man took over his machine. Early in the afternoon the foreman burst into Davie's office. His normally ruddy Hibernian features were as white as nature would allow and his eyes were so prominent that they seemed to be perched on his nose.

'We've found Thomas,' he said, once his breath had steadied. 'I think you'd better come, but be prepared for a shock. He wasn't all that pretty when he was alive, but he's a damned sight uglier now that he's dead,' he added unsympathetically.

Davie went to a filing cabinet and took out a bottle of brandy and poured a generous measure which he handed to his foreman. The man tilted his head back and swallowed the raw spirit in two large gulps. 'Almost as good as Irish whiskey,' he smiled as he handed the glass back. Davie noticed that his eyes weren't even watering and wondered what kind of throat was needed to cope with punishment like that.

'I've sent a man to get word to the police camp,' the foreman explained as they walked out towards the edge of the site where Davie could see an idle bulldozer.

'That is, or rather was, Thomas' own machine. The driver was using it to fill up a hollow when two vultures rose almost in front of the blade. He got off to see what they had been at. This is what he found.' the foreman ended as they got to the front of the machine. The cloud of flies buzzing over the naked body made Davie think of bees in the act of swarming. Before the bulldozer had stopped it had pushed forward soil which covered one leg up to the knee. Vultures had been at work on the face and one eye was missing but there was enough of the features left for Davie to recognise Thomas. A panga had slit the breast to pelvis bones and vultures had almost completed the process of evisceration. The smell was overpowering and almost tangible. Davie turned, leaned against the bulldozer and was sick. He still looked the worse for wear when he got home that evening.

'But who would do a dreadful thing like that?' asked Elaine after he had told her an edited version of the story.

'The police are certain that it has a Mau Mau connection,' he told her. 'It turns out that they have had an eye on Thomas for some time. They think that this was the result of an internal squabble.'

'That must mean that they are active around here then,' said Elaine and told him of the three men that she had seen and of Samuel's reaction.

'You should have told me,' he said angrily.

'Oh, Davie, I know and I'm sorry, but I was afraid that you'd send us home and I don't want to go and leave you on your own out here. I'd just worry about you all the time. At least when I'm out here with you I know what is going on.'

Davie was mollified.

'We'll both talk to Samuel in the morning,' he decided. 'I think that he'll have a fairly sensitive finger on the local pulse. Meantime I think that you should pour me a dram of Glenmorangie.'

'Yes, I heard about Thomas Jomera,' Samuel told them the following morning. 'He was a foolish man. Something of a peacock.'

'Do you think that it was terrorists who killed him?' asked Davie.

'Oh, yes. He had been boasting of the power that he was going to have after independence. They do not like someone like that. He was dangerous. They would have to kill him. He could have named names that at present are unknown to the security forces. The Kikuyu are not normally a savage people. I married one,' he finished with a smile.

'Are there many terrorists around here?' It was Elaine who put the question.

'Only men like Jomera who have come to the area. They try to recruit the young bloods but we can usually control that. Young people here have work and the chance of education if they seek it.'

'Samuel,' Davie was serious. 'I'm sorry but I have to ask you, do you have any sympathy for the terrorists?'

'As terrorists, none at all,' Samuel answered levelly. 'To take Jomera as an example, he was an educated man who infiltrated a building site posing as a driver. Jomera had been a school teacher, but he wanted power and influence. He had been well treated by white men. He had no need to rebel. But there have been cases of injustice. There's no doubt about that. Man is the only animal who always seems to want more than he can eat and the person who suffers must be his fellow man. The men who are resorting to violence in Kenya are not doing so to further the long term good of the country. The men with that goal are not being violent although some of them are being blamed for being behind the violence.

'I do not think that that is true. If these men were behind it the violence would be much better organised. They are clever men and hopefully will yet be given the chance to save Kenya. It is a beautiful country. A land worth saving. And not with the gun or the panga,' he ended.

'I want to send Elaine and Donald back to Scotland. Am I right?'

Samuel paused for so long that they thought that he wasn't going to answer.

'That is a question that I cannot answer with a yes or no,' he said slowly.

'I think that there is very little danger, but there is a background of danger. Otherwise we wouldn't have been discussing the late Thomas Jomera. But whether the danger is sufficient to justify splitting up your family, I'm not so sure. These troubles have been going on, publicly, for four years. The security forces now have a reasonable grip of the situation. Also the death of Jomera will draw attention to the people who were trying to establish a unit in this area. They will scatter. We are well rid of them. We do not like them corrupting our young men.'

Davie sat in silence for a long time after the older man became silent.

'Samuel, what would you do if you were in my shoes?' he asked.

'I would remember the man who would not enter a motor car in case it would have an accident. He was kicked to death by a camel.'

Elaine burst into laughter at the look on her husband's face. Samuel permitted himself the luxury of a smile before going on. 'If it is decided that your family stays on here, I will make a bed in the stable. Each night I, or one of my people, will sleep there. Also, we will bring Archibald. There will be no trouble.' The last was said with conviction. The young couple looked at one another for a moment.

Elaine's eyes were glistening.

'Samuel,' said Davie indignantly, 'if you are going to do that you will sleep in the house.'

But the wiry, grey head shook. 'No,' said Samuel. 'It would defeat the purpose. Besides, Archibald has never been in a house. He would be uncomfortable. Say no more until you have had a chance to talk to one another. You can tell me tomorrow morning what you have decided.'

Next morning it was Elaine who told Samuel that she and Donald would be staying in Kenya for the period of Davie's contract. 'I really don't know how I can repay you,' she said. 'If it hadn't been for you I'd have been packed off home. I would have hated it.'

'You are repaying me just by being here. Kenya needs men like your husband and young men do their best work when they have a mate. It is the way of nature.'

They stood on the step looking south to where the view became lost in the morning heat haze; Samuel continued, 'Kenya will one day be a great African nation. When Donald grows up I hope that he will have reason to be proud of having been born here.'

Early next morning Elaine fed and changed her son before preparing breakfast for Davie. Donald had regained his contented nature but his mother had painful proof that some teeth had come through his gums. All mornings seemed to be beautiful in Kenya but now that she knew that she wasn't leaving this one seemed particularly pleasant. Idly, she looked over the wooded area. The sun was already making its presence felt and she could feel its heat through the glass. On the patio the overnight dampness was rising as a mist which clung reluctantly to the ground. Suddenly an ugly tawny head rose above the level of the mist followed by the upper part of a large dog. For a second or so, two large brown eyes regarded her, then the head turned towards the stable door from which appeared Samuel.

He waved and started towards the patio. Elaine went to the back door to speak to him. When she opened the door he was standing on the step with the dog beside him. The two front paws of the animal were on the step but its rear end started at ground level. Samuel was a big man, but, as he stood upright, he was able to comfortably rest his hand on its head.

'Allow me to present Archibald,' Samuel said with a smile. 'Archibald, say how do you do to the lady,' he commanded.

A large right paw was presented. Unhurriedly Elaine bent to shake it then presented the back of her hand to the dog's nose. A coarse tongue licked from knuckle to wrist and she turned her hand to fondle the large head. The breed of the animal puzzled her.

'I can see the Alsatian in him, but there's something else that I cannot recognise,' she told Samuel. 'If it wasn't for the length of his hind legs I would say that his mother had enjoyed a night out with a hyena. He must be the most powerful dog that ever I have seen. He seems to have a lovely gentle nature. Just as well for a dog of that size.

'His mother was Alsatian but his father was a Rhodesian Ridgeback,' said Samuel. 'He is five years old. Both his parents were of good temperament otherwise I would never have kept a pup of that cross. He is very strong. If he was bad natured he would be unmanageable. Could you call your husband to come to the door so that they can meet,' he ended.

Davie was greeted as Elaine had been. When he dropped the paw the big dog flopped on his haunches in a sitting position and leaned his head against the man's stomach. Davie found that he had to brace himself to support the weight.

'Is he good with children?' The question was inevitable from a young father who had grown up with dogs and Samuel had obviously anticipated it.

'He is good with the children of the village,' he said without hesitation, then added, 'but he has known them all of his life and if their play becomes rough he has room to escape. He is a large, powerful animal and in a confined space such an animal can cause hurt even if he is trying to be protective.' He smiled. 'It is indeed unwise to allow the bull into the china shop. I will take him home now. He will be back in the evening. If he is displeased he has a deep growl which can increase until it becomes almost a roar. Do not worry if you hear him during the night. We will have the situation under control.'

Samuel made a chirping noise with his tongue and turned away. The massive dog rose to his feet, sniffed at both Davie and Elaine as if refreshing his memory, and then followed. When Elaine was closing the curtains at the onset of darkness, she glanced out of the window. Archibald lay on the cooling concrete of the patio with his head resting on his outstretched paws. The following morning a black man who was a stranger to her was walking towards the wood with the big dog at his heels. Samuel's rota of sentry duty had obviously been established. On intermittent occasions during the following months Archibald could be heard registering his disapproval. Then would come the soothing voice of a man followed by silence.

Davie found that his job was progressing very well. The Irish general foreman was a garrulous humorist who was able to get the best out of his men. On most days the dust on the site was terrible, but everybody worked cheerfully.

CHAPTER XX

Despite being kept in step with his progress by a regular supply of photographs, Marie longed to see her grandson. One Saturday evening in late summer Jock was servicing her car and she sat on the low garden wall engaging him in conversation as he worked. The Kenyan letter from Elaine had arrived in that day's post. They had been studying the latest batch of snapshots over a cup of tea before Jock had started work and inevitably the talk had continued on the same theme.

'Why do ye not go oot there for Christmas?' asked Jock suddenly.

'Oh, Jock, I couldn't do that,' Marie was taken aback.

'For why wid ye not?'

'Oh, it's an awful long way. And it would be an awful lot of money.

Mind you, it would be nice to see where they live.' Jock could see that she was wavering.

'Wid ye like me tae fintoot mair aboot it?' he asked.

'Yes, but how will you do that?'

'Och, there's a young fella has started up a travel agency in the toon. Things wur a bit tight wi' him. He has an auld Austin car an ah've been breathin' life intae it till he gets on his feet. Ah'll ask him.'

A fortnight later, Jock had accumulated a lot of information which even included a brochure of 'things not to be missed while in this beautiful country'. Most importantly, he had a list of prices and flights on which seats were available.

'Ah'll leave these wi' ye an' ye can hae a think,' he told Marie. 'Ah'll come doon a night in the middle of the week an' if ye've decided on a date ah'll make the bookin'. Whatever ye decide, ah'll leave ye as far as Glesca.'

By the middle of the week Marie had prepared a short list of possible dates and times.

'There's a flight out of London on the twenty third of December which would be ideal,' she told Jock.

'The only snag is that I would have to stay the previous night in London and I would have to miss the school Christmas party.'

'Have ye ever travelled on a railway sleeper?'

'No, I don't think that I could sleep with the noise.

'Ah thocht that tae, but when ah went tae the London motor show an slept like a top - baith ways. The last train oot o' Glesga doesna hae any stops so ye've got a smooth run. Ye can stay in yer berth tae half past seven an' hae a wash an' a cup o' tea before ye leave the train. Ah think ye should try it. Ah enjoyed it. Ah'll book that bit o' the journey for ye.'

'No, Jock, you mustn't,' Marie protested. 'You do more than enough us as it is.'

'Ach, away wi' ye. That can be my birthday present tae wee Donald.'

Thus in the middle of October, Marie's weekly letter to Kenya contained a welcome bit of news. 'I am coming out for Donald's first birthday,' she wrote. 'I am booked to fly out of London on the twenty third of December. I am being allowed four days extra holiday at the start of January term. I will be with you for fifteen whole days. Tell Donald not to speak until I get there so that I can hear his first words. Incidentally, his father's first recognisable word was "bugger". I often wonder where he heard it'

In a state of high excitement, Marie found herself, late on a cold December evening, being escorted by Jock down the platform of the Central Station in Glasgow. As they had waited at the ticket barrier, she had been aware of Jock in conversation with another man, but she had taken little notice.

'That wis yer steward,' he told Marie. 'He's on duty all night. If ye need anything, juist ring for him.'

'The only thing that I'll need may be a sleeping pill and he won't be able to dispense that,' laughed Marie.

'Ach, ye never ken. He might,' said Jock cryptically.

After a further few yards he opened the door of a carriage, but Marie drew back.

'No, Jock, this is a first class carriage.'

'Aye this is where ye're booked. In a first class carriage ye're given a berth tae yersel' In a second class ye might huv tae share. Besides, ye're makin' this journey fur a first class reason. In ye get.'

After he had passed her case in the carriage door, she gave him a quick cuddle. The plan was that on her return she would go to Edinburgh to give Katherine first hand news and that Jock would go through to Edinburgh to fetch her.

'Look after yourself 'til I get back,' she said as she kissed his cheek.

'Ach, ah'm good at that. Tell thay young yins no' tae wait too long awa fae civilisation,' the voice was hoarse and unnaturally gruff.

Marie was barely settled in her berth and the train hadn't yet started when there came a knock at her door. She opened it to find a white jacketed steward bearing a tray on which was placed a tray of sandwiches, a glass and a half bottle of chilled white wine. A white envelope was propped against the bottle. After the steward had left, she opened the envelope. Inside was a plain white card on which, in a neat hand was written the words 'Sleep well. Give my grand-nephew an extra cuddle for me'.

Sandwiches disposed of, she sat up in bed to enjoy a last glass of wine before snuggling down, although she didn't really expect to sleep. But it really was surprisingly comfortable and so lovely and warm, and the sheets were so crisp and fresh. She awoke to find the train stopped and switching on the light she looked at her watch. 'Damn,' she thought, 'It must have stopped the previous night and I didn't notice.' It read a quarter to seven. Why had the train stopped? Everything was very quiet until she became aware of the sound of a slow moving train. They must have stopped to let another train go through.

She glanced irritably at her watch as she wondered how far on the journey they had progressed. But her watch had also made progress. It now stated the time as being twelve minutes to seven. Marie suddenly realised that she had slept all night and was now lying in bed in Euston Station in London. She had just finished dressing and was brushing her hair when the steward knocked on her door with her morning cup of tea and toast. As he picked up the tray from the previous night, Marie reached for her purse, but the man waved her aside. 'No need for that, Mrs Sinclair,' he said. 'Your husband was very generous to me already.'

For long afterwards, Marie was to wonder what had gone through the mind of the steward when she burst into a fit of giggles.

She took a taxi from the station rank direct to the airport and this gave her plenty of time for a casual breakfast. After her night's sleep she felt good and found to her own surprise that she was looking forward to the flight. It was a frosty morning and there had been a hint of fog in London, but the airport was clear and her flight was called on time.

Leaving the ground was frightening, but the easy drifting sensation of smooth high level flight was marvellous. Even more marvellous was the first sight of her grandson. Davie had come to the airport on his own to meet her. He looked older. More mature.

Elaine had been listening for the jeep and came out to the stoep to meet them... slowly. Beside her, grasping tightly to her hand and moving with an exaggerated duck-waddle, was the most beautiful, perfect skinned, fair-haired boy that Marie had ever seen. She stopped at the edge of the stoep, her knees at floor level. Elaine gently disengaged her hand. Donald started forward, but stumbled and fell forward with his hands on the floor.

For a moment he hung suspended like a pond-feeding swan then pushed himself upright, chortled, aimed and stumbled forward into the arms of his grandmother. Marie wept copious tears of pure joy.

'He's been navigating his way round the chairs for a few days, but that was his first solo effort,' Elaine explained later. 'I don't suppose there will be any stopping of him now. Ornaments will have to rise to a new safety level too.'

Marie told them about her journey and the railway steward referring to Jock as her husband.

'I wonder why he never got married,' said Elaine. 'He's such a kind hearted man. It's a waste.'

'I think that when he was younger he saw his role in life as looking after his mother,' Marie told her. 'When she died while still in harness it left him a bit lost. Men like Jock need somebody to look after. I'm lucky that he never married. I just don't know how I would have coped without him.'

Elaine laughed. 'I remember saying something like that to him and he told me that the graveyard was filled with people that the world had thought were indispensable and things were going on just the same.'

'Yes, he said something similar to me once when I embarrassed him with thanks. He's right up to a point. But some are missed more than others.' Marie was wistful.

'I hardly slept at all on the plane,' Marie admitted. 'There's so much to see, even at night, that it seems a waste of time to sleep.'

Even tired as she was, Marie lay listening to the night sounds for some time before sleep took over. While it was still dark she awakened to the sound of Donald crying. Then she heard the soft soothing murmur of his mother's voice.

It seemed a very short time later that she opened her eyes to find Elaine standing by her bed holding a cup of tea. Even filtered by the curtains the sun was strong enough to cause her to shade her eyes with her hand. 'Merry Christmas, Gran,' said Elaine.

Davie had gone to work on Christmas morning as usual but had promised to be home in the early afternoon for Christmas dinner. Mid morning Marie and Elaine were sitting on the stoep while Donald played around their feet. As they sat, Samuel appeared round the corner of the house and, at a call from Elaine, came forward to meet Marie.

Marie was obviously impressed by the tall Masai who courteously shook her hand. As they spoke, Donald staggered forward and grasped Samuel's knees. Without interrupting the conversation, Samuel bent at the waist, picked the boy up and perched him on his shoulder. Donald laughed happily and buried his stubbly fingers in the grizzled grey hair.

'I've heard so much about Archibald that I'd like to see him,' said Marie. My husband always had dogs but now I've only got one. He's eleven years old now. I don't know if I'll get another one when he dies, but I think that I probably will. He's such good company.'

'I will bring Archibald myself this evening. It is necessary that you should meet and he can identify you,' she was told.

Christmas dinner was over. The women had left Davie and Donald to play and taken the dishes and debris through to the kitchen.

Marie was at the sink by the window when suddenly two large paws appeared on the window sill and she found herself the subject of a pair of brown eyes which were at a level with her own. Her gasp of surprise made Elaine turn around.

'If that's not a wolf it can only be Archibald,' said Marie. 'I see what you meant about his size. He's more like a Shetland pony than a dog.'

'He's less likely to bite you than a lot of the Shetland ponies that I've met,' replied Elaine. 'Come to the door and meet him. Samuel won't be far away. He never allows the dog to come here on his own.'

Samuel was crossing the patio as they opened the door and his dog had fallen in at his heels. Marie duly shook the proffered paw then smoothed her hand over the broad head.

'My husband used to say that dogs were like people, the big ones were gentle and the small ones aggressive,' said Marie. 'Archibald looks so placid.'

'He is good natured but he is also a very good watchdog,' Samuel told her. 'He would attack if told to do so, but only on command.'

As they were talking, the light was rapidly fading. Elaine, standing a step higher than Marie, became aware of the figure of a man approaching from the direction of the wood and she mentioned this to Samuel.

'Yes,' he said after a glance, 'that is Paul. He will be staying here tonight and I will leave now. There is something else to which I must attend.'

As he turned away, the dog moved to the middle of the patio and flopped on the concrete. He was almost invisible.

The following morning after Davie had gone to work, Marie was dressing Donald and heard a tap on the outside door. She looked up from her struggle to see a tall black girl enter the room.

'Hullo,' the voice was rounded and rich. 'You must be Mrs Sinclair. I am Ruth, Samuel's daughter.' Then to Donald. 'I'm glad that you weren't as big as this a year ago, young man.'

'You're not alone in that,' said another voice and Elaine, half clad, ran into the room. The two girls embraced tightly.

'So this was the something else that your father had to attend to last night,' said Elaine when she had settled down. 'I thought that there was a strange smile on his face when he said it.'

'Yes,' Ruth's smile fascinated Marie, 'I asked him not to tell you that I was coming, but I wanted to be here for Donald's birthday if I could.'

'Now for my piece of real news. This is really a form of what soldiers call embarkation leave. Oh, Elaine, I'm moving to Edinburgh. I'm joining the tropical diseases unit at the infirmary. I start at the beginning of February. Isn't that great! Dad doesn't want me to come back to Kenya just now,' she explained. 'He says that it could take ten years yet for the country to find its feet. One of the specialists from Edinburgh was in London on secondment. He told me about this post and that he would recommend me if I applied. So I did. I got it. I'm going to live in Bonnie Scotland.'

She spent the rest of the morning with them.

'I'd better go and give my mother the chance to ask all the questions which she forgot last night,' she said as she left. 'But I'll be back tomorrow and, if not, certainly on the day after. I must see this boy passing the first milestone on his journey.'

'Try to come tomorrow, we have so much to catch up on,' said Elaine.

'And I think that you should stay here the following night. I want you here to have your dinner with us and I do not like you going home afterwards in the dark.'

In the event it was the early afternoon of the birthday when they saw her again. She explained that a young boy in the village had, on the previous day, sustained a bad cut on his leg.

'He was lucky,' she said. 'Twenty years ago, or even much less, such an injury could have cost him his life. As it was I cleaned and stitched it and gave him an injection on each buttock and off he went. When he came back this morning to let me check his wound he was quite indignant. He had been trying to show off his injection sites to his pals and there was nothing to be seen. He couldn't convince them of the extent of his suffering and felt cheated at their lack of sympathy!'

Elaine laughed. 'I find that whenever people hear that I am a vet they give me a blow-by-blow account of all the horrendous illnesses which have attacked their pets. I often wonder if meeting a policeman makes that type of person confess their crimes. I suppose that you will get quite a bit of extra work when you are on holiday.'

'Oh, yes. A lot of the older people would never think of going to a doctor but because I am Ruth, daughter of Samuel, they trust me as one of their own. Fortunately, because of modern antibiotics, my success rate is higher than that of the witch doctor. He tries to voodoo me but so far it hasn't worked.'

The star of the birthday party became tired and had to go off to bed halfway through the dinner. His father, by the coffee stage, was also showing the signs of a busy day and Marie and Ruth elected to do the clearing up and let the parents go to bed. When tidiness again ruled they sat down to a last cup of tea and a blether. Marie's journey through university had been quite simple. She had been able to live at home and commute. Her parents had been comfortably off and able to provide for her and when she left university after the dreadful trauma of the 1926 general strike, she had been fortunate enough to find a job waiting.

Ruth, by contrast, had had many obstacles to surmount. Her colour was no problem in her early education which had been at mission school, but the ambition which drove her to seek further education made her an oddity. There was no available transport to take her to and fro so she had to find somewhere to stay. When teachers discovered how bright she was they became very helpful, but some of the white people, particularly the boys, resented being beaten by the only black pupil, who also happened to be a girl. One boy, the son of a white farmer, was particularly cruel in his taunts and the last straw came on a day when he left a bunch of bananas on her desk with a label attached which read 'Ape food'.

The rest of the class were obviously awaiting her reaction when Ruth got to her desk but she spoiled the joke by slipping the bunch beneath her desk before the lecturer entered the room.

After the class the boy was waiting for her. By this time Ruth was sick of the whole business, so, when he apologised and fell into step beside her she was civil to him in the hope of future peace.

When they came to a quiet part of the road where there were neither houses nor people, it became obvious that if he couldn't humiliate her in one way he would try another. He pulled her into the scrub and attacked her.

'I was big and strong even in those days, but even so he might have succeeded if he hadn't had trouble with the belt of his trousers,' she told Marie. 'This gave me a moment to get my breath back. I doubled up my legs and drove both feet into his rib cage and winded him completely. Before he could recover I hauled off his trousers and used them to tie his hands behind his back.

'I didn't know what to do next, but while I was still wondering the rest of the class arrived. Evidently he had boasted to some of them about what he was going to do. Some of the girls decided that this was really going too far and they had recruited a couple of the more decent boys to come

148

after us to stop him.

'I had just hauled him to his feet when they caught up with us. When they saw him they laughed and made a complete fool of him. I wanted to untie his hands when they were there to protect me but they made him walk back home as he was. If I had reported him to the principal he would have been expelled. When I didn't, the rest accepted me as one of them and life was different I still keep in touch with some of these girls. Christmas and birthdays. I've been to the weddings of three of them as well.'

'Do you ever hear what happened to the boy?' asked Marie.

'Yes, it's quite sad really. His father was killed by the terrorists. The son, who had always been spoiled, couldn't run the business so he lost the farm. He now works at Nairobi airport. I see him most times that I pass through. I feel quite sorry for him. He is a much nicer person now than he was,' she ended.

As Marie was preparing for bed she parted the curtains and looked out of the window to see Archibald standing in the pool of light. His big head turned as he looked at her for a moment, his tail wagged and he continued on his patrol. Feeling contented and secure Grannie fell asleep. On the evening before she was due to leave she was walking in the garden, with Donald by the hand, when Davie joined them.

They stood watching the sinking sun for a time.

'Have you enjoyed yourself, Mum?' he asked.

'Oh, yes, Davie, I wouldn't have missed it for anything.' She hesitated before going on, 'But I wish you were back home.'

'Well, don't tell Elaine because I don't want to raise her hopes too much, but we did an assessment of progress today. The job is going well. We could be home for next Christmas.'

CHAPTER XXI

Marie arrived back in Britain at midday on a Friday and following the pre-arranged plan she flew to Edinburgh to spend the night with Katherine and bring her up to date with first-hand news. Jock had said that he would collect her from there on the Saturday, unless there was danger of snow. The weekend turned out to be mild and about eleven o'clock on the Saturday morning the two women heard the noise of a car on the gravel. Going to the door together they saw Jock stepping out of a shiny new black Ford Consul. The wee man had left home in the dark of the winter morning before six o'clock. He hadn't told Marie that the reason why he was so keen to come to Edinburgh to meet her was that he had bought his new car for registration at the beginning of January and that the journey to Edinburgh offered him the ideal chance to run it in properly.

As he had driven through the deserted Saturday morning villages on the west Kintyre coast, he savoured the luxury of the inaudible heater and the soft murmur of the radio and allowed his mind to wander. Despite the relative hardship of her life, his mother had always managed to save a little money and had taught her son the value of thrift. Her ambition had been to 'to buy a wee Ford to tak yer faither for wee runs oot the toon an' intae the country'. After her death her son, despite knowing of her thrift, was surprised to learn that after the funeral expenses she had left slightly in excess of a thousand pounds, all in National Savings Certificates in which she had also encouraged her son to invest.

After Jock had gone to work in the garage one of his regular customers was a local bank manager who was particularly proud of his car. Once, as Jock was fitting a new set of spark plugs while the owner waited, they fell into conversation and the upshot was that for the first time in his life Jock paid a visit to the office of a bank manager.

'What I'd like to do, with your permission, of course, is hand this over to our investment department,' he told Jock. 'I would be in favour of giving them a fairly free hand, knowing as I do that they would do their very best for you, but that being said, is there any share or any type of share in which you would particularly like to invest?'

Jock told him the story of his mother and her 'wee Ford' and how pleased she had been when he had, as an apprentice, saved up enough money to buy her first and only washing machine, a Hoover.

'If ah'm gaun tae invest money in buyin' shares ah think it wid hae pleased the auld yin fur me tae hae some o' them,' he finished with a smile.

The bank manager laughed. 'If your mother was still alive I would offer her a job,' he said. 'You've just named the two shares which are being tipped at the moment. Anything else?'

'Well ma auld man wis a rivetter in the ship yairds an' ah've aye been a mechanic so anythin' tae dae wi' ships or road transport. Ah'm fit enough tae earn mair an' ah hope tae be for a long time yet, but juist tell yer boys tae keep aside enough tae gie me a reasonable funeral an' no tae lose the lot.'

'I'll pass on your message,' said the manager as Jock rose to leave. 'Come to see me as often as you like, but make a habit of spending an hour with us at least once a year so that we can review your share portfolio.'

That had been more than seven years ago. The original bank manager had retired and been succeeded by a younger man, but before he had gone he had seen Jock's original capital increase by a multiple of six with no change in the little man's pattern of saving.

'It's not often that I advise clients of the bank to spend money,' he said when Jock visited him just before his retiral. 'But you are a single man and you are now in a very comfortable position. If you feel like allowing yourself some luxury you can well afford it.'

'Ah'll think aboot it,' promised Jock solemnly.

The manager kept a straight face with difficulty.

'I wish we had more clients like you, Jock,' he said. 'The old motto of looking before you leap has been forgotten. Nowadays too many of them jump, then shout for help when they are in mid air.'

His friend's words had prompted Jock to make a will and now, several months later as he drove along the quiet road he reflected on the fact that his car had cost a sum which represented roughly half of his mother's legacy. He thought of his friendship with the Sinclair family, beginning with Davie's appendicitis and how it had provided him with the joy of family involvement which otherwise would have been denied to him. He thought of John Stark and how the tragedy of the death of his younger daughter had affected him. He thought of the families he had known in Clydebank decimated by the blitz. Yet those who were left had gathered together the remnants of their lives and steadfastly carried on. He thought of Ian Boyd whose father had died in war before his son was born and whose mother had died outwith the memory of her son. Yet some compensating factor in life had allowed Ian to become attached to a caring family before his guardian aunt had died while he was still a teenager.

He tried to anticipate the reaction of Marie and Katherine when they saw his new car and hoped that they would not think him pretentious. He had never before given an indication of his true financial position.

Darkness had given up the fight with grey winter sunlight when Jock turned under the shadow of the church steeple into Byres Road. There he parked and visited a café which was run by a family of Glasgow Italians. It was a place which he had frequented fairly regularly when he had worked in the city before the war and he was pleasurably surprised when the patriarch recognised him instantly.

When he came out he visited a florist to buy a bunch of flowers for Katherine before rejoining his route through the city towards the Edinburgh road. A haze over Edinburgh told him that there had probably been an early morning frost, but there was none now on the road. As he turned into Morrison Street to avoid the centre of the city, he took up station behind two horse drawn milk floats and screwed down his window to listen to the clop of the hooves on the cobbles before they turned off into the yard of the dairy. The tyres of his own transport made barely a whisper as he drove up Lothian Road until, some ten minutes later, he crunched onto the gravel of the drive of Katherine's house.

He had worried needlessly about his reception. The two women went round and through his car like delighted children and it was some time before they went into the house.

'Now, what are your plans, Jock?' asked Katherine as they waited for a kettle to boil. 'Can you stay here for tonight and then go home tomorrow?'

Jock looked from one to the other.

'Ah had Ian and Jean on the phone last night,' he said. 'They thocht that you two wid hae plenty tae speak aboot and didnae want tae disturb ye. Their plan wis that we should all go oot tae them for the night. We could swing back this wey the morn an' drap you off.'

Katherine hesitated. 'Jock, I'd love it. But it wouldn't be fair to ask you and Marie to come all this way back with me tomorrow. Both of you have to work on Monday.'

'Well, how aboot this. If we were tae turn doon at Lochearnheid we could drop you at Stirling an' you could get the train. By cuttin' through the Carse tae Balloch oor journey widna be any mair than half an oor langer.'

Katherine and Marie looked at one another and both nodded in pleasure.

'Right, could wan o' you phone tae Jean tae tell her tae peel half a dozen extra tatties. It'll be nice tae see the sun gaun doon ower the braes o' Balquidder.'

Young John, confident in his eight and a half years, came running to meet them with a half-grown collie pup on tow at the end of a rope but his sister, at just a month past her second birthday, took refuge in the folds of her mother's skirt for a time until curiosity prompted her to come out.

Ian and Jean were obviously very happy in their village where they had now lived for over ten years and where they had become active members of the community. Ian was an elder in the local church and had just turned down an invitation to stand for election to the County Council. Jean, because of her nursing experience, was often called on, if a doctor wasn't immediately at hand, in an emergency. Their son attended the local two teacher school where he was already showing academic promise. Since Ian himself had had to take a roundabout route to university, he was determined that his children should find the road easier if that was their choice.

The evening passed quickly, comfortably, in the warm glow of the coal fire. Naturally, Marie had to do most of the talking until, in a lull in the conversation, Jean, who was sitting opposite, saw her head nod and realised that post-travel tiredness was having an effect so she rose and went through to put on a kettle for a last cup of tea.

Jean had wanted to decant her son in order to provide a bed for Jock but that worthy had insisted that he could be comfortably accommodated on the sofa in the sitting room. After the house quietened down he lay for a long time cocooned in warmth and contentment until the dying fire surrendered the room to darkness and he slept.

The next morning there was a skin of ice on Loch Lubnaig and thick hoar hovered over the Carse of Stirling. As Jock and Marie purred through Arrochar and climbed the Rest and Be Thankful, heavy snow began to fall and Marie thought of the contrast to the weather which she had left just three days before. The snow followed them well beyond Inveraray, but by the time they were crossing the neck of the Kintyre peninsula from East to West Loch Tarbert, the sun had reasserted its authority. The colours over Islay as it set had to be seen to be believed.

Marie found that most of her first few days back at school were taken up answering her pupils' questions about her trip, but the novelty eventually wore off and normal study was resumed by the end of the week. She had enjoyed her trip and it had been nice to see how and where Davie and Elaine lived, but it was nice to be home. On the Saturday she went into town, bought a bunch of flowers and on her way home put them on Donald's grave.

That night, before going indoors, she stood for a time in the fading light looking over the North Channel to the snow on the east coast hills of Ireland. Her mind drifted comfortably over the past month... the things she had done... the people she had seen... the marvellous first sight of her grandson. Smiling, she entered the warmth of her home and closed the door.

In Kenya, Ruth had spent that Saturday afternoon with the rest of the family Sinclair. She was leaving early on the Monday morning to take up her new post in Edinburgh and had come to say goodbye. Elaine had gone to bed before Davie saying that she was tired and when he came through to the bedroom she was lying with her back towards him and appeared to be asleep.

Quietly he undressed and turned out the light, but as he settled in bed he heard his wife sob. Like most men Davie could deal fairly competently with material crises, but a tearful wife was an impossible problem. He lay without moving until the sound was repeated on a higher note.

'What's wrong, Elaine?' he asked, turning towards her.

She whirled round, scattering the light covers and buried her wet face in his chest.

'Oh, Davie. I hate this bloody country. Your mother's gone home, Ruth's gone to Edinburgh, you go off to build your stupid, bloody aerodrome and Donald and me have damn all to do all day but swat bloody flies.'

As her sobbing burst into the open, the strange thought went through Davie's mind that in one breath she had just used more swear words than in all of the rest of the time that he had known her. Not knowing what else to do, he gently gathered her in his arms. Soon her breathing became even. She slept. Davie was not so fortunate. Eventually exhaustion defeated anxiety and he too drifted into an uneasy, tossing slumber.

Elaine never brought up the subject on the Sunday morning and Davie was content to let it lie. The day passed pleasantly enough and, trying his best to suppress a feeling of guilt, he escaped to his work on Monday morning. After a drive round the site he sent for the general foreman and the two of them worked until the mid-day break reviewing progress and trying to work out a rough completion date. Although the heat was at times a problem, Davie enjoyed the country and the dependability of the climate which meant that work could be planned for weeks in advance without worry about vagaries of the weather.

Since the birth of their son, Elaine had seemed to be so happy that it never occurred to him that she might have a longing for female conversation. As he sat at his desk, a sudden trick of memory took him back over some four thousand miles of distance and almost fifteen years of time. He remembered the summer before he went to secondary school. He remembered himself and Jock sitting on a rock above the rough shore of the Moil on a beautiful summer's day. He could hear the wee man's warning about the coming difficulties in asking people to 'bide at the back o' beyond'.

That day on the rock, Davie had decided on the course of his secondary education. They had resolved to go back to the same rock after five years to plan the next steps in his career. They had gone back but not to the rock at the head of Glenamoil. The pre-university plans had been laid at the top of Cnocan Lin. Suddenly Davie remembered that September Sunday morning and the roe deer hind and her calf. Tears of pure home-sickness welled out of his eyes. He understood his wife's loneliness and longing for home.

CHAPTER XXII

That evening Davie was able to assure Elaine that their next Christmas Day would be spent in Scotland. She linked her hands round his neck and drew his head down.

'I'm sorry, Davie, I didn't mean to put pressure on you. I don't want to be one of those wives who can't take the rough with the smooth. It was just the thought of Ruth going away, and to Edinburgh of all places, so soon after your mother left us. I felt as though I was abandoned out here for the rest of my life. I'm sorry.' She kissed him. 'Donald's still asleep. I think his Daddy deserves a sweetie,' and she led him towards the bedroom door.

Late that night he confessed his own tears as he thought of home.

From time to time they heard reports of terrorist activity but the death of Thomas Jomera seemed to have caused any local cell to abandon activities. Davie put this theory to Samuel.

'Fortunately, they hadn't a chance to get organised in this area, the tall Masai told him. 'Jomera made two mistakes which in the end was fortunate for the rest of us. Firstly, he was boastful and talked too much which meant that even the young men were reluctant to join him.

'Secondly, he had a liking for young girls. It was, I understand, the father of one such girl who killed him and not the terrorists as I at first assumed. Either way, a good job was done and not a moment too soon. He could have made much trouble.'

'Do the police know about this, Samuel?'

The black man smiled. 'Officially, no,' he said. 'The local inspector is a sensible man who knows his job. If the terrorists were to know that Jomera's death was merely the result of a father making sure that justice was done he might be replaced. We do not wish that to be done. The next man might be more efficient than he was.

'But the murderer won't be punished,' Davie was indignant, but Samuel shook his head.

'He is not a murderer,' he said evenly. 'He is a man who performed a service to Kenya despite that not being his motive. Had he not done so there are others among us who would have found it necessary.'

The expression on the good-natured black face was quite calm, but Davie felt a chill travel up his spine. While in the RAF he had read a book about resistance fighters in German occupied countries during the war.

He now had a better understanding of the patriotism which had motivated these people to take the risks which they had taken. Despite his homesickness he knew Kenya to be a naturally beautiful country. It would be wrong if the future of such a land had to be settled by terrorists and not by democracy. Very wrong.

Over the years there had been settlers who had undoubtedly exploited the land and the native population, but there also had been people like the Scots Missionaries who were foster parents to Samuel and helped to make him the man that he was. It was to be hoped that the work done by such people, often at great risk to themselves, would prove to be sufficient to allow the prevalence of right over wrong. Davie felt that he had a vested interest. It was the land of his son's birth.

Later that day as he was making a leisurely and satisfied inspection of progress of work on the site, he recalled what Jock had told him and he had later quoted to Elaine's father, about the long-term worth of the work of a civil engineer. He hoped that the job he was doing here would be helpful to the long term prosperity of Kenya and that his aerodrome would not, in the future, be simply used to allow tourists to come to gawp at a dying culture.

As Donald steadied on his legs he spent more and more time with Samuel. The older man had endless patience and didn't seem to mind raking out small footprints in his flower beds and replacing plants that infant curiosity had caused to be pulled out by the roots. Samuel's English was so precise that by the time he was eighteen months of age, Davie and Elaine found that their son was learning to speak with an accent which owed nothing to Edinburgh or Kintyre.

'Savour it while you can,' said Davie when Elaine drew attention to this. 'We won't be long at home until Jock has him talking with a Glasgow accent.'

The word 'home' had been used sparingly for some time. Privately, they were both longing for the hills and the luxury of a variable climate which laid the dust and forced the flies to hibernate.

Donald's increasing independence also meant that Elaine was finding time on her hands. This she found, had a two pronged effect. On the one hand, she longed for the excitement of her own profession. Alternatively, she became broody. She had never had a brother but she now had a son. Since Kay's death she, like Davie had grown up as an only child. Many times during her father's later years she had longed for someone close in whom she could confide. Davie had always had Ian who had been big brother to him in everything but blood. And then there had been, in time for his adolescent years, the ever practical Jock. She smiled to herself as she recalled Marie's story about the steward on the train who had thought that Jock was her husband.

She blushed when she recalled how her father in his drunkenness had gibed at Davie about taking advice from Jock and how he had referred to him as a street pundit. Why did some people assume, like her father had done, that education automatically bestowed some form of moral superiority. Davie's mother had been to university, but his father had barely progressed beyond primary school. Yet they enjoyed great respect in their community and had produced a well balanced and sensible son.

She glanced out of the window to see her own son perched on the broad shoulder of his friend. Would he go to university when he grew up? Yes, probably he would. Anyway, he was going to have a wee sister.

She had made up her mind. She would put the matter in hand as soon as possible. She sang to herself as she began to prepare an evening meal for her husband.

Sometime during that night Elaine woke to the restless murmuring coming from Donald's cot. A half moon shining through the open curtains gave her sufficient light to go to the cot and stand with a comforting hand on the firm young shoulder until he settled. After a brief glance out of the window to the quiet garden, she went back to bed and had just achieved that comforting serenity between sleep and wakefulness when a piercing scream from just outside the window wrenched her fully awake. Davie had been in a deep sleep but as the scream faded to be replaced by scuffling sounds, he leapt out of the other side of the bed and ran to the window.

A young black man was huddled on the ground in a whimpering heap and another was fleeing across the flowerbeds with little regard to the damage he was causing. He had almost reached the perimeter fence when the dark, pursuing form of Archibald became airborne and struck him squarely between the shoulders.

The weight of the big dog combined with the velocity of impact propelled the man forward in an arc and his feet left the ground. His throat landed squarely on the top wire of the fence, His head jerked forward and Davie clearly heard a horrible crunching snap. For a moment he hung on the fence like a discarded rag doll before slowly sliding backwards to collapse motionless on the ground. Archibald stood over him briefly before coming back to join Samuel who has hauling the first man to his feet.

The scream had disturbed Donald and as Elaine stayed to comfort him, Davie opened the door leading on to the stoep where he met Samuel and Archibald with their captive. The left arm of the young man had obviously been subject to the attentions of Archibald and it hung limply by his side with blood dripping from the wrist.

'I am sorry that you were disturbed, but I wanted to be sure of catching them both,' said Samuel. 'If I had interfered sooner one of them might have escaped.'

'I must summon the security forces,' Samuel went on and Davie noticed that he seemed to be speaking slowly and clearly. 'Meanwhile I will leave the dog to guard this gentleman.'

The man gave a gasp of terror and cowered against the wall. Samuel showed his white teeth in a smile. 'Ah so we do understand English,' he said before turning to Davie. 'Could you take a torch and go to the end of the stable building. There is a rocket fixed high up on the wall. If you put a light to it, it will summon help.

'They will not be long. We have been expecting something like this for some time. While we wait this man is going to tell me the story of his misspent life.'

'I won't,' muttered the man as he nursed his injured arm, 'I won't say a word. You can't make me.'

'Indeed,' Samuel was calm. 'Archibald'. The command was sharp. The big dog growled as he rose to his feet.

The man collapsed on the edge of the stoep and began to babble.

Davie found the end of the fuse and applied a match. There was a hissing sound as the fire travelled upwards then a rocket exploded high into the night sky to burst in a shower of sparks.

On his way back to Samuel, he used his torch to check on the man by the fence. The head was turned at an unnatural angle and the man was obviously dead.

Samuel was standing over his captive who was now silent. The big man was holding the handle of a panga in his right hand with the back of the blade resting in the palm of his left. Archibald lay with his head resting on his front paws, but his eyes were open and alert. Samuel's glance went to the figure by the fence then travelled back to Davie who shook his head. The glow of headlights appeared in the distance and soon they could hear the sound of vehicles that were being driven to their limit. Two Land Rovers jerked to a stop and several men tumbled out and ran towards the group at the house.

Samuel spoke quietly to Archibald and the dog never moved. Their leader looked for an identifying moment at the man who was sitting on the edge of the stoep then looked at Samuel who answered the silent question by pointing towards the fence. Two men went and looked at the body before one of them went towards the vehicles and the other came back.

'No trouble with that one, sir,' he said. 'Jones has gone for a stretcher and we'll cart him off. What about this fellow? Do you want us to take him as well?'

'Yes, sergeant. Better take him to hospital to get that arm seen to and leave a couple of men to keep an eye on him. We don't want to lose him again. I'll get some details and meet you back at the depot.'

'These two were escaped prisoners,' the officer explained when they were seated in the house with Archibald again on guard on the patio.

'They broke out almost a fortnight ago from a camp about sixty miles north of here killing two guards in the process.

'A couple of nights ago somebody tried to break into a farmhouse about ten miles from here. A dog kicked up a racket and they gave up, but we were pretty certain that it was them. They would be desperate for food. We had some guards posted at a few of the farmhouses, but we knew that it wasn't necessary to have anyone here.' The last was said with a glance at Samuel.

'Were they terrorists?' It was Elaine who asked the question.

'Oh, yes. They were captured during a raid on a farmhouse. The family had been warned that a raid might take place and were evacuating the place.' He hesitated, glanced at Elaine then went on. 'There was a little girl of four. She ran back into the house because she had forgotten a favourite doll. These two had broken in from the back and were in her bedroom by this time.' The expression on Samuel's normally impassive face made him stop.

'Do you know about this?' he asked.

'Yes, but only after I had asked Davie to set off the rocket. Had I known earlier I would not have troubled you until the morning. He told me it was white troops who captured them. That was unfortunate. My people are more efficient in dealing with such animals.' The quiet voice of the dignified old Masai chilled the atmosphere of the room.

Elaine sobbed quietly and reached for Davie's hand.

At the beginning of September, Davie announced that he expected his job to be completed in three more months at the outside. Elaine threw her arms around his neck and he clasped her in a bear hug.

'Careful, boy, careful,' she said. 'I can stand it all right but you may be squeezing more than me now.'

He held her at arms length and looked at her.

'Are you sure?' he asked, his smile threatening the safety of his ears.

'Not sure. No, it's early days yet. But suspicious. You see, there's this man who shares a bed with me,' then she laughed and came back within the circle of his arms and laid her head on his chest.

'Oh, Davie, I hope I'm right. Donald will just be about two years and four months, just the age to look after a wee brother or sister. We will be at home. It will be born in Scotland.'

The following Sunday morning she rose from the table in the middle of her breakfast, went to the bathroom and was sick.

The sickness in the mornings lasted for about a month and by the end of that time, Elaine was finding her waistbands constricting.

Out of habit, Davie had added a bad weather factor to his estimated date for finishing the aerodrome, but by the middle of October it was obvious that less than four weeks would see all the loose ends tied up. When he went to see the lawyers who were factors of the house they were able to tell him that the owners intended to return to Kenya after the New Year. This news helped to take the edge off Samuel's sorrow at their leaving. The family left Kenya on the afternoon of what was a very hot day. They arrived in Edinburgh the following evening, to a full moon and the first hard frost of the winter.

Katherine met them at the airport. Davie drove her car through the evening quiet of the city. Elaine sat by his side and grannie and grandson sat in the back. When they arrived at the house, Ruth had a meal ready.

Davie phoned his office in Glasgow in the morning and told them that he would be through on the following day.

'Are you bringing Donald?' asked the girl.

'No '

'Then bring the photographs.'

At the office he was hugely welcomed. As young men, he and Damn had been adopted by the female office staff and now, his return after the successful completion of his first major contract and as a young father to boot, was greeted with prodigality.

Davie then spent more than two hours in a meeting with the managing director before being taken out to lunch. He had been surprised to find few changes in the office staff after his two and a half years absence and he mentioned this over lunch.

'It has always been one of the main strengths of this company,' his companion said. 'They have always treated their staff fairly and as a result have got loyalty. Did you know that the founder, like yourself, was the son of a shepherd?'

As Davie, whose mouth was full, shook his head, the man went on.

'Yes, he started off doing farm drainage work and repairing farm roads. With his first savings he bought a young Clydesdale horse and a cart. He used to say that the horse was his first employee and the cart his first machinery.

'As he got more work he started to take on a number of men. One Saturday morning he found one of them abusing the horse. The men normally got their wages in cash at the end of the Saturday morning and had the afternoon off. By the time of this incident he was employing three men. On this Saturday, before paying them he beat this fellow up in front of the other two. He then paid them and dismissed them for the weekend. All of them, including the fellow who had been disciplined, turned up on Monday morning.

'The horse-beater stayed with the firm for the rest of his working life and became general foreman. Later on, his brother joined the firm as its first engineer and then his son in turn started work with the firm. That first engineer, of course, was the father of our Mr McLeod and the son, who has devoted all his working life to this office, is your old friend and mentor Mr McLeod himself.'

'I didn't see Mr McLeod this morning in the general excitement,' said Davie. 'I'll make a point of looking in on him this afternoon. How is he?'

'You won't see him in the office I'm afraid. He took a stroke three months ago and won't be fit to come back to work. He is paralysed right down his right side.'

'Oh, that's terrible. Is he in hospital?'

'He was, but his wife took him home a fortnight ago. That wasn't a good idea but none of us could talk her out of it. They live in a tenement, one of the older ones, and have to share a toilet with the three other flats on the landing. It's ridiculous.'

'Couldn't they have moved to a house that was better adapted to people of their age? Mr McLeod has always worked and they have no family. They should be reasonably well off.'

Davie's tone had been conversational but he noticed his companion assuming a purplish hue.

'Reasonably well off,' he spluttered. 'Davie, that man owns fifty thousand shares in this company.'

'He what?' Davie was incredulous. 'But that must be worth a fortune.'

'That is, and on top of that he always had a good salary. He's not just comfortably off, he's wealthy, very wealthy. You just can't persuade the mean old bugger to spend any of it on his own comfort.'

'How did he come to have so many shares in the company?'

'He inherited them from his mother. When the company went public, the founder gifted them to her because her husband and indeed her brother-in-law, who had never married and was also dead by this time, had put so much work into building it up. This company repays its loyal servants, you know, young man.

162

'The idea was to keep her in comfort without the degradation of accepting a pension. Our company has always paid a good dividend in shares so the idea was good, but Mr McLeod is the last of his line and it's just plain stupid for him and his wife to be living as they do when they can afford to live so much more comfortably.'

CHAPTER XXIII

As a family of three and a bit would have put too much of a strain on the facilities available at Damn's flat, Elaine and Donald elected to stay with Katherine while they were house hunting. Davie had to spend time in the office tidying up the financial side of his contract and, except for some of the worst nights of the January freeze up, was able to commute. Katherine occasionally hinted that she would like them to stay with her on a permanent basis, but both Davie and Elaine felt that they would be better with a place of their own, even accepting that neither Katherine nor Marie were interfering mother-in-laws. Before they had settled on the house that they wanted to buy, Davie was summoned to the office of the managing director. 'Have you bought a house yet' he was asked.

'Not yet, but we are hoping to go to see a couple this weekend. There are plenty on the market but after the baby is born Elaine is hoping to set up a small animal practice which she can run from the house so we need a place with a garage or outhouse of some kind that she can adapt as a surgery.'

'Would you be willing to live in Edinburgh?'

'Well, yes, I certainly think that given a choice Elaine would prefer it but my work is here,' Davie was surprised at the question.

'At the moment, yes, but that may be about to change,' before Davie had time to panic, his boss continued. 'Keep this under your hat at the moment, but we are negotiating to open a branch office in Edinburgh. If we are successful, and we will be eventually, we would like you to run it.

'Talk it over with Elaine and let me know on Monday. We think that you will be the right man for the job and you don't need me to point out that it will be a tremendous opportunity for you.

'If you decide to take it then go ahead and look for a house through there. If you have to commute to Glasgow while you are waiting for your office we will make it as easy as we can for you.'

As Davie had expected, Elaine was enthusiastic about his news.

'I would have gone with you to Glasgow, I would go with you to the North Pole, but Edinburgh is home to me,' she said. 'We'd better tell Mum, then phone your mother. I know that they are both worrying in case we take off again to some corner of the Empire where they won't be able to see the children.' She laughed, 'It's losing the children that worries them - not us.'

By the time they phoned Marie, Katherine had provided a codicil to the story they had to tell her.

'Why don't you two take over this place and let me look for something smaller,' she said and as Davie started to protest, she stopped him. 'Believe me I can well afford it and all I've got is willed to you anyway. Talk it over,' But from the look on the face of his wife Davie knew that there was no need for discussion.

On a beautiful spring morning and to the chorus of the romancing blackbirds in the grounds of the maternity hospital, Katherine Marie Sinclair made her uncomplicated way into this world.

'She looks like an orange,' said her big brother.

'Aren't you clever,' was the comment of mother to father. 'If there was a third sex I would let you try again for a full house.'

'We'll call her Kay,' said Davie.

When Davie had joined the firm he found office work tedious and repetitive and something to be avoided as much as possible. Necessity, however, is an efficient tutor and the period stationed in Kenya without Mr McLeod and his team had shown him not only the value of running an efficient office, but also that, surprisingly, he quite liked it. Mr McLeod's successor was a woman, a tall red haired lady of pleasing appearance and bubbling humour whose husband had been killed in the war in the Far East. Her two daughters were both at Edinburgh University studying medicine so, when Davie was given the keys of his new Coates Crescent office, he had no difficulty in persuading her go to Edinburgh for a month to help him to set things in motion and interview suitable staff.

Katherine had bought a two bedroomed bungalow less than a mile from her former house. The previous owners had been an elderly couple who grew masses of roses in the small sheltered garden. She and Ruth had developed a firm friendship and the black girl divided her spare time between the two houses.

At first Davie's staff consisted of one engineer and an apprentice plus two office girls, but by the time of Kay's third birthday, which coincided with Donald starting school, two more young engineers and another office girl had been added. Elaine's problem had been solved by the partners of her old practice who, when they knew that she was back in the area and available for work, had invited her to rejoin them on a part-time basis. Katherine had retired to enjoy her garden and her grandchildren and was an enthusiastic baby sitter whenever she was required.

Marie had bought herself a new car and as experience had made her a more confident driver, she visited both her family in Edinburgh and Ian and Jean in Perthshire on most school holidays.

The double income and the gift of a house made the young Sinclairs very well off and their obvious prosperity was noticed in Davie's calf country as they spent three weeks holiday with Marie each summer. Jock delighted in the children and on Sunday mornings would set off with Kay on his shoulder and Donald running in front to follow the course of the burn, drink cold water from the spring and stand eventually on the summit of Cnocan Lin with a pride no less than that of Hillary and Tenzing on the summit of Everest.

Davie was tackling the build-up of business at his Edinburgh office as a matter of personal pride. At first he found himself staying to work later than his staff on odd evenings, but as time went on this became a more frequent occurrence until it seemed that he never left the office before eight o'clock. He was leaving home in the morning before the children were up and arriving back after they had gone to bed. As a consequence he saw very little of them. At weekends, he was tired and irritable and on frequent occasions Elaine would put the children in the car, pick up her mother and Ruth and take them off to the beach or the zoo.

The family, at Elaine's insistence, still took their three week annual holiday with Marie, but even then it was several days before Davie felt relaxed enough to join in the fun with any enthusiasm.

Things came to an abrupt head on an evening shortly after Kay had started school. Davie didn't arrive home until just before ten o'clock. Elaine had a drink sitting poured for him and his meal ready. As had become usual, when he got home, the children were already asleep in bed. Elaine sat quietly reading a book while he was eating. When he finished, he rose and turned towards the door, but was halted by a sharp 'Davie, sit down,' from his wife.

Her voice sounded strange and as she looked up he saw that her eyes were red from crying.

'What's wrong now?' he asked in a puzzled voice, then added irritably, 'I'm tired. What's the matter with you?'

'Yes, you're tired,' Elaine's voice rose. 'Of course you're tired. I'm tired. But I'm also bloody well fed up. Well, can you cast your tired mind back five-and-a-half years? We had a baby daughter then. We called her Kay. Remember?

'Yes, of course. But I don't see that as an excuse for a tirade.'

'Oh, you don't. No, of course, you don't. You see damn all but your office nowadays. Well, let me explain,' she went on bitterly. 'For the past three nights she has sat up until her eyes were closing so that she could show her new school reading book to her Daddy. She got a dirty mark on

166

it today at school.

'When I went to tuck her in tonight she was crying to herself. Her book isn't new any more and Daddy hasn't seen it. I hope you're proud of yourself.'

'Elaine, that's unfair. I have to make money.'

'No, it isn't. It 's what you 're doing that 's unfair. Don't you see that for me this is just history repeating itself. I remember when I was ill before Kay went off to go to Canada. The night before she was due to go off, her favourite teddy had lost its leg. She sat up for as long as she could to get her Daddy to mend it for her. By the time that he came home, she had gone to bed. Do you know what he did,' her voice broke into sobs, 'I'll tell you,' she went on when once again she had control, 'he was off to work the next morning before she was up. He hadn't mended her teddy. He left her a pound to buy a new one. He couldn't understand that she didn't want a new one, She loved her old one and had depended on her Daddy to make it well again.' In a renewed burst of sobbing she ran from the room.

Davie lay on his own side of the bed and spent most of the night staring at the darkened ceiling.

Next evening, Elaine heard his car on the gravel before six o'clock. She ran to the door to meet him.

'I just never realised what I was doing,' he said as they embraced. 'I'm sorry. Where's the weans?'

'They're waiting for you in the sitting room. But don't go in yet. Run upstairs and change out of that suit. You'll then look more like a Daddy and less like a director.'

Knowing her man as she did, Elaine had expected him home in time for his meal with them on that night. She had put thought into the menu, being careful to select things which were favourites with the children and which could be disposed of with forks and fingers.

Davie came down to find a picnic laid on the carpet in front of the sitting room fire. Elaine came through and handed him a dram of whisky and water. 'Kay has a reading lesson,' she told him. 'If you listen to that I won't be more than five minutes. Donald has his homework finished.'

Kay climbed on to his knee and opened her book.

The meal had been cleared away, the children had gone to bed and the parents in close and companionable silence were sitting watching the flames of the fire when, after a tap at the door, Ruth walked into the room from the hall.

'Oh,' she laughed when she saw the scene before her, 'I'm sorry. Would you like me just to go away again?'

'No, you idiot, come in,' said Elaine as she jumped to her feet. 'I'm glad to see you. You're just in time to prevent this man from getting ideas which might prove to be beyond his capabilities.'

'I deliberately waited until the children would be in bed,' said Ruth when she was settled with a cup of coffee. 'About six weeks ago I phoned Jock and asked him to look out for a car for me. He phoned back last night. He has bought me a two-door Morris 1100 that is less than a year old.

'My plan is to take the train through to Glasgow on Saturday morning and fly down to collect it. I'll stay with Granny Marie on Saturday night and drive back on Sunday.' She paused before going on. 'What I wondered was, would the children like to come with me? I have checked that there are seats available on the plane.'

Davie and Elaine looked at one another before Elaine answered, 'They would love it, I know they would, but,' she hesitated, 'would the two of them not be too much of a handful?'

'No, no. Jock is going to meet me at the plane and we can take as long as we want to drive back on Sunday. I just have to get them from the train to the airport bus in Glasgow and I won't have any luggage except an overnight bag.'

'I've got a better idea,' said Davie looking at his wife. 'We can take you through to the airport from here on Saturday morning then we can go up to Perthshire and spend the Saturday night with Ian and Jean. By the way, does my mother know about all this yet?'

'She knows that I'm coming, but I never said anything about the children in case it wasn't going to be suitable.'

'I'll phone her now and leave you girls to have a blether' said Davie as he rose form his chair. 'It's a while since I've spoken to her. Anytime we call her now Donald and Kay monopolise the phone.'

There was a low lying fog over Edinburgh when they left on the Saturday morning but by the time they got to the airport they found a clear autumn day.

Donald claimed veteran status on the strength of having flown from Kenya when he was less than two years old. He settled in a seat in front of Ruth and Kay, but when the engines were run up before take-off he looked round anxiously and Ruth leaned forward and placed a reassuring hand on his shoulder.

When they were airborne and had circled out over the Clyde estuary he forgot his fears. The flight path led round the north end of Arran to touch the Kintyre coast at Skipness and Kay scrambled over Ruth to join her brother at the window and watch the patterns made by the ships on the calm water far below. Ruth found their excitement infectious and leant forward to thrust her head between theirs.

As the plane taxied up towards the reception area, they saw Jock standing and waving beside a lovely little dark green car. He had obviously spent a good part of his morning with a polishing cloth. Jock insisted on Ruth driving her purchase into the town where he and Donald transferred to his own car and the girls followed out to the quiet country road. It was barely mid-day when they drew in behind Marie's car at the croft.

Kay tumbled out of Ruth's car and ran to greet her grannie. Donald, as befitted a big brother, walked round the corner with Jock in a more dignified fashion, but as he got closer decided sensibly that he wasn't yet too big for a cuddle and he too broke ranks and ran forward.

When the children had settled and the two women had greeted one another with a similar enthusiasm, Marie looked round. 'I've prepared picnic things since it was such a lovely morning,' she said. 'But we can eat here if the children are tired.'

A duet of protest assured her of their fitness.

It was decided that as Jock's car was the biggest they would use it to go up to the viewpoint above the lighthouse and there find a sheltered spot.

After the meal, Jock and Donald climbed out the hill to Glen's grave from where they could look down towards the house where Davie had been born. The bracken on the more exposed parts of the hill had faded to a deep brown but was still green in the shelter of the bottom of the glen. The afternoon sun was behind the man and the boy and despite being barely nine years old, Donald was obviously impressed. 'It's beautiful, Uncle Jock,' he said taking the older man's hand.

Before they went to bed, the children ganged up to persuade Jock to wait overnight. 'We want a walk in the morning,' said Kay. 'Grannie's too old to take us and Auntie Ruth doesn't know the way.'

Marie was sensible enough to recognise a diplomatic argument and burst into laughter.

'I'll wait at home and make the breakfast and you can all go. But I'll expect a cup of tea in bed before you go,' she ended.

Jock rose early next morning to check that the weather was dry. By the time Ruth and the children appeared he had tea and hot buttered toast ready for them. Hostilities threatened over who was to take Marie's share through to her but peace prevailed by means of a compromise whereby Donald carried a mug of tea and Kay took the toast on a plate. As they passed through the gate leading from the road onto the hill, Kay took Jock's hand. Donald proceeded independently for a time until, after a glance at Kay to make sure that he wouldn't be teased, he slipped his left hand into Ruth's right one.

When they came to the spring, Kay ran forward, filled the jam jar with water and passed it round with a grandeur befitting a chalice of the finest wine.

When they wound their way through the whin bushes towards the rough hill, Jock and Kay were in the lead but as the climb got steeper, they fell back and Ruth and Donald were first to gain the top. Ruth loved the view, but as the children excitedly pointed out the various places of interest, she glanced round at Jock who sat down on a rock behind her. His breath appeared laboured and there was a slight tinge of blue at the corner of his lips. Quietly she sat down beside him. 'Are you feeling alright, Jock?' she asked softly.

'Fine, Ruth. Aye ah'm fine, dinna fash,' and he rose to his feet as the children turned back towards them. Ruth saw that there was nothing to be gained by pursuing the subject at that moment.

Her new car performed satisfactorily on the road back to Edinburgh and the children travelled well. They were wound up after their weekend and bursting with the stories they had to tell, but exhaustion defeated them quickly. After they had gone to bed, Ruth confided her fears about Jock's health to Davie and Elaine.

'I don't want to sound alarmist. It might have simply been that we set too fast a pace. The children were full of beans and I wasn't paying too much attention but I'd feel happier if he had a check up.'

'Can we ask what you suspect?' It was Davie who broke the silence.

'At his age, and if he wasn't such a wiry wee man, I'd be worried about his heart. But if he had a pain he certainly never admitted to it. He never even gave me a chance to take his pulse.' She paused before going on. 'He doesn't smoke, but against that he has worked for most of his life in an atmosphere of exhaust fumes. Och,' she ended, 'maybe living in Scotland is making me fey.'

Davie thought for a moment. 'If you like, I'll get Angus Graham on the phone and you can talk to him,' he said and on her nod he rose to his feet.

Ruth spoke on the phone for about five minutes.

'We're in luck,' she said when she came back, 'Jock's doctor worked as a houseman with Mr Graham and they still keep in touch. He's phoning him now. He promised to let me know how they get on, but it may take a day or two for the doctor to get a hold of Jock.'

On the Tuesday evening, just over a week later, Davie was sitting by the fire watching the late evening news on television. Elaine had been called out to an emergency and the children were both in bed. Over the noise of the television, he heard the noise of a car on the gravel and assumed that it was his wife.

Suddenly the room door burst open with such force that it banged against the sideboard. Startled, he jumped to his feet just in time to catch Ruth as she ran into his arms.

Sobs racked her body and it was some moments before she could speak. When she eventually did so, he felt tears well up into his own eyes. 'Mr Graham's just off the phone. He had an emergency operation and hadn't time to call me earlier. Oh, Davie, Jock has carcinomatosis. He'll be dead in less than three months.'

She leaned backed and looked at him. Tears ran in rivulets down her black cheeks. Suddenly, she pounded his chest with her fists so hard that it hurt.

'It's so bloody unfair,' she cried. 'Such a good and kind wee man. He would never hurt anyone. How can God do this to him?'

CHAPTER XXIV

A merciful embolism intervened and five weeks later Jock died without pain. After the original prognosis, he had taken a week's holiday and cheerfully visited both Ian and Jean in Perthshire and his friends in Edinburgh. On a crisp Saturday afternoon just ten days before he died he and Marie had set off for a walk and to their surprise reached the top of Cnocan Lin and admired the view of the Irish coast. A week later he was in hospital. He had left instructions for his funeral including the number of the plot in the small cemetery by the shore where he wanted to be buried.

He had also ordered that the mourners were to be given a dram and a cup of tea at the nearby hotel 'after they've got me planted'.

Before the dignified elderly lawyer left the hotel after the funeral, he called Davie and Ian aside.

'Could you two gentlemen call at my office tomorrow morning?' he asked.

'Would ten o'clock suit both of you?'

The following morning they were shown into the small comfortable office. During preliminary small talk, a lady secretary brought in cups of coffee and the older man offered cigarettes which they both refused. He slipped the case back in his pocket without taking one himself.

When the secretary had left and the door was closed, he picked a document from on top of the pile on his desk.

'I have here a will which I prepared a month ago on the instructions of the late Mr Spence,' he said. 'It is a straightforward document which contains just five bequests. The joint executors are Mr David Sinclair and Mr Ian Boyd.' He took a sip of tea before going on in his unhurried West Highland voice. 'There are bequests of ten thousand pounds to Mrs Marie Sinclair, ten thousand pounds to Mr Ian Boyd, ten thousand pounds to Dr Ruth MacLeod and ten thousand pounds to Mr Angus Graham.' He looked over his glasses at Davie. 'After the settlement of funeral expenses and any small debts which may have been incurred, the residue of the estate goes to Mr Davie Sinclair.

'At present there is about three hundred pounds in current account at the bank, ten thousand pounds plus accrued interest on deposit and the remainder is invested in a portfolio of shares which were administered by his bank.' Again he sipped his cup. 'It will be some time before the will goes to probate so it is impossible at this point to give an accurate figure. However, I have done a rough sum based on last night's closing share values as reported in this morning's press. This indicates that after the sums which I have mentioned the estate will have a credit balance in excess of one hundred thousand pounds.'

If the old man had wanted his statement to have impact he wasn't disappointed. Davie had just taken a casual sip of tea which he spluttered all over the carpet. Ian, unable to speak, only gasped. With the aid of a handkerchief, Davie restored some order to his person. The lawyer sat smiling across his desk.

'We knew that Jock was fairly comfortable, but never dreamed that he had wealth on this scale,' said Davie eventually. 'How on earth did he do it?'

'It's quite simple really. He made so much money because, personally, he just wasn't interested. About fourteen years ago he gave his bank an entirely free hand with his account. His only instruction was that they set aside enough for his funeral expenses.'

'Did he know himself how much he had?' asked Ian.

'Only after he asked me to prepare his will. I suggested that I go with him to visit his bank manager. Yes, Mr Spence was rather surprised.'

'Can you think of anything that he might have wanted us to do ?' It was Davie who put the question.

The lawyer hesitated for some time before he replied. When he did so he was obviously weighing his words carefully.

'Maybe I can best answer that by quoting to you something that Mr Spence said as we were preparing his will.' To their surprise, his voice dropped into the broad Glasgow accent which Jock had never lost.

'If Davie an' Elaine wurna such a sensible pair ah wid lea' a thoosand or two on trust for their weans, but they've baith got their heids well screwed on so there's nae need. If ah lea' it as a lump sum then they're free tae buy anythin' that they think might be a good investment.'

He smiled as his voice returned to normal. 'Does that answer your question?'

Davie felt tears behind his eyes.

The lawyer glanced covertly at his watch then rose to his feet.

'Tell me,' he said as he saw them to the door, 'how did Dr MacLeod come by her surname?'

'Her father was orphaned when he was a baby and brought up by missionaries,' Davie explained. 'They belonged originally to Lewis. He grew up speaking Gaelic in the middle of Kenya.

'I see. It was interesting to meet her. When Mr Spence was making his list of bequests he told me a little of how he came to know her. "Ye ken," he said, "if ah'd been a wee bit longer and that lassie had been a wee bit shorter ah wud hae merrit her." Good day, gentlemen,' he shook hands. 'I'll be in touch.'

Davie and Ian said little to one another as they drove back to the croft. When they got there the only person to show no surprise was Marie.

'He spent the evening with me after he had been to see the lawyer,' she told them. 'He seemed so pleased with himself that I suspected he had left a nice surprise for us. I've never known a man who got so much pleasure from doing things for other people.'

After she had waved them off in the afternoon Marie found herself reluctant to go inside. She had much to think about.

She would soon be sixty years of age and the long day of teaching was becoming tiring. At sixty she could receive both her superannuation and state pensions.

Shortly after Davie's graduation she had started putting a monthly sum into National Savings. This combined with Jock's bequest would add up to a comfortable nest egg.

Her own needs were simple and apart from her car, inexpensive. Now she even had the assurance that her grand-children would have a good start in life. As so often happened when she was in blessing-counting mode her thoughts turned to Donald. She felt proud. She knew that when she had married her parents had been doubtful of her choice of husband. Fortunately they had been well aware of her happiness before they died. She, like her own son had been an only child.

From the corner of the house she could see the start of the Glen road.

As a bride she had walked up that road. She remembered the motherly welcome she had received from Mrs Bennett and how when she had been little more than a week in the Glen the old lady had walked the three miles up the rough road to visit her. She remembered her own tears at the sight of another female face.

Suddenly she realised that she was cold and went into the house. She sang softly to herself as she prepared a tea which she could take by the fire.

Not wanting the intrusion of television on her thoughts but still seeking company she turned on the radio as she settled.

The heat of the fire was soporific. Vaguely she was aware of the flat voice of the announcer. Her head nodded. Contentment pervaded the warm room. But the noise of the radio was obtrusive. Lazily she arose to switch it off, then paused, smiling.

The FT Index had risen on the day. Jock would have been pleased.

As she reached out her hand again the road traffic report was just beginning. This was never a worry in Kintyre. She pressed the button, and the voice disappeared.

A few minutes of the gently waltzing flames was sufficient. Marie slept.

She awoke to the jangling of the phone. This would be Elaine to tell her that they had arrived home. Or maybe one of the children would be given the job of phoning Granny.

'Mrs Sinclair ?' the voice was that of a man.

'Yes,'

'Mrs Sinclair, this is the West Lothian Police. I'm afraid that I have some bad news. There's been a serious road accident.' Marie fell to the floor in a deep faint.

Through the mist of returning consciousness she heard a car scrunching on the gravel then hurrying footsteps. The opening door revealed her doctor. His anxious face cleared when he saw her move.

'What has happened?' she asked as he grasped her wrist and replaced the hanging phone.

'Davie's car had an accident with a lorry, somewhere near Edinburgh. As far as I know none of their lives are in danger. Once we get you in a more dignified position I'll phone the hospital.'

The doctors voice was calm and Marie allowed herself to be helped to a chair. As he moved back out to the phone a policewoman met him at the sitting room door. This was a girl who had recently been at the school to talk to the pupils and while the doctor was out of the room she filled in some of the gaps for Marie. The policeman in Bathgate had heard the clatter when Marie fell. When nobody else had come to the phone he phoned the station in Campbeltown and they had phoned the local doctor as well as sending somebody of their own out.

'I'll just wait a moment till the doctor comes back then I'll switch on the kettle,' she finished.

When the doctor came back Marie anxiously scanned his face but his expression gave nothing away.

'None of their injuries are life threatening' he began and then went on to explain.

Davie and Elaine both had concussion but should be out of hospital within a few days. Donald had a broken left forearm as well as fairly extensive bruising.

Kay had fared worst. The rear door of the car had burst open. She had been thrown out and landed on the road. A following car couldn't avoid her.

'She has multiple fractures of both legs. She is in the operating theatre just now.' He paused before continuing in a level voice.

'It will be a few days before they can be certain that they can save both her legs.'

Marie turned her head into the policewoman's shoulder and wept uncontrollably.

The phone rang. The doctor went to answer it.

CHAPTER XXV

'That was Mrs Stark' said the doctor on his return. 'Dr MacLeod has gone to the hospital. She will phone later tonight, Mrs Stark is pretty upset' he went on 'but I will tell you the same as I told her. All that can be done is being done. A high percentage of the admissions to that hospital are road accident victims. They know what they are doing.'

The doctor left soon afterwards. The policewoman phoned her station to be told that things were quiet and they would call her if she was needed. Marie was grateful for the company and as they talked it emerged that the girl's mother had been among the older pupils in the local school when Marie started teaching there.

Ruth phoned after a long three hours. Davie and Elaine were sore but fairly comfortable. Donald was asleep under sedation. His arm would be set the following day. Kay was back in the ward but would need further surgery. Anxiety made Marie question further. She forced herself to be calm as she listened.

The surgeon had shown Ruth the first X-ray plates. The right leg would not present too much of a problem. The news of the left leg wasn't so hopeful.

'But she's young, healthy and determined. Now you try to get some rest. I'll spend the rest of the night with Katherine.' The phone went silent.

Some periods of time seem protracted. Some periods of time are interminable. Such a night stretched before Marie.

She lay fully dressed on top of her bed. She rose to make yet another cup of tea. She stood out on the gravel watching the lights in the North Channel and on the Irish coast. At length, exhausted she slept fitfully, but wakened when the early morning light fell on her face.

Should she phone the hospital? No, that would only be troubling them selfishly. Ruth had promised to call her as soon as she knew anything further.

For the first time in many months she was glad that she had work to go to. As she was ready to go out to her car the phone rang.

As she struggled to see the road to drive through the waterfall of tears she thought of Ruth's voice. Emotion had been fighting a losing battle with calm professionalism. The hospital were a bit concerned. Kay was restless and running a temperature.

'I'll phone you at the school at lunchtime. Try not to worry, Marie. She's young and strong.'

Lunchtime came at last. There was little change but at least the temperature hadn't risen any further. They had decided not to operate on her legs until the following day.

Davie managed to phone her from the hospital early in the evening. His voice usually so positive was tired and strained but the news was slightly better. The temperature had gone down a little and Kay appeared to be sleeping naturally.

Donald's arm was set satisfactorily and he had little pain. Both father and son were going home tomorrow but Elaine would wait to be near Kay. 'Try not to worry mum.'

He phoned again the following morning. Kay had had a good night and her temperature had continued to ease. He and Donald were going home. Elaine would phone in the evening.

But it was Ruth's voice that came over the wire. Where was Elaine?

'Is something wrong?'

'Kay has some pain and Elaine is sitting with her to try to get her to sleep. But her temperature is down. They should be able to operate tomorrow.

'They took some pictures this afternoon. Her right leg is going to be alright. By this time tomorrow I hope to have good news about the other one. Courage, Marie.'

Another sleepless night was followed by a day which wasn't helped by the fact that it was Saturday with no school. She couldn't even go to the town in case somebody phoned. The wife of the neighbouring farmer dropped in but could only wait for a short time.

The lawyer who had been at Jock's funeral called in on his way home from golf in the afternoon. Quiet kind and dignified, accustomed to family traumas. 'Such a bright wee lass. If there's anything that I can do please give me a ring.'

The next phone call was from Elaine. While Kay was in the theatre Ruth had taken her home for a few hours so that she could soak in a bath and pick up a change of clothes. She was now back in the hospital.

The surgeon had told her that he was pleased with the operation but that the next few days were critical. Ruth had been close by and took over the phone for a moment.

'You take a strong toddy and get to bed early tonight,' was her advice.

'I've told Katherine to do the same. Grannies are going to be very important in the next few weeks.'

The next week was one of desperate anxiety. When Donald had been ill Marie had no thought that his life might be in danger. At the worst he might not regain the full use of his limbs but her man would cope. Anyway, she had a good job and would be able to keep the two of them.

Then Donald was dead.

The old must die, whether they be man, beast or plant. That is necessary for the survival of the world. But the fit should not. That was waste.

Now she had a fear for the life of someone very young. Even the fear was tragedy. Coming so soon after Jock's death Marie felt herself unable to cope.

For the first two days after the operation all was well. Then an infection developed in the wound. This caused a temperature which raged at fever level. The resultant shivering meant that it was difficult to keep her leg still and this maintained a pain level which otherwise could have been controlled.

The phone was a tenuous link, but vital. 'We have to depend on antibiotics' Ruth told Marie. 'The operation itself was a success but compound fractures always carry a risk of complications.'

Time crept to twelve hours, and on to twenty four with little change. Then the fever broke and the temperature began to go down.

Two nights later Marie had a surprise when Kay's voice came on the phone. 'I'm in a wheel chair, Granny Marie. It's magic. When are you coming to see me? You'll need to come to write your name on my plaster. Here's Daddy – bye.'

'That's probably the best phone call that ever I've had,' Marie told her son when he came on the line. 'Is she as good as she sounds?'

'To us she's amazing,' confessed Davie 'but Ruth tells us that such a quick improvement isn't all that unusual in a healthy child.'

Davie went on to explain that if the surgeon remained pleased with her progress Kay would be allowed home in about a weeks time. For the first time in what had seemed like a lifetime Marie went to bed happy and slept soundly.

The news continued good and on hearing a car on the gravel and going to the door on the following Saturday Marie was surprised to see Ruth taking an overnight bag from the car. When they were settled with the inevitable cup of tea Ruth explained the reason for her unexpected visit. There was a fear that Kay's left leg might be shorter than her right.

'We didn't want to tell you over the phone she told Marie. After all the trauma of Jock's illness and death and then the car crash we thought it better that somebody should come down. Anyway, I wanted to see for myself how you were and as far as Kay's concerned we may be worrying needlessly.'

Ruth had brought flowers to place on Jock's grave and after they had done this they walked along the beach and climbed the rock of Dunaverty. As they looked west towards the setting sun over the Mull of Kintyre a pair of golden eagles could be seen hovering above the glen.

'Davie and Ian want to put up a headstone for Jock' said Ruth as they retraced their steps over the sand. 'They want you to choose an inscription.'

That evening Marie told Ruth that she was going to retire from teaching at the start of the summer holidays. She had done her sums carefully and the arithmetic looked comfortable. But the accident had been the bubble which popped the cork. She had felt both helpless and useless depending on the phone for news and unable to do anything to help. Now she could see how she could make amends and get pleasure from so doing.

Donald's broken arm wouldn't cause him to miss too much school and he should soon catch up but Kay was going to be off for sometime. The two of them would spend their summer holidays with her on the croft. She would set aside time to bring their school work to a level where they wouldn't start the autumn term at a disadvantage. The rest of the family would have to commute from Edinburgh at the weekends. They could share a car. All four of them could drive.

Marie was once again aware of a feeling essential to the happiness of most women. She was needed and could contribute.

CHAPTER XXVI

The gutta percha resilience of the very young now took over Kay's recovery. At the mid-term break Marie flew to Glasgow where Elaine picked her up and took her on to Edinburgh.

The sight of metal calipers on the small legs brought a lump to her throat. When it came to bedtime, however, Kay took pride in showing Granny Marie how she could climb the stairs without help.

She was attending physiotherapy sessions twice weekly and although Ruth said that this was bound to be giving her some pain she never shed a tear.

Marie was more concerned at the appearance of her son. When Donald had died he had hardly a grey hair on his head but Davie's hair had gone almost white. To add to her worry his features were grey and deeply lined.

'He blames himself for the accident,' Elaine told her when they had a moment on their own. 'But of course that's complete nonsense. If he hadn't reacted so quickly we could all have been killed.'

But as the two women conversed it became clear that Elaine had another worry. Davie was working much too hard and like many more professional men was resenting the fact that the younger minds were grasping the new technology much faster than he was. Civil engineering had come a long way since the days of the firm's founder with his horse and cart. Elaine could remember all too well how loss of confidence had affected her father and she couldn't bear the thought of something similar happening to her husband.

Marie's weekend passed all too quickly. She returned home with mixed emotions. Relief because of the progress of her grand children was overshadowed by the worry about her son.

She remembered how she, but more particularly Donald had wanted their son to go to university and how proud she had been on the day of his graduation.

Had they made a mistake? Then she thought of the worldly-wise Jock and his advice to Davie – no education was ever a waste of time.

For several days she brooded, then early of an evening Ian phoned from Perthshire. He and Jean were coming down to stay for a couple of nights.

'We'll be with you late afternoon tomorrow. Sorry for the short notice. Bye.'

Their news did much to lift Marie's spirits. The Laird was now in his eightieth year and becoming very frail. He had never married. His nearest living relative was a nephew for whom he held neither respect nor affection.

'I didn't care much for his mother either' he had told Ian. 'To be perfectly honest I've often thought that my brother was a father more by appointment than by creation. This lad just doesn't resemble our family at all. But I'm stuck with him.'

'Fortunately he married an otherwise sensible woman who was a bit younger than him. They have a son who resembles his mother.'

He went on to explain that this boy was just ten years old. The terms of entail allowed him to leave the estate in trust for his grand nephew. He wanted Ian to take over the management of the estate until the boy had the necessary experience to run it himself. The trust was to be in power for a minimum of fifteen years from the date of signing which was planned for the following week.

'I hope to live for a while yet but I would die a happier man if I knew that you were in charge' the old man said. 'If you have to sell some of it to make the rest more efficient then the trust gives you the power to do so. Just preserve as much as you can and don't allow anybody to smother the place in sitka spruce.'

The first contact had been through the estates lawyers. The salary was attractive. Ian and Jean had taken a few days to talk it over before reaching a decision. Their son was going to university in Glasgow in the autumn. Their daughter was finishing primary school.

'We always said that we would come back when we retired' said Ian. 'Perthshire has been good to us but this was always home.'

The lodge house on the estate was going to be made available to them but they planned to sell their own house and buy whenever a suitable house became available locally.

The Edinburgh branch of the Sinclair family arrived on the first weekend of July, but on the evening before their arrival Marie heard a car on the gravel outside. She went to the door to see a tall distinguished looking man coming towards her.

'Mrs Sinclair?' he asked.

At Marie's nod he introduced himself as Archie Gillespie. 'I'm the orthopaedist who has been looking after your granddaughter,' he told her.

His visit lasted over two hours and during it Marie heard the story of this lonely man. His wife had died five years previously after a long illness. After her death he had tried to smother grief with a blanket of work but had only succeeded in driving himself into a nervous breakdown. He had now cut down his work load to a more sensible level. He and Angus

Graham had gone through university together and still remained friends; Angus had recommended Kintyre as an ideal place for a quiet golfing holiday and he had taken a two month let of a house near the village.

He had arrived the previous evening and Kay was the last patient that he had seen before leaving Edinburgh. His daughter and two grandchildren were joining him on the following day. But the real reason for his visit delighted Marie. During the summer he would call at least twice a week to adjust the brace on Kay's left leg. Any X-rays that he needed could be done at the local hospital. If all went well she could have the whole summer without needing to go back to Edinburgh.

'Her right leg will only need a support bandage and we will soon be able to dispense with that as well' he told Marie. 'But we must be very careful that she doesn't develop a rock. In a child this can so easily become a subtlety which develops into a permanent limp.'

After he left, with a promise to call back on the Monday morning Marie realised that for two hours she had listened with hardly a need to utter a word. The man had visibly relaxed as he talked. One of Jock's homilies came into mind. 'Its amazing the good ye can dae for folk if ye have an open lug anta closed mooth' the wee man had said.

Despite her anxiety she had forced herself to refrain from asking if Kay would eventually have two legs of equal length.

During the next few weeks Marie was given a demonstration of how the resilience of youth could overcome the trials of life. Kay found some difficulty with rough ground and had to tackle stairs a step at a time but otherwise treated her caliper as part of her normal furniture.

'How long can you and Elaine stay?' Marie asked the gaunt Davie after they arrived on the sunny Saturday afternoon.

'Oh, we'll have to go back tomorrow' began Davie only to be interrupted by his wife, 'We leave here at eight o'clock on Monday morning.' Elaine said in a no-argument tone, 'tomorrow is going to be a day for a picnic on the beach.'

Marie was pleased to see that her son still had enough sense to recognise a fight that he wasn't going to win and Elaine's plan was carried out on the following day. When they got to the beach Elaine eased the brace off Kay's leg and Davie carried her into the water for a swim.

'Well, how are things?' Marie asked as the two women sat watching the three in the water.

'Alternating between fair and hellish' said Elaine after some thought. Davie was lapsing into moods of depression and at times retreating into a shell of silence which she couldn't penetrate. He really enjoyed his work when he was going out to sites every day but his seat on the board meant sitting in an office and seeing nothing but papers and people. About a month ago one of the younger men had misread a plan. Fortunately an experienced ganger noticed that something was wrong before too much harm was done. Davie was on the site for four days getting it sorted out.

'It was the happiest I've seen him in ages.'

There was silence for a time and they became conscious of the laughter of father and children as they sported in the water.

'As a family Jock's money has taken us from being well off to wealthy' Elaine went on, 'both you and Mum are comfortable and will never need help from us. But there's damn all sense in being financially secure if you're unhappy.'

Marie couldn't remember ever hearing her daughter-in-law swear before.

The return of the swimming party changed the topic of conversation.

184

CHAPTER XXVII

Davie and Elaine left the following morning with a promise to phone in the evening. Their children cheerfully waved them off. When Archie Gillespie arrived he had his two grandsons, aged six and eight, with him and Donald took them for a walk while their grandfather attended to his sister. When he had finished Kay wanted to go out to join the boys and he raised no objection.

'The bone has knitted well and the caliper will give support' he told Marie. 'The nearer we can keep her to a normal life the better. A romp with the boys will do her as much good as physiotherapy.'

After a cup of coffee in Marie's kitchen he left saying that he would call again on the Wednesday and the Friday. 'After that twice a week should be enough.'

Elaine phoned in the evening from her mother's house. After she had spoken to the children Marie took over the phone again.

'Davie is going to try to arrange holidays tomorrow' she was told.

'If all goes well we'll see you in a fortnight. Can we stay with you for three weeks? Here's Mum. Bye.'

Katherine's news delighted Marie. Ruth had accumulated a week of days-in-lieu by working through weekends and public holidays. She and Katherine could come down next Sunday and stay for a week.

'Why don't you stay longer?' asked Marie, 'surely you don't have to rush back.

'I might just take you up on that. Yes, I might.' Katherine had a laugh in her voice which puzzled Marie slightly.

As Marie put down the phone it rang again.

'The Boyds are coming back to Kintyre on the fifteenth' Jeans voice told her. 'Ian takes up his new job at the beginning of August. He'll be there to sell the top draw of the Glen lambs.'

The orthopaedist spent over an hour with Kay on the Wednesday and kept the conversation on general subjects afterwards while he and Marie drank coffee.

Relaxed, he was a very amusing man and Marie enjoyed his stories. As a young man working with a rural teaching practice he had accompanied a group of men going out to a hill to carry in an injured shepherd. He had been bringing in a gather of some hundreds of sheep when his foot went into a rabbit burrow. The resultant fall not only broke his shin bone but left the broken bone protruding through the skin. When they found him he was sitting with his back propped against a rock and directing his two dogs to hold the gather. As his dogs wouldn't work for anyone else he insisted on sitting up on the stretcher as they were carrying him in and they brought the gather in ahead of the stretcher party.

'Did his leg mend alright?' asked Marie.

'Oh yes, and he lived to a ripe old age. We used to visit him whenever we could. He was a really interesting character. Well, I'll see you on Friday morning' he added, as he rose to leave.

Marie was setting aside a little over an hour each evening for Kay's lessons. Donald hadn't missed much school time but she set him a task as well so that Kay wouldn't feel that she was being victimised.

'Mr Gillespie seems to be a nice man' she said as Kay settled her leg on a footstool.

'Yes, he's funny, he makes Granny Katherine giggle' said Kay and demonstrated.

Ruth and Katherine arrived as promised and, nearer the end of their week, Marie had little difficulty in persuading Katherine to wait longer.

The Boyds' flitting arrived escorted by three of the family. Young John had taken a summer job before going to University and would only be down for a short holiday prior to full time study.

On the first two mornings after Davie and Elaine arrived Davie rose early, walked to the top of Cnocan Lin to see the sun rise then spent the rest of the day restlessly doing jobs about the croft. Then he began to relax, lie longer in the mornings and generally look more like his old self.

Archie Gillespie invited the women folk to his holiday house for afternoon tea.

'Let the children bring their bathing togs' he said.

The house was a beautiful bungalow overlooking the beach and they had tea in the garden. Elaine and Archie's daughter just had a quick drink and then went off to play on the beach with the children. As the remaining trio sat in the sunshine the gentle surge of the lapping waves was punctuated by the sound of happy children. It was the man who eventually broke the companionable lull in conversation.

'The lady who owns this house has offered to sell it to me' he told the two women. 'I must say that I find it very tempting. It's the most restful place that ever I've known.'

He went on to say that his son-in-law who had been on a business trip abroad was arriving the following day to join the family for a fortnight's holiday.

'I'm really very lucky. He's a sensible lad. I'll discuss the situation with them after he arrives.'

The subject was then dropped and they went on to talk of other things.

On the Sunday afternoon Davie was constructing a bogie under the supervision of his children.

The three women in his life were sitting in chairs on a square of concrete which had originally been the floor of a sizeable shed. Over the years Jock and Marie had with the help of plant tubs, converted the area into an attractive sheltered patio.

Young Jean Boyd arrived on her bicycle. 'Dad and Mum are squabbling over the laying of a carpet so I cleared out' she explained. 'Why people can't agree over a simple wee job I'll never know.'

Marie laughed as she rose to her feet. 'I'm going to put on the kettle for coffee' she said, then added to Jean, 'I'll phone your parents and invite them up for their tea tonight.' The sound of raised voices came from the old blacksmiths shop. 'Meanwhile I think you should go and referee among my descendants.'

This has just been like old times, thought Marie as she tidied away the dishes that Jean and Katherine were washing. Young Jean and Elaine had gone to put the children to bed and the two men had strolled out to enjoy the evening air.

Early the following evening Ian arrived back.

'I don't know if its fair to ask you this' he began to Davie with a glance at Elaine.

He went on to explain that they had planned to gather the south side of the Glen hill on the following day. One of the shepherds had twisted a knee and was fit to do a little work about the fank but not able to go out on the hill. This left them a man short on an awkward gather where three people were essential.

'My own straight leg rules me out of that type of walking so I wondered if you'd like a day on your old haunts,' he finished rather hesitantly.

'I'd love it but I haven't a dog.'

'Oh, we can get over that snag easily' replied Ian. 'The Laird, as you know has always kept a good dog, partly for work and partly as a pal. He'll work for you if you just keep a lead on him till you're clear of the steading.'

'OK. What time?'

'They'll start to walk out at five o'clock. Better have some radox for his bath tomorrow night' Ian said to Elaine as he left.

Davie arrived back the following night tired, smelly but happy. The fact that the Laird's dog had been a descendant of the collie family which had been owned by his father had added to his enjoyment of the day.

When Davie and Elaine's holiday ended Marie had little trouble in persuading Katherine to wait on. The younger couple went home cheered by Archie Gillespie's report on Kay. He had carried on the thrice weekly visits and could now see real progress. The weather continued kind with many sunny days when the children could swim in the sea.

The two grannies were also enjoying themselves with Marie particularly so after joining her grandchildren in the water. It became accepted on good days that they changed in Archie's house and then went down the bank to the sand. After each swim he massaged Kay's leg before refitting her caliper.

Before her parents next weekend visit he announced that he could see an end to the use of the caliper.

'At this point I cannot be sure about the length of her leg' he said 'but if you were to ask me to guess I would say that any difference will be in the end very slight. Now for a bit of personal news. I've decided to buy the house here.'

He would need a few months to tidy up his retirement in Edinburgh but he hoped to be back by the beginning of next spring.

On the third weekend of August Davie and Elaine arrived to take the Edinburgh contingent back to the city. The children cried because they didn't want to leave. Katherine wasn't much better. Marie cried after they left.

Archie came to say a temporary goodbye. He would see Kay regularly for the next few weeks, but after that he felt that she wouldn't need him. There would be check ups every few months but there had been no muscle wastage and he didn't foresee any problems. Elaine phoned regularly. They were all much the better of their summer. Davie still spoke about his day on the Glen hill as being the happiest in years. They would all be back for the September weekend including Katherine.

Jean was doing some part time district nursing and dropped in regularly for coffee and a blether. But it was her husband who came to see Marie on the night before the next Edinburgh visit.

The Glen was going to be put up for sale. As the old Laird became less fit to manage things the estate had been losing money and the bank was becoming noisy. Fortunately, the Glen had been a later acquisition and wasn't part of the original entail. The Laird wasn't keen to sell but wanted to secure the rest of the estate for his grand nephew.

Ian wondered if Davie would be interested and whether he shoul dare to mention it to him. If he did would Elaine's first thought be to strangle both of them?

Marie thought long into the night and couldn't make up her mind. She would love to have her grandchildren close to her as they were growing up but didn't want either Davie or Elaine to waste their qualifications.

But unknown to them all, including Davie and her own mother, Elaine was two steps ahead of them. She had seen how the summer holidays in Kintyre had benefitted her husband and children. Her first move had been to contact the practice where she had worked as a student. The partners were still there and remembered her. Brucellosis eradication was going to mean an upsurge in work. If she wanted to come back they would be happy to have her.

Meanwhile she had perused the job adverts in the papers. A local construction firm had expanded and they were now looking for a civil engineer. The salary wasn't as much as Davie was making but she knew that in a remote area there was often consultancy work as it was much cheaper to employ somebody locally than go to the expense of taking somebody down from a big city firm. All this she had planned before hand and was going to tell Davie over the weekend. When Ian told his story she ran forward and kissed him.

CHAPTER XXVIII

'There is a tide in the affairs of men which if taken at the flood leads on to fortune.'

Marie thought of the quotation from Shakespeare's *Julius Caesar* as she carried in the turkey for Davie to carve at what was a mammoth Christmas dinner.

Things had moved swiftly. When the Laird heard that Davie was interested he had insisted that he be offered the Glen without it being advertised. He then called in a firm of estate agents to make a valuation of the property on a lock, stock and barrel basis. When a figure was struck he reduced it by twenty per cent. He said that as the estate owed its existence to the founding work done by Davie's great grandfather this was only fair.

The young shepherd who had been tending the farm for the estate had announced that he was getting married. Subject to some repair to the house and the access road he was willing to stay on in Davie's employ. Ian recommended him. Not only was he a good shepherd but he was also a skilled tractor driver and fencer.

All this had been more than a year ago. Young John Boyd was studying civil engineering at Glasgow University. He had spent his summer break working at the Glen. He had the natural enthusiasm and energy of the young but he also had a good eye, something which Davie said was invaluable in site work for a civil engineer.

The total area of the Glen was slightly over two thousand acres. Much of the farther out land was naturally dry and could be greatly improved by using modern machinery to spread lime and phosphates. A grant had been obtained for an access road which would bisect the hill. John had chosen the route. Davie had had reservations but wisely kept them to himself. The road had been completed in record time with the only imported materials being reinforced pipes which were used in the crossing of half a dozen ditches.

'I would have kept to a lower line' Davie confided to Ian 'but the route John has taken has meant that all the displaced rock has been used with nothing wasted. That boy will go far' he predicted.

During the spring Katherine had provided a bit of news which was a surprise to everyone except her own grandchildren. Marie's phone had rung late one evening.

'Archie has just asked me to marry him' came the excited voice.

'Och, I knew this would happen' said young Donald with all the wisdom of his half score years. 'She giggles at all his corny jokes.'

Only Ruth had been less than enthusiastic.

'It's not fair' she complained 'I'm going to be left all on my own in Edinburgh.'

'Just you keep visiting us. There's plenty big hunky young farmers here who are looking for a wife' Marie told her.

Preceded by young Kay, Marie carried the huge turkey aloft in the manner of someone bearing a haggis at a Burns supper. She and Ruth had joined two tables together to accommodate nine adults, one teenager and two children.

The meal had been a joint effort. Elaine had created a starter, Ruth and Marie provided the main course, Katherine had arrived armed with a Christmas pudding. Pressed for their contribution the men said that they would provide approval and the young folk volunteered to wash up.

Cold winter relinquished the fight with cheery spring which subtly gave way to a warm summer. The middle generation of Sinclairs had adapted well to their more relaxed lifestyle. For the first few months they had rented a house, then were able to buy a beautiful stone built villa on the edge of the village. A view over the golf course had persuaded them both to take up the game in the light evenings, but although the competence of his shepherd meant that there was little need, Davie liked to walk round his estate at the weekend.

The children were attending the school where Marie herself had taught and where their father had received his primary education. On their holiday times they had a choice of grannies and Elaine was expert at watching that they didn't favour or indeed pester one more than the other.

On a bonny summer Saturday when she was on her own Marie decided to drive her car to the Glen house then walk out the hill a bit from there.

It was a journey which she had done several times since the road had been improved. As she was parking at the side of the old barn the young shepherd came round the corner. He invited her in for coffee but Marie said that she would walk first to develop an appetite for his wife's baking and come in on her way back..

'Take your car up the new road to the end' he told her. 'that way you'll get further with less effort.'

Thus after a gentle walk and a short climb Marie found herself standing at a height of some fifteen hundred feet above the shore with sufficient breath left to enjoy the view.

She sat on a warm rock for a time alternately looking out to sea and then back towards the hills which she had known so well as a young woman. Glancing to the right she saw her son standing on the top of the Smokers Knowe. He looked tall and straight silhouetted against the blue haze of the Irish Coast.

Suddenly she remembered something Jock had said to her just after Davie had gone to University and she had been missing him badly.

'Don't you be worryin', Marie,' was the advice of the wee Glasgow man. 'A good boy lake yours, he'll nivver forget ye. He'll aye come back.'

At the time she had had the comfort of knowing that this was true. But she hadn't known that he would quite literally come back to the Glen.

THE END